Arden

Nick Corbett was born and raised in the Royal Town of Sutton Coldfield, England. He studied urban design at Manchester and Oxford Brookes Universities, with a stint at Amsterdam University. He served as the urban designer for the Royal Borough of Kensington and Chelsea for eight years, and has helped to regenerate many other places. In addition to *Arden*, he is the author of *Revival in the Square* and *Palace of Pugin*.

Praise for *Palace of Pugin*
"A compelling historical novel"
Lady Wedgwood

Praise for *Revival in the Square*
"A thoughtful book"
The Rt. Hon. David Miliband MP

Arden

a novel by
Nick Corbett

Gateway to the Journey Home

TRANSFORMING CITIES

But let justice roll on like a river,
righteousness like a never-failing stream!
Amos 5:24

1 Friends

The universe opens over the warm earth. Sky and earth merge as one. Stars dance upon water. There is a primordial silence. Ripe fruits are testimony to a long, hot summer. Beside a sandy beach, a rowing boat sways. This is the Forest of Arden. Trees have grown here since the retreat of the Ice Age. The air holds a woody fragrance.

Deep within the forest comes a rushing sound of wind. A red fox darts into the undergrowth. The wind becomes a screaming engine. An Audi Quattro hurtles down the dirt track towards the water. Headlights dazzle through the trees and flash across the pool, revealing an island with two stubby trees. The car skids out of control dangerously close to the water. Black dust engulfs the scene.

For a moment all is silent and then a second engine roars from within the forest. The box shape of a Mini springs from the trees. It is being throttled to its limits in a low gear, bounding down the dirt track in hot pursuit. The brakes have locked. It is on a collision course. Three men pull themselves into an emergency brace position, eyes tightly shut, expecting the impact. Miraculously, the Mini stops so close to the Audi's back bumper it looks as if the two cars are kissing. Dust settles.

Two young women stagger out of the Audi. They run to the water's edge, laughing, breathless, and giddy. They lean forwards, hands on knees, catching their breath, a giggling heap of blonde and red hair.

The three young men clamber out of the Mini and stand in amazement pointing at the tiny gap between the cars. The excitement of the race injected a fierce energy into all of them, but now they are all relieved that no damage has been done. The adrenalin rush has passed. Joe shakes his head.

"I can't believe we missed it Luke, the mighty Mini survives again!"

"I know mate, I really thought we were going to crash again."

The young men are anxious to save face because they have lost the car race from town to the pool. They have never lost a race to the girls before. They scratch their heads, searching for an excuse. Their other friend, Archie, looks very pale, in fact he is turning green.

"Maybe we should say we had to slow down because he was being sick," says Luke.

Archie is bent double leaning against a wall of the boathouse.

"Are you being sick *again* Archie?" shouts Luke.

Archie retrieves a finger from down his throat and wretches but nothing comes out.

All eighteen years old, Joe, Luke, and Archie are best friends. Joe is dark and a bit of a dreamer. Luke is a fair-haired golden boy. Archie is ginger and the girls say he is a "loon".

"We won! We won! I beat you Luke, at last!" cries Cathy, the driver of the Audi, from the water's edge, hands firmly on her hips. A slightly plump, pretty red head, Cathy is a little powerhouse. She has an artistic temperament and is constantly changing her wacky hairstyles, much to the disapproval of her parents who are wealthy and live in a large detached house on the edge of town. Tonight, Cathy is dressed in dandified regency copied from Adam and the Ants, plus lots of jewellery. She is a true New Romantic.

Standing beside Cathy is her best friend, Hannah, who is tall, thin, blonde and beautiful.

"So who's the fastest now? Face it Luke, you're never going to beat the ace Audi again!" shouts Hannah, holding aloft a victorious clenched fist.

"Didn't you see me flashing my lights at you? Archie was being sick, we slowed down ages ago!"

"That's a lie, imbecile and you know it!" snaps Cathy.

What follows is an ill-tempered discourse on the girls' lack of care for Archie and the boys' lack of fair play. They all take it too seriously.

"Oh, come on, I need to get away from these little boys, they're absolute imbeciles," says Cathy.

"Hey, what did you call us?' asks Luke.

"Imbeciles!"

"Oh, that's alright then."

Cathy grabs Hannah's arm and escorts her off to the little beach.

Archie joins his mates. "I really do need to make myself be sick. I know I'd feel better if I could just throw up."

"Blimey, your face is completely green!" says Joe, alarmed. "Are you alright? Do you want me to poke you in the stomach?"

Archie shakes his head with a worried look. They turn and notice that Luke is already strolling off towards the water's edge. They turn on their heels and follow him.

"How come we always follow Luke?" mumbles Archie with a grimace.

"I'm not following him," replies Joe. "I just want to look

at the water too."

Luke is good looking and popular. Joe and Archie often find themselves in orbit around him. He has star quality and a strong gravitational pull. He is self-contained and can happily go a week without seeing the others, while they want to be in almost constant contact. Luke rarely makes phone calls. He knows his friends will make the necessary social arrangements and that he will find himself in the middle of it all. In their sports lessons at school, Luke would always be one of the first to be chosen out of the line. He wasn't much better at football than Joe, and yet Joe would always be a much less popular selection. He had less gravitational pull. Poor old Archie was often the very last to be chosen, especially when Greenie was off sick. On one occasion when Archie was the last boy standing in the line, the two team captains actually argued about which one would have to take him. He stood there, humiliated, looking at the ground, feeling like toxic waste. But all that is in the past now; school is finished.

At the water's edge, breathing deeply, Joe smiles at Luke.

"It's all over now. No more school, ever! It's weird, isn't it? It's going to take some getting used to."

"Oh, I'm used to it already. I've been waiting years for this. No more tyrants!"

"That's true."

"Freedom!"

All five friends stand together upon soft sand at the edge of the pool. A fragrant, warm, forest breeze blows over them; their tempers are soothed. They drink in the silence and absorb the wonder of the night.

For each of the friends, their teenage years brought a degree of estrangement from their families. They found sanity and security in each other. Over the previous eight hours they have been to several pubs and parties with their wider circle of friends, a convoy of cars making its way from one venue to the next. Cathy and Luke, both driving, have been more or less sober all night, but the others have been very drunk. Now they are sobering up again.

They stand, gazing into the shallow water. William Shakespeare and his friends had stumbled upon the same pool half a millennium ago, but now this Forest of Arden belongs to Joe and his friends. This is their time. Joe looks over the pool. He is at one with the world and imagines he is merging into the water. He wonders if the others can feel the same urge to be submerged. He turns to look at them. These are the people he is most at ease with in the world; nobody is missing. He nods almost imperceptibly at Hannah and she smiles back, approvingly. She kicks off her red high-heeled shoes. The boundaries are few between the friends, and the boundaries are few between the friends and this old forest. Joe breaks the silence.

"Oh come on! No time to worry about wobbly bits!"

He takes off his shirt and trousers. Cathy stares at his athletic body. Hannah looks away. Her attention is drawn to the solitary rowing boat, tethered to a dead tree a few metres from the shore. She takes off her jeans, folds them neatly, then deposits them on the beach. She paddles out into the water, cautiously to begin with, and then more confidently, her smooth brown legs striding through the dark water.

"Where's she going?" whimpers Archie.

"To get the boat," replies Luke.

"Oh, right. Hey, she's had a lot to drink. That red wine we were supposed to be sharing, I hardly drank any of it."

The others ignore Archie and strip off.

Hannah, balancing herself carefully, reaches forward and grabs a slippery rope that ties the boat to the dead tree. The water is cold around her ankles. She grapples with a frayed knot. Something distracts her. Water is tinkling and tumbling behind her. She turns around. The stars are bright but it is still dark and difficult to see. Hannah can just make out the faint outline of a stone archway under the boathouse. Beneath it flows a stream of water, overflowing from the pool. The water passes over large stone slabs and then disappears into blackness. Hannah regains her focus. Nothing is going to delay her further from getting that boat and taking it out to the island in the middle of the pool. The knot unravels. Hannah grabs a handful of rope, oblivious to the green grime that coats it and now her hand. She drags the heavy boat into deeper water. A v-shaped ripple flows in its wake. Little waves wash over the sandy beach where the friends have stripped down to their underwear.

"Come on you lot, I've got it!" yells Hannah.

"Coming Hannah!" replies Cathy, stepping into the water before letting out a squeal.

"It's freezing!" She runs out again.

"No it's not, come on!" says Luke, manfully.

They all paddle through the shallows and then wade into deeper, darker water, where they climb aboard Hannah's heavily swaying boat. They are five laughing teenagers, splashing around on a pool in the middle of the Forest of Arden, under a numinous sky.

"The mission's to get to the island and back before sunrise, alright?" says Hannah assertively.

"Yeah, let's do it. I'll row!" says Cathy, and she paddles the boat surprisingly well, using a small oar, found under the seat.

Steady progress is made on their outward journey to the

island, it is a small hump marked by two stubby oak trees. Joe lies back with his head resting upon Hannah's legs, soothed, comforted, and warmed. He looks up, marvelling at the night sky. He has never seen the sky illuminated like this, with millions of pulsing stars stretching from horizon to horizon.

"Are the wispy bits the Milky Way?" he asks.

"Yeah," murmurs Hannah sultrily, as if she knew.

Cathy doesn't look happy. Desperate to interrupt whatever is happening between Joe and Hannah, she interjects with the first thing that comes into her head - a question about Joe's underwear.

"Why on earth are you wearing paisley Y-fronts, Joe? I thought you'd be the kind of guy to wear trendy boxers."

The wind is taken out of Joe's sails. "All my other pants are boxers, actually, and it's just that my grandad hasn't got around to doing the laundry yet," he answers, clearly rattled. He refuses Cathy's request to help her row the boat. He regains his comfortable position resting upon Hannah, and he stares again at the sky. Cathy remains huffy about Joe and Hannah being so close. The group continues its journey to the island in silence. Archie surreptitiously looks at Cathy's large breasts, which wobble in her black bra as she paddles. Then, to everyone's surprise, Luke stands up, shakily, and with one hand holding his Calvin Klein boxers, he dives into the black water as cleanly as an otter. He leaves behind a heavily swaying boat.

Over the last summer whenever the friends have been together beside water, Luke has always been the first to get into it, and the others have followed. And so it is now. Remnants of drunkenness are blown away by a second wind. Being eighteen, the friends are no strangers to lethargy and yet at other times they get these wonderful bursts of bouncing energy. One by one they enter the water, but all less impressively than Luke. The water is deep and cold. Archie is the only one left in the boat.

"Come on, Archie, you wimp!" splutters Cathy, treading water after swimming a few strokes.

"Come on Archie!" echoes Hannah, and then she screams. "Agh! I can't touch the bottom!" She disappears under water, then emerges, laughing.

Joe does a valiant front crawl, catching up with Luke who is treading water about ten metres away from the boat.

Meanwhile, Archie remains unconvinced. His complexion has returned to its usual white rather than alarming green, but he is not a strong swimmer and he fears the dark water. He is also very short-sighted, so taking off his glasses is a risky business. His large, thick, tortoiseshell spectacles cost him a lot of money, which he earned by working on a boring summer job, stuffing envelopes. He mulls the situation over, evaluating the risks: *Could I actually wear my glasses in the water? If I leave my glasses in the boat, will I be able to see the boat when I'm in the water? Would the others help me? Would they duck me? If I become submerged could I forget which way is up? Are pike a threat?*

Archie's desire to join his friends in the water is greater than his anxieties. He places his spectacles under the wooden seat in the boat and steadily prepares to launch himself. Suddenly, he slips on the edge and for a split second he is flying through the air with a panic stricken grimace. There is an impressive backwards summersault, legs pass over head and then he plunges into the water with a very loud splash. Water rushes up his nose, stinging. There is cheering and hysterical howling from the others. Joe punches the water with delight. In the blackness, some instinct tells Archie which way is up. He emerges gasping for breath, shocked and disorientated. His nose hurts, but he is also exhilarated and grins inanely.

After a few more minutes of swimming and fooling around, the friends clamber back into the security of the boat, dripping and laughing. The pool becomes still and silent again. The leaves rustle on the stubby oak trees. One by one, the stars renew their dance upon the water. After a brief rest, Cathy again paddles the boat, very gently. Slowly, they resume their journey to the island.

For the boys it's been a summer of discovery; drinking to excess, fumbling with girls at parties, and one-night stands. They have fire in their bellies and sex on the brain.

"You're staring Archie," whispers Joe with a wink and a nod. Archie turns away from Cathy and he crosses his legs tightly.

With Cathy pursuing a steady course, the boat soon pulls up beside the island, but only Joe can be bothered to get out. He climbs up the earth mound and leans against one of the oak trees. He claims the island for himself and his friends. The others lay content and restful in the gently swaying cradle of the boat. Cleansed of all worries, they are at peace with the world and with each other.

"Shooting star... just went by," says Archie with a disinterested yawn.

Luke is more excited, he points up at the night sky.

"Hey! There's loads of them!"

"Where?" asks Hannah. "I want to see one. I've never seen a shooting star, where are they?"

"Just look up there," replies Luke.

Hannah sits upright and her eyes follow the line of Luke's pointing finger.

"Wow! There's lots of them, look Joe!" she calls over to the island. Joe moves away from the trees and looks skywards. His jaw is agape as he counts one, two, three, four, five shooting stars darting across the firmament.

These shooting stars could be portents of change. The living has been easy for the friends over the long, hot summer, but their time together, at least in this place, is coming to an end. Tonight is the climax of their season together and a new day is dawning. Short bursts of birdsong are already breaking out from within the forest. The vulgar squawk of a crow echoes over the pool.

On the journey back from the island, the dawn chorus gains momentum. Joe looks up at the changing sky. He feels his spirit lifting on the growing crescendo of warbling, whistling, chirping and cooing, until every atom in the air is resonating with birdsong. As he helps Cathy paddle the boat with his arms, his eyes follow frenetic blackbirds, darting across the pool, rejoicing in their territorial claims.

Cathy and Joe continue to paddle, Joe lunges his arms fearlessly into the dark water. The boat glides in the direction of the boathouse. After a while, Archie is the first to speak. He moans about his new job, which annoys the others, and so the girls tease him about his growing beer belly; then they tease him about Tanya, his educational one-night stand. Archie skilfully shifts the conversation to Joe and his embarrassing cricket skills.

They have soon covered half the distance between the island and the boathouse. Archie speaks again, but in a more serious tone.

"It's time for me to go away. I'm not sure where yet, but I want to leave..."

There is a pregnant pause.

"You're going to have to walk on water if you're leaving us now mate," chuckles Joe.

Archie continues unabashed. "I wish I could take a year off like you Luke, and go around the world, then study... what is it you're doing, again? Fishing studies?"

"That'll be ocean science, at Portsmouth University,"

replies Luke. "Hey, why don't you come with me on my gap year?"

Archie is genuinely flattered, but he hasn't got any savings and he hasn't got rich parents like Luke. His bright ginger hair is cropped short because the real world of work has arrived early for him. He had hoped to be going away to university like his friends but he didn't get the A-level grades required. Universities aren't too impressed with one grade E and three "Unclassifieds".

Joe steers the conversation towards what each of the friends will be doing in ten years time.

"So, what'll you be doing then, Archie?" he asks.

"I'll be in New York, in a penthouse apartment, where the thinkers live," Archie replies snootily.

"Pompous carrot," mutters Luke with a half smile. "But what will you *actually* be doing Archie?"

"I'll be in advertising with *loadsa money!*" Archie gestures with his hand as if he's got a big wad of cash. "And I'll have a bevy of beauties waiting for me back in the penthouse."

"Where does he get it from?" Cathy asks, turning to Joe who shrugs his shoulders. Joe turns to Hannah. He speaks in a gentle voice, he is very fond of her.

"What about you, Hannah? What'll you be doing ten years from now?"

"Don't ask me, Joe." Hannah brushes off the question initially, but then she continues. "Well, I did read this book recently about a woman who travelled to Africa and worked with children with AIDS. I'd like to be like her."

"I don't believe AIDS does you any harm. It's ignorance that kills you," states Archie alluding to the recent television advertisement campaign. Hannah looks over to Cathy for affirmation of her career choice, but Cathy's face is blank.

"So, how about you Cathy?" asks Hannah.

"Well, as much as I'd like to be with you, I couldn't possibly work in Africa because of the flies," she replies with a smile. "Instead, I'll just have to be the editor of a fashion magazine. I'll marry a very rich man, we'll have a big house, a cleaner, two Porches and enough babies for you lot because I can't imagine any of you will ever get married."

This comment about marital status leaves Hannah looking worried. Cathy then turns to Joe.

"Okay paisley pants, you started this, what'll you be doing ten years from now?"

"He's going to be a journalist, I reckon," says Luke. Joe looks baffled. Luke continues. "Well, you're always getting your letters published in the local newspaper aren't you? You're like disgusted of Tunbridge Wells!"

Archie steps in. "You need to be careful about that, Hitler started off with letters to the local newspaper."

"Thanks for the warning," replies Joe. "I'm not sure what I'll be doing. I'd like to save the rain forests... but, I'd like to be rich too. It's boring being poor. So, maybe I'll be a property developer."

Luke rolls his eyes, but Joe continues.

"I don't know where I'll be doing my developing, maybe in the South of France. Yeah that'll do. I like French women."

"Well, why are you doing gardening or whatever it is at uni, dick head?" Archie is surprisingly agitated; he goes on. "Anyway, you'll be living back here in ten years time with a bossy little wife and you can forget about her being French. No such luck. Oh, and she'll have very small tits."

"No she won't! She'll be French, gorgeous, and have juggernormous baps!"

Joe gets a laugh with his new word but he is clearly a bit

flustered by Archie.

"I know you're mentally handicapped, but it's landscape architecture I'll be studying, not gardening! There's a big world out there waiting for me too, Archie!"

Joe takes a deep breath and then turning to Luke he forces a smile.

"How about you Luke, what'll you be doing ten years from now?"

Before he can answer, Archie interjects again with a loud whisper to Cathy, followed by a furtive look down her bra.

"He'll be working for his dad."

"I won't be working for my dad that's for sure, ginger pubes."

"Why not?" asks Archie, ignoring the insult.

"I'll be doing my own thing..." Luke takes a moment to think about what he wants to do most in the world. The previous year he went sailing around Cornwall with his dad and his cousin Jamie, in his uncle's fifty-foot yacht. When they were a mile offshore they saw a pod of killer whales. For Luke, that was a mind-blowing, life-changing, spectacle.

He continues with his train of thought. "Marine research or maybe I'll just be painting boats in Cornwall. I like it down there. I could be a lobster fisherman!"

The boat glides back to the shore and the friends clamber out with unsteady legs. The sky is distinctly lighter now, bereft of all but the brightest stars. Luke wades through the water, pulling the boat by its sodden rope. He ties it to the dead tree with a proficient sailor's knot, which later mystifies the boat's owner. The others make for the beach where their clothes are piled on top of each other. Hannah beckons Joe to join her. She smiles and presses her body against him. He feels her pert breasts against his chest.

Their lips meet in a long kiss. Hannah meant for this to be a quick friendly farewell, but she and Joe are taken by unexpected passion. Hannah manages to break off, she stares into Joe's eyes.

"We all love you, you know that don't you?"

Cathy dresses quickly. She walks over to Hannah and Joe carrying a large bundle of clothing under her arm. Ignoring their intimate embrace, she grabs hold of Hannah's arm, roughly.

"Come along please! I've got your clothes here. We need to go right now. I've got to get that car back!"

Hannah only has time to smile at Joe before she is escorted off, still in her underwear. Sitting back in the Audi Quattro, she lowers the electric window and shouts to Joe.

"See you!"

Cathy settles into the driver's seat and turns the stereo on. It is her favourite song, the number one in the charts: *The Only Way is Up!* by Yazz and the Plastic Population. She turns it up full blast, shattering the peace of the forest. The car pulls off with a wheel spin. Hannah blows Joe a kiss out of the window. There is a cloud of dust. Joe is motionless, standing there in his paisley underpants. All around him are trees, water and burgeoning birdsong.

When Joe eventually returns to Archie and Luke, they are already dressed and waiting for him expectantly on the beach. Archie stands with his hands on his hips looking like a parent waiting for an explanation from a naughty child. Luke just gives Joe a knowing nod.

"Who's a big boy then?" says Archie. "That was a turn up for the books wasn't it? Have you got off with her before without telling us?"

Joe smiles, but then he lets out a yell.

"Aaaargh! Cathy's got my clothes! No wonder she raced off!"

Either for a lark or maybe by accident, Cathy has taken Joe's clothes. He is left feeling angry and cold.

"We'll call at my house, it's on the way, you can borrow some of my clothes," says Luke reassuringly.

"Okay, thanks."

Joe tries not to sound too pleased, but going to Luke's house is always a treat. Lullingdon Manor, Luke's home, is a very old and special place, right on the edge of the Forest of Arden. The friends were last at Lullingdon for Luke's eighteenth birthday party. What a brilliant night that was; party games, a barn dance, and Luke's intriguing, entertaining family. Joe anticipates borrowing some particularly cool clothes from Luke. The three friends climb back into Luke's Mini. They race up the dirt track with U2's *Joshua Tree* blasting out of the windows.

2 Wellspring of Life

Shafts of light penetrate the canopy giving the woods a mysterious glow. Green and gold trees shroud the road, there is dappled light and shade. The Mini speeds through with the windows down. "Turn the music up!" shouts Joe from the back seat. It's his favourite U2 track: *I Still Haven't Found What I'm Looking For.* There is Bono's voice, the speed of the car, wind… freedom.

They are on the main straight road through the forest. Luke accelerates to almost seventy miles per hour. He always drives fast, despite a history of minor crashes. Archie sits in the front passenger seat, occasionally looking at Luke. Archie was present when the last crash happened. He has noticed that Luke always has a mad look about him when he is driving too fast.

"He's got that look again," says Archie, turning back to face Joe, but he doesn't get a reply. Joe's feet are up on the back seat, knees tucked into his body. He looks like a naked hostage in the confined environment of the back seat; he is smiling serenely as he stares out of the window, lost in the music. Archie finds Joe's unintelligible smile as troubling as Luke's manic grimace. He scratches the back of his head and mumbles on about slowing down.

Joe can't put into words just how happy he is feeling. He has shed an old skin; he is emerging into the first day of the rest of his life. An electric riff emerges from harmonious chords. Then the electric guitar storms in like an attack helicopter. Joe feels the power. He is totally free. He doesn't need to know where he is going; he doesn't need to go home again. It is as if the car is racing him to a bigger country where he can stretch his wings and soar. For the first time he is excited about going away to university, but then what of this new possibility with Hannah?

The forest becomes copses, meadows, hedgerows, fences, paddocks and ancient red brick garden-walls. Dark green cedars of Lebanon with unfurled trembling arms herald the arrival of Lullingdon Manor. This is glorious Warwickshire under a pale blue, ever-lightening sky. The car slows down.

"Okay, windows up and music down," orders Luke as they turn off the forest road. They pass a picturesque brick-built lodge house. The car rattles over a cattle grid and passes lichen covered granite gateposts. On more than one occasion, Luke returned home from school to find nervous, giggling girls waiting for him at these gateposts. They turn a corner and cross a bridge over a moat, then up a steep gravel drive. There it is: Lullingdon. The ancient manor stands on raised ground at the edge of the forest. Luke pulls up beside the grand entrance.

"Come in for a drink," he says with a wink as he gets out of the car. Joe looks pleased but Archie looks ill again. His face is so white that his ginger hair, by contrast, appears radioactive.

"I'll wait in the car... feeling a bit queasy," he says.

Joe is smiling, lost in his own sense of well-being. He steps cautiously upon the crunchy gravel with his bare feet. In the past, he has struggled with the fact that Luke lives in such a grand mansion, but now they have all been through so much he doesn't think twice about past insecurities. In fact as he makes his way to the house he has forgotten he is only wearing paisley Y-fronts.

There is an all-pervading sense of peace at Lullingdon. Joe savours the quietness of the place, which unsettled him on his first visit. That was when Joe and Archie were passengers in another friend's car. Luke was being dropped off and he invited them in for a coffee. For Joe, a teenager living on a council estate on the edge of Birmingham, the beauty of Lullingdon and the Forest of Arden had been overwhelming. Archie was very drunk on that first visit and embarrassingly he had sworn a lot in front of Luke's father, David Rogers, who had been reading on the garden terrace.

David Rogers's life is quite a story. Growing up in the back-to-back tenements of Birmingham, he went on to become a self-made multi-millionaire. He speaks with a Home Counties accent. His wife, Annie, Luke's mother, has a completely different story. She is from an established well-to-do family and grew up in a Georgian rectory near Guildford in Surrey. Her only sister, Rosalind, married a Labour Peer and they have one son, Jamie, who is seven years older than his cousin, Luke. Jamie, a former day-boy at Charterhouse School, has followed his father into politics. Joe and Archie met all of these people at Luke's eighteenth birthday party.

Lullingdon stands serenely in the pale morning light, surrounded by long, timeless shadows. Joe stares at the white stucco house and recalls a conversation with Luke's father, who had said the house was unusual, architecturally speaking.

"The main part of the building is classical, dating from the eighteenth century," Mr Rogers had explained as he took Joe on an impromptu tour of the property.

"The building has various idiosyncrasies, a steeply-pitched slate roof, which doesn't fit with the classical idiom. The stucco, heavy cornices, full height pilasters, tall sash windows, all an attempt by a Georgian to make the place look grand. Fortunately, they'd been restrained by budget and simplicity won the day."

Now, many months later, Joe ponders that Lullingdon Manor really is a fascinating amalgamation of different styles. His eyes rest upon the jewel of a timber-framed building that is attached to the main part of the stucco house. Like the main house, it has two levels, but the upper storey projects forward of the ground floor. Luke's father had said that it was "jettied". This was the original "hall house", a very ancient manor built from great oak trees at a time when wolves roamed Arden.

Red bricks, glowing crimson in the morning light, are set between ancient timbers, turned silver-grey by many centuries. Some distance beyond the timber-framed building and on the other side of a lawn, lies a range of farm buildings under gables and rusty red corrugated metal roofing. Black paint has peeled off large tongue-and-groove doors. A stable block has been converted into garages. This is where Luke's father keeps his collection of cars, including a stunning black 1969 Bentley. When he was a boy, Luke would fall asleep on the back seat of the Bentley with a blanket thrown over him, on long adventurous journeys.

Joe has always been baffled that such a fine car is kept in a rather dilapidated building.

Massive stones underpin the walls of one of the old barns. These stones have been reused in many buildings through the ages. Bales of hay are stacked against them, fodder for the wild ponies that live in the forest. Centuries ago, the ponies were cross bred with Arab horses to produce strong, fast animals, used in the logging industry, but now everything is mechanised so the ponies run free. One of the walls of a barn has partially collapsed, bricks are left in a heap upon the dew soaked grass. Joe likes the fact that these outbuildings are almost derelict. It is comforting for him to think that Luke's parents can live with something that has failed.

Joe and Luke enter through the wide, oak front door of Lullingdon. Luke whispers.

"Joe, keep quiet, I'll get you some clothes, everyone'll be in bed, just follow me." Joe follows cautiously, tiptoeing, as if he were a burglar. He follows Luke up the grand oak staircase onto a wide panelled landing, past an ornate doorway. They are walking on a thick cream carpet with grubby bare feet.

"Wait in there. I need a piss," whispers Luke.

He pushes Joe, quite hard, through an elegant doorway. Joe lands in the room, his feet thud onto the floor and he almost falls over. He turns to scowl at Luke, but he has already gone. Joe pulls himself together. He has never been in this room before. It is as high as it is wide; a perfect cube shape, all in opulent shades of green and cream with a grand stone fireplace as a focal point. Joe's mouth is wide open with surprise; he has never seen a room as splendid as this, at least not in a private house. His attention is immediately taken by the view from the three large sash windows. Through irregular, wavy panels of glass, he sees a moat overgrown with reeds, and there are meadows. Beyond, is the vast green forest merging into a golden horizon. Joe is mesmerised by the view.

"Blimey," he mutters to himself, resting his elbows against the window sill. Suddenly, there is a cough from behind. Joe, startled, jumps and turns around.

"Is that you Joe?" David, Luke's father, stands before him clutching a large leather-bound tome in one hand as if he is about to swat Joe with it.

"Eh? Um, oh, yeah, good evening Mr Rogers."

"Well, it's morning actually. Are those leaves that are stuck to you?"

Joe looks down and sees several bits of aquatic plant are attached to his underpants. He is also alarmed to see that his body is covered in smears of mud and that his feet have marked the cream carpet.

"Sorry! We've been swimming." Joe tries to say this in a-matter-of-fact kind of way and he adds a beguiling smile.

"Where? I can't imagine the municipal pools are open at this time."

"In the lake, in the forest" replies Joe.

"Swimming in the lake in the forest?"

After a thoughtful pause, David smiles and then he allows his large, bear-like frame to fall back into the old battered green leather armchair. Soon comfortable, he tries to find his page again. Joe has disturbed his time of early morning study and now he feels awkward in sharing his space. He thinks surely some further explanation for his presence in underpants is required, but apparently it isn't.

David is aged sixty but he looks considerably younger, dressed in casual blue jeans and a blue hooded sweatshirt; similar clothes to what his son Luke might wear. He is a cool, slightly Italian looking man, with a sharp, hooked beak of a nose. He goes sailing and skiing with Luke a few times a year. Joe likes David because he always seems to be so relaxed and down to earth. It is confusing to Joe that Luke's family are so easy to be with, and yet they are so wealthy. He doesn't normally feel particularly comfortable with the better off. But then Luke's family are in a league of their own, at least compared with anyone else that Joe has ever met. Although Joe likes David, he is relived when Luke barges in waving a pair of jogging bottoms and a sweatshirt.

"So you're up Dad."

David looks up from his book; a bushy eyebrow is raised.

Luke continues. "I'm going to make us a drink Dad, do you want a coffee?"

David smiles and nods. Luke throws the clothes over to Joe and disappears again. Joe struggles to maintain some dignity as he put the clothes on.

As soon as Joe is dressed, David looks up from his book.

"It's good to see you this morning, Joe. How are things with you? How've you been coping, since the loss of your parents I mean? I hope you don't mind me asking?"

"That's a long time ago now," replies Joe in a quiet voice.

"Well, yes, I know, but I lost my parents in the war. That's a very long time ago but I still think about them, surprisingly often actually."

"Well, I do think about them. I dream about them too."

David nods reassuringly and he smiles warmly. "My mother was quite a character, she claimed to be the great, great, granddaughter of the Earl of Shrewsbury, perhaps it was true, but she and my father were quite penniless. It's your grandfather that you live with now isn't it?"

"Yeah, that's right. There aren't too many rules so it's okay."

"I see, and you live on the…Broadway estate, don't you?" David appears to be slightly uncomfortable as he asks this. Joe feels a shudder go through him. He had been prepared to share about the loss of his parents given David's similar loss, but now the ground beneath his feet begins to move. The question has made him feel uncomfortable. In fact, it is almost like a betrayal for David to pry into the Broadway estate, especially when he lives in such splendour. Joe feels old insecurities coming to the fore. That one question has brought his two worlds colliding. He feels a need to protect himself from embarrassment, even to protect David from the brutal reality of what the place that he calls home is really like. Joe decides not to give much away, he won't mention his grandfather being made redundant from his job as the estate's caretaker. Joe tries to control his face; the ends of his mouth are pulling down. It's been such a good night, why does reality have to arrive so brutally?

"It's not too bad," he lies.

Joe feels exposed. In an attempt to salvage some dignity he decides to mention his most important piece of news.

"I leave for university in a few days."

"Ah. Now that's exciting. What are you going to study?"

"Gardening. No! I mean landscape architecture."

"Interesting. At which university?

"Sheffield."

Joe feels he is moving onto firmer ground. "Aren't you an architect, Mr Rogers?"

"Well, in a way I suppose. I'm a developer really. I'm just a simple builder. Do call me David by the way."

"I'd like to make sure we never build anything like the Broadway estate again," says Joe, a little more confidently.

David shifts uneasily in his leather chair. He looks away and scratches the back of his neck. Joe wonders if he has said something wrong, or is this another sign that landscape architecture isn't a good choice? Joe mulls it over and then decides to change the topic of conversation.

"How big is the forest?" he asks.

David sits forward in his chair. This is one of his favourite subjects.

"Our surviving bit of the forest is about two thousand acres. That might sound big, but it seems to be getting smaller as I get older. Shakespeare used to visit this part of Arden, you do know that don't you?"

"Yeah, he got caught for poaching didn't he?"

"That's right. Lullingdon would've been pretty remote back then, a day's ride from town." David looks downcast. "Now you can see the lights of the city from our attic windows. I'm sure those lights are getting a little closer every year."

Joe feels a shudder of disappointment go through him. Of course, he knows it is just a remnant of the old forest, and that the city with its run-down council estates, and his own home in one of them, isn't very far away. But the summer has been spent with his friends in the forest and they have had little need for anywhere else.

Joe is feeling hot and bothered, and the borrowed clothes are uncomfortable. He turns around and for a moment leans against the window sill, staring out at the brightening world. He looks over manicured lawns and garlanded borders tumbling down to a lily-filled moat. The morning sunshine glitters on the water. Beyond the gardens are open meadows, bathed in gold. A sudden movement catches Joe's eye. He watches a brown pony cantering effortlessly through the meadow, tail held high like a banner. It is one of the wild ponies from the forest, with pleasing Arab proportions. Joe feels the same sense of physical energy as when they were driving through the forest listening to U2.

David leans further forward in his chair.

"Humble beginnings can be a great blessing you know, Joe. I guess you must be eighteen now, the same age as Luke. You're young men. Here, let me read you this, it might help at university."

With considerable effort, Joe breaks away from watching

the pony. He turns around and nods.

David continues. "It's a proverb of Solomon. 'Above all else, guard your heart, for it is the wellspring of life.'"

There is an awkward silence. David turns a page.

"Thanks," says Joe, searching for what to say next. He scratches his head. "You know, I'm not sure landscape architecture is a good choice."

David raises his eyebrows. "Well, choose what brings you joy, so you don't have regrets when you're as old as me."

There is another awkward silence. Joe looks puzzled. He is trying to digest David's words.

"How do you mean, like…?"

David looks exasperated. "Try to be clear about what you enjoy doing, that could show you the way to go. Life's all about the heart. If your motives are good, everything works out in the end."

David shuts his book; the interview has come to an end. Joe is touched by David's kindness, even though he is unsure how helpful his advice has been. He feels that he can trust David, as if he could confide in him, about his struggles in life, and even that he has come to the conclusion that he's got a hole in his heart, that will never be filled.

Luke comes bursting into the drawing room, grinning, with a tray of steaming coffees. David gets up from his deep, comfortable seat with considerable effort, and he takes his coffee in a mug with *Dad* written across it. He walks over to Joe, places a strong hand upon his shoulder, and looks him in the eye.

"I asked about your estate earlier because I had an odd dream about it last night."

"Oh, what was in the dream?" asks Joe, cautiously.

"It was all very strange as dreams often are." David turns

and stares out of the window, as if contemplating whether or not to continue. He turns back to face Joe.

"I do remember, there was a river flowing by your estate, by an impressive Gothic gatehouse. There isn't a river there really of course, but in the dream you and Luke needed to cross this raging torrent. One of you was reluctant to cross it. I wouldn't have mentioned it but it was so vivid and it's such a coincidence to see you here this morning, dripping wet! Anyway, look Joe, do remember, you're always welcome here at Lullingdon."

With that, David leaves the room. Joe is uncertain how he feels about featuring in that dream; he wonders what it could possibly mean. Do dreams actually mean anything? The words he remembers most clearly are: *You're always welcome here at Lullingdon.*

Luke speaks up, shattering Joe's introspection.

"Don't worry about my dad. He's always going on about his dreams and weird things. Just the other day he was telling me about death; you can imagine what a cheerful chat that was!"

"What's this about you being related to the Earl of Shrewsbury?"

"Did he tell you about that? Nothing is proven, I shouldn't mention it."

Luke and Joe make their way outside. They find Archie sitting on the bonnet of the Mini. Some colour has returned to his face.

"I've been sick," he announces proudly.

Luke is curious. "Really? Did you put your fingers down your throat?"

"Yeah," Archie replies, sounding earnest.

Luke and Joe look at each other, eyes wide, eyebrows raised. They turn back to Archie, who is much more cheerful now he is getting proper attention. There follows a detailed conversation on the colour and content of Archie's vomit. There is some relief from Luke that he doesn't need to clean it up. Archie has already covered it all with gravel. Then an unexpected silence descends. The three friends just stand there, staring at the ground in front of them. It's beginning to sink in; this isn't just the end of a night out, it's the end of a major chapter in their lives. Joe breaks the silence. "It's hard to believe isn't it? We'll be going our separate ways in a few days."

Archie nods. "Yeah, I know, end of an era."

Luke looks up and he chuckles.

"What you laughing at?" asks Joe.

"Nerdmobiles!"

They remember back to school, when the three of them first got to know each other. It was utter madness in the technology class, something close to a riot. Joe and Luke shared a drawing board and they used to draw imaginary vehicles on it, the so-called nerdmobiles. They were invalid carriages, designed to give their teacher, Mr Walters, a degree of mobility and dignity should he ever meet with a terrible accident with the circular saw. For example, if he were to lose his legs, or even his head. There was some precedent for this. Mr Walters had already lost three fingers in a messy accident with the dreaded circular saw, which brooded in the corner of the workshop. The boys used the saw with extreme caution, but Mr Walters continued to treat it with a rather cavalier attitude, as if he knew it would be fatal to show it any fear.

Their nostalgia continues as Luke and Joe recall binding Archie to their drawing board. This incident occurred when Mr Walters was delayed and there was the usual mayhem in the technology class. Archie said the pivoted drawing board reminded him of a medical operating table. To illustrate his point, he had reclined across the board. Joe and Luke then used a whole reel of masking tape to ensure he didn't get up again. They also attached straws to Archie's nose in imitation of drip feeds. When Mr Walters's lanky frame loomed in the doorway, Joe, Luke and the rest of the class scrambled back to their seats, leaving Archie stranded. Mr Walters screamed hysterically at Archie.

"What the hell are you doing, boy?"

He had never bellowed in such a commanding voice before. Stunned silence. Then the drawing board started squeaking. Archie was trying to escape, kicking his legs wildly into the air. His head turned so purple you could see his scalp through his ginger hair. Mr Walters had to cut him free. Joe almost wet himself he laughed so much.

They reminisce about their walks home from school, through the fields, into town. The fifteen-minute walk took them hours.

"We used to have such a laugh," says Joe.

"Getting home was an odyssey," splutters Luke.

"What's an odyssey when it's at home?" asks Joe.

"It's Greek isn't it, for a long journey," explains Archie.

Luke smiles at Archie and he slaps him on the back. "Come on you, no more school for us!" With that, they all clamber back into the Mini. Luke races them into town at break-neck speed.

Archie is understandably agitated by Luke's very fast driving. They are hurtling around tight bends and narrow streets fronted by an assortment of terraced houses and small industrial premises.

"Slow down, Luke, will you? A lot of cats live around here!"

"I haven't killed anything yet, have I?" replies Luke, irritated.

They are getting close to where Archie lives. When Archie asks why he is the one who always has to be dropped off first, Luke replies impassively.

"It's so me and Joe can have a meaningful conversation without you."

Archie isn't sure if that is meant to be a joke. He goes very quiet. Luke takes a tight corner with a screech of the wheels. They get thrown to the left. They are driving through an old part of the town. The narrow streets are huddled around the town centre. It's an untidy place, but has a certain charm. Everyone knows their neighbour around here. They spin around another corner and they all get thrown to the right. Now they're on Holland Street, which is where Archie lives.

"Okay, windows up and music down," says Luke.

"I'm not bothered about that," replies Archie, sounding dejected. He is still thinking about what kind of conversation Luke and Joe are going to have after he's been dropped off. He is also thinking about how he's going to say goodbye to Joe. This will probably be the last time he sees him before he leaves for university. Archie fidgets nervously with his ear, then he pretends to sort through the music cassette case.

They drive past a little factory that makes boiler parts. Tucked in beside it is the bowling green, popular with older people during the day and at night serving as a hang-out for Archie and his mates. They pass the little Holland Street theatre, sandwiched between red brick terraced houses. Over the years, the little theatre has grown and taken over several of the neighbouring houses. Archie's dad is a hospital clerk, but he is also involved with amateur dramatics in that little theatre. Luke finds a place to park the car. The only sign of life is a milk float, pulling up in front of Archie's house. The house has a tiny front garden;

you could easily lean over and tap on the glass of the living room window. The sprightly milkman jumps out from his float and deposits two pints on Archie's doorstep. Most of the terraced houses look the same, except for Archie's, which stands out with tacky stone cladding and irregularly shaped plastic windows. Archie has the small box bedroom at the back of the house, where he sleeps on a foldaway camper bed, a temporary measure that has gone on for several years. Beside Archie's camper bed is a basket, where his dog sleeps. From Archie's bedroom window you can see the neon lights of the town centre, including the glaring "M" of the McDonalds burger bar, a place that's been a regular haunt for Archie, Joe and Luke, especially when they have been asked to leave pubs for being underage.

The three friends sit in the car, nobody's sure what to say. Eventually, Archie puts the music cassettes down.

"I can't wait to leave this place," he says.

"Why? It's alright here," replies Luke.

"It's posh compared to where I live," adds Joe, trying to be supportive.

Both Luke and Joe know Archie's house well. They used to call in virtually everyday on their way back from school. They would watch *Neighbours* on the telly and fantasise about Kylie Minogue.

Archie has made up his mind, there will be no goodbye speeches from him. It is just not his style. He gets out of the car, smiles briefly at Joe, and then he slams the door shut.

"Hey! I was going to get in the front seat!" yells Joe. But it is too late. Archie has gone.

A dog is barking madly. It is in the front living room of Archie's house. The milkman says good morning; he gets a gruff response.

Archie is well known in this neighbourhood and people often recognise him. He has usually got his cute dog with him, Deefor, a wiry little terrier who is barking in the window now. Archie is also known as a troublemaker. In his earlier teens, the police brought him home a few times after being cautioned for alcohol-related offences. His friends are a civilising influence on him, but his moral compass still drifts all over the place. The trouble is, he takes in everything from his older brother, Douglas, like a sponge. It's usually about drinking, drugs, and sex, information that Archie, Joe and Luke have found fascinating. Archie's gone through times of being almost feral.

Joe opens the front car door from the inside and he struggles out. Archie turns on his heels and walks back to the car. He grabs hold of Joe in an awkward hug and then he walks off again, fumbling in his pocket for his house key. When he disappears behind his front door, he buries his face in Deefor's fur. The dog yelps for joy, its tail a wagging blur.

3 Leaving Home

After a few minutes of speeding down main roads and careering around the suburban lanes of Sutton Coldfield, Luke and Joe are approaching the Broadway estate. This is the 1960s local authority housing estate where Joe lives. The car turns a bend. Standing before them is a splendid early Victorian Gothic gatehouse, built from fiery orange Staffordshire bricks. It is an architectural masterpiece. It appears otherworldly next to the brutal housing estate. Set within its frontage is an arched, oak door. Nobody can remember it ever being opened.

Some distance behind the gatehouse, hidden from view by mature beech woods, is a seminary; another Gothic masterpiece. The beech woods are luxuriant and they provide a splendid backdrop, but the grey blocks of the Broadway estate are malicious teeth, ready to bite. The beech woods can be seen from Hannah's bedroom in her parents' house, which is not far away, on top of a hill. Hannah marks the passing of the seasons by the trees; lush green to resplendent gold. For her, there is an air of mystery about the Gothic gatehouse, and she longs to know what is on the other side of those trees but, even in winter, the trees keep the seminary hidden.

Joe notices that Luke hasn't taken the usual route into the housing estate. Instead, he's pulled up on the main road, next to a bus stop and a pedestrian alleyway. Luke used to drop Joe off outside his home but on the last visit he got a puncture from the broken glass. This new dropping-off arrangement doesn't bother Joe. He's grateful for the lift and while he doesn't mind Luke seeing where he lives, it's just as well that any other friends don't get to see the condition of the estate full on.

"Hey, that was a record time," says Luke.

"Well done," replies Joe. "Anyway, I'd better get off now. Thanks for the lift."

Joe is surprised to see that Luke is also getting out of the car; he is walking around to him. Luke looks Joe in the eye and smiles.

"Some friends are forever. You're one of those friends."

Joe smiles, looks down at his feet. He remembers they won't be seeing each other again, for a year, while Luke is off travelling around the world.

"I should have tried harder. I mean to take a year off too. I wish I was going with you."

Luke nods sympathetically. He gives Joe a hug, and then he's back in the car. The window is lowered.

"Get to know the nurses in Sheffield. I want to hear about some results!"

Joe promises he won't disappoint, he raises a hand to bid Luke farewell. The car screeches off, leaving black tyre marks.

Joe walks down the alleyway and enters the estate. He looks around the place. More smashed glass and litter than usual, some new graffiti on a wall. He scans the tenements. His eye is drawn to the looming tower block at the end of the estate road. It is built of stained concrete panels. It has been empty for two years, awaiting demolition. Joe is an arrival from another world. Since last night he has become accustomed to beautiful things. This scene offends him. The weather is worse here and a heavy greyness covers everything.

The Broadway estate hasn't always been so run down. In the early years it was quite a cheery place with a sense of community. Mums stood gossiping on their doorsteps. At the end of the day, they would give tonsil-rattling screams for their kids to return. The children would then appear, back from the wild, with grazed knees, runny noses, and glowing faces.

Joe hasn't always lived on the Broadway estate. He used to live in a semi-detached house with his mum and dad at the bottom of Hannah's hill. In his early childhood, Joe and his family enjoyed visiting his nan and grandad, who did live on the Broadway estate. Joe played with the estate kids. Some of them were almost like brothers and sisters for Joe, who had no siblings of his own. They played their games in the communal gardens; football, cricket, rounders, water fights on hot summer days. Mums and dads joined in too. Joe's grandparents were at the heart of the new community, right from the beginning. Grandad was appointed resident caretaker in 1969. He was also a father figure to the fatherless kids. He was always fixing their bicycles. Nan helped out the single mums as the informal resident baby sitter.

The newspapers heralded the Broadway estate as a vision of modernity. An old manor house and cottages were swept away, replaced with Le Corbusier's deck-access walkways in the sky. At ground level, the landscaping was supposed to be inspired by Capability Brown, but it didn't really seem to belong to anyone. That is why the council caretaker and gardeners were needed. The estate was part of a government-funded housing initiative. The homes were built quickly, using an innovative, standardised production technique. Novel features included under-floor heating, and big swivel windows that were easy to clean. People queued up to take one of the futuristic homes. The Mayor opened the estate. Grandad and Nan had been at the opening ceremony. In his speech, the Mayor said the estate was part of a "brave new world" that would solve the housing crisis. He had specifically said that the resident caretaker would be its "custodian". Those words meant a lot to Grandad. He took the responsibility seriously.

Now Joe stands at the end of the alleyway on this grey morning. He spots Grandad in the distance, off for his shift in the local shop. Grandad stops to inspect the communal garden outside his home, where Nan's cherry tree has pride of place. When he was a younger man, Grandad was particularly handsome. Now what is left of his receding hair is silver, he has a double chin and a slight stoop. He sees his grandson and waves cheerfully. A boy and a girl are skipping towards Joe, empty crisp packets blowing at their feet.

"Hi Joe!" The little girl shouts with great enthusiasm. She is wearing a long pink jumper and pink leggings; her hair is platted into pigtails.

"Hi Belinda!"

Joe is always happy to see little Belinda, aged six, and her brother, Owen, aged twelve, who is dressed in a smart red shirt and denim jeans. These are good kids. They are Joe's neighbours, from a poor family, with a dad out of work, but they are always well turned out and very polite. Today, however, there is something wrong with Owen. He's got a black eye.

"How did you get that?" Joe asks.

Owen looks at his feet. "Jimmy Stokes hit me," he

whispers.

Joe makes a mental note to himself, *Have a word with Jimmy Stokes*; he is one of the estate's brutalised bullies.

Joe recalls the shooting stars from the previous night. He wishes these kids could see such a wondrous thing. He turns to Owen.

"Have you ever seen the stars, really clearly?" he asks.

"Do you mean like Jimmy Tarbuck?"

Joe tries to explain what he means, but he gets a blank response.

"Don't worry about it. So, where are you going so early, anyway?" he asks.

"I'm taking Belinda to her dance class," replies Owen, and then he turns to the main road to check if their bus is coming. He turns back to Joe. "Hey, will you play football with me later?"

"Sorry mate, I really need to get some sleep. I've been up all night."

"Bus! Bus!" shouts Belinda, yanking Owen by the arm. They run off towards the bus stop. Joe watches them board the double-decker. He can see them through the dirty windows as they take the front seat, upstairs. They wave as the bus pulls off. It disappears down the straight, tree-lined main road. There is very little traffic. Joe heads for home. He is the only person around.

Two days later, Joe has enjoyed some very long sleeps. He has packed his gear and he is ready to leave for Sheffield University. The sky is overcast with heavy grey clouds; looks like rain. Something wonderful has happened, though. Grandad has used his savings to buy Joe a car. It is a second-hand brown Skoda, it runs well, and it's Joe's. It is freedom to go wherever he wants. It is a gift that far exceeds his wildest expectations. The car has made Joe feel more excited about the future, not least because he'll be able to take girls out in it. Mingled doubts about leaving home, and even leaving Hannah, have faded.

The Skoda is parked next to a couple of old bangers on the estate road. Black tape holds up its wing mirrors. It is now packed full of everything Joe needs for his new student life. The car's suspension is weighed down by dozens of tins of food, provisions from Grandad and the neighbours. Joe laughs at Scruff, their old cat, who is curled beside the tins. Scruff is a character. He often followed Joe to school. "Not this time little fella," he whispers. Scruff purrs as soon as Joe picks him up, stops when he is deposited on the pavement. Scruff looks around, wearily. Happy there is no impending danger, he looks up; bright green eyes meet Joe's blue eyes. It's hard for Joe to pull himself away, but he must. Everything is packed. He's said goodbye to Grandad, and given him a big hug. Scruff scampers off back home, tail in the air. Joe is ready for his new adventure. He starts the car, it rattles into life, and then he pulls off, swerving around a broken bottle. He beeps the horn triumphantly. Grandad leans out of the lounge window, waving enthusiastically. Belinda and Owen and their parents are waving from next-door. Joe glances sideways and waves back, and then the car disappears around the bend. Grief engulfs Grandad. Nobody sees the tears. Joe passes the empty tower block and then the Gothic gatehouse. He is off!

Joe turns his car onto the busy dual carriageway. After a few minutes, it's the roller-coaster flyover. His heart beats faster. He is climbing into the sky. Hands grip the steering wheel, more tightly. Lanes merge. The urban fringe whizzes by with industry, sprawling housing estates, and marching pylons. It is all fragmented under a metallic sky.

The traffic is heavy. There are beeping horns and aggressive hand gestures. Joe's eyes bulge at the highway signs and the gantries displaying ominous warnings. The towering lighting masts appear to be designed to search for escapees. It is all utilitarian and ugly. Information overload. Beads of sweat are on Joe's brow. He has never driven alone before, he is totally inexperienced, and has certainly never driven in such heavy traffic; but he is excited. Even in these testing conditions, every now and again he puts his foot down hard on the accelerator to feel the power. Butterflies are in his stomach but all obstacles are surmountable. A big blue sign says, *The North.*

Urban detritus passes away and it is soon time for Joe to pull off the motorway. Now he follows country roads along a route carefully planned with Grandad. He drives through Staffordshire at fifty miles per hour, with rural sights passing by. A westerly wind blows the clouds away to reveal a bright blue sky. Joe is passing through a landscape of wide-open barley fields and scattered green hedgerows. Combine harvesters, gathering in a late harvest, are silhouetted on a ridge of hills. Farmsteads appear and vanish like isolated worlds. The dark, wooded hilltops are all new to Joe. How can he have been a stranger to all of this for so long?

Half an hour later, there are rich green pastures and herds of Frisian cows, but no more barley fields. Joe has his cassette player turned up, loud. *Kiss me* by Stephen "Tin Tin" Duffy covers the sound of the Skoda's labouring engine; it is climbing a long, steep, hill. The car keeps climbing. The song finishes and the landscape changes again. Sheep are dotted randomly in rough hill grazing country. Stone walls border the road, blocking the view. A field gateway suddenly reveals a panorama but vanishes in a blink.

The Skoda rattles over a cattle grid. Joe is now driving through a wild, bleak, open moor. The sky is darker and it feels colder. There are swathes of pink heather and brilliant flashes of yellow gorse. Higher and higher, the car keeps climbing with its noisy labouring engine. Streaks of grey mist gather across the moor, obscuring Joe's view. The windscreen wipers are on but they don't help. The road narrows and the growing darkness feels ominous. Streaks of mist are coagulating into a murky fog. It is no ordinary fog, it is becoming a thick black smog. Through a clearing, orange flickering flames can be seen. The moors are being consumed by fire. Joe panics. He is shouting out loud.

"What do I do? What do I do? Should I go back?"

"No! No!" Joe answers himself in a calmer tone.

"There's no going back now."

The car disappears into the smoke. Joe's life will never be the same again.

4 Kensington

Joe feels as if he has been stuck underground for ages. In reality, it's only been an anxious seven minutes, so far. He turns to avoid the foul breath of the tall man standing next to him.

Is he really reading that book? Joe wonders, crossly.

The man is leaning over Joe's head, holding a handle attached to the ceiling of the train carriage. With his other hand he is holding a book to his face. The book is positioned at the end of his nose. Surely his eyes can't focus on the words.

Is he just hiding behind it?

The poor man can't hold the book any further away because other people's heads are in the way. Joe is feeling very grumpy. As far as he is concerned, that book is far too close to his own face; it's in his air space. He imagines how one jolt of the train could result in it poking him in the eye. He fantasises about grabbing hold of the book and stamping on it, but there isn't enough room on the train to stamp on anything. Joe can't even lift his leg. The carriage is absolutely packed with commuters. Joe breathes steadily and closes his eyes. The air is humid and dirty. It is only Monday morning but the weekend is already a distant memory.

It is ten years since Joe left home for Sheffield University and more than six years since he arrived in London. On arriving in the big city his priority was to experience everything it had to offer. It's been a very long time since he last saw his grandad. The old gang of Joe, Luke, Archie, Cathy and Hannah, haven't been together for ages, although Joe still sees Archie regularly in the West End.

Joe's thoughts drift. He remembers sending a postcard to Hannah recently with a picture of Trafalgar Square on it.

I wonder why she hasn't replied? She's probably got herself a boyfriend.

Joe's eyes open and dart around the carriage, looking for something pleasant to rest upon. Suddenly, the stuffy silence is broken by news from the world beyond the tunnel. A train driver's voice crackles through the carriages via the intercom system. Commuters listen, intently, to each word delivered in a rolling West Indian accent.

"The queue for a platform at Earl's Court's gettin' shorta. We'll be der in about five minutes. Tanks for your patience folks."

Commuters digest the message. The carriages resound with huffing and puffing and the angry rustling of newspapers, but the relief is tangible. Still, five minutes sounds a very long time to Joe. He tries to reassure himself. *At least we're not forgotten.*

Joe's eyes settle on a turquoise bag, hung over the shoulder of a businesswoman. The colour is mesmerising. He imagines it is the colour of the Caribbean Sea. His imagination wanders further. For a moment he is lying with the girl from the Bounty advert on a golden beach. Then the scene clouds over and he frowns. Coming forth like a sea fog is a memory of his first day at university. That first morning, he awoke to the sight of grey breezeblocks and fog outside the window. He had not expected dreaming spires but his halls of residence really was awful. It was like a prison block. He was also disappointed with his flat mates. He had expected his fellow students to be stimulating; at least as interesting as Luke, Archie, Hannah and Cathy. No such luck, the students were dull in comparison.

On that first night away at university, Joe felt homesick and bereft of friends. He slept fitfully. It was a long, starless night that offered no dreams. He overslept. It was a rush to get dressed and prepared in time for registration.

It was a crisp, autumn morning, the fog lifted, but it remained misty. Joe crossed the campus lawns for the first time, scanning the windows of the nurses' residence. He glanced over to his brown Skoda and was grateful to see it safe where he had left it. The air buzzed with excited young students, away from home for the first time. Joe walked quickly, along a busy main road lined with old grit-stone terraced houses and shops. As he continued towards the landscape architecture department, a bit of blue sky appeared. He felt excited and a little nervous, like a boy about to enter the big school for the first time. He passed an imposing church, and then turned off the main road. And there it was, the landscape architecture building. He was actually early. The department was in an impressive, stone Victorian mansion. *This is more like it!* Joe spent a lot of time in that building over the following four years.

The woman in the carriage with the turquoise bag looks sideways. She notices that Joe is staring at her bag and that he is wearing a big smile. He is remembering an old man in a tweed jacket, standing by a red Volvo estate, next to the landscape architecture building. The old man was bent double as he loaded tree saplings into the back of his car. He turned and stared at Joe, like a crow about to stab a worm.

"Morning," he snapped, breath visible in the cold air.

"Do you need a hand?" Joe asked, cautiously.

"I did," the old man sounded flustered. "But this is the last one."

With considerable effort the old man straightened his back. He softened when he saw Joe's beaming face and shining eyes. Joe peered into the back of the Volvo. Even though he was about to become a landscape architect, he knew embarrassingly little about green things.

"What kind of trees are they?"

"Do you want their Latin names or common?"

"Common."

"Thank goodness for that, they're silver birches, oh, and a few beeches." The old man seemed pleased that Joe had taken an interest in his trees.

"Are they for your garden?"

"No, they're for anywhere that needs them."

"How do you mean?"

"Are you a fresher?"

"Yeah."

"For landscape architecture?"

"Yeah."

"Oh, right, I'm Donald Oakes, what's your name?"

Joe. So you're Professor Oakes?"

"That's right, Joe. Let me tell you, it's always a good idea to have a few saplings in the back of your car, if you've got a car…"

"I have."

"Well, it's probably hard for a well off student like you to appreciate it, but a lot of people who live in flats will never plant a tree!"

Joe looked aghast, although he'd never actually planted anything in his life.

The professor continued. "Someone's got to plant a tree for them, Joe. Think about roadside verges and roundabouts."

"Okay."

"Well, eighty per cent of open space in our cities is highways land. We need to merge utility, with beauty!" The professor had a wild look in his eye.

Joe scratched his head. "So, you're just going to plant your trees anywhere?"

"Correct!"

"What about if you get caught?"

"Don't worry about that, I'll be planting them in the middle of the night."

Joe looked impressed. "And you've never been caught?"

The professor winced. "Well, there was one incident."

"What happened?"

The professor continued, cautiously. "Well, it was when I was planting a Scots Pine beside a railway station. A stupid police officer thought I was planting a bomb."

"What did he do?"

"He arrested me. I spent the night in the clink."

"Wow, and that hasn't put you off?"

"Not at all. It's still easier to beg for mercy than to ask for permission."

Joe liked to imagine the professor charging through the night like a comic superhero, secretly making everything beautiful.

On that first morning the professor invited Joe into the landscape architecture building for a coffee. As they walked in together Joe thought that landscape architecture might be the right choice after all.

The woman with the turquoise bag is attractive. She is standing very close to Joe in the packed train carriage. With two dainty fingers and a thumb, she clasps the pole. Fatter, sweatier hands with stubby fingers also grasp it. Suddenly, the train clanks into life, it jolts forward. As soon as it is started it stops again with a screech of the brakes. The man with the book pressed against his nose is catapulted into the back of a businessman, who yelps. There are mumbled apologies and then the man with the book quickly resumes his reading position as if nothing has happened. The woman with the turquoise bag loses her grip on the pole and somebody else's hand takes her spot. She has to lean upon Joe, her hands resting on his shoulder. She avoids eye contact, but Joe is aware of her breasts pressing against him. The woman can't even put her hands down by her side because other commuters are pressing against her. All she can do for the moment is to hold onto Joe, her body pressed against his. Resigned to this awkward position she briefly looks Joe in the eye and smiles. They both begin to laugh. It is such a ridiculously intimate situation for strangers to be in. Joe is thinking. *Perhaps being packed like sardines is a turn up...*

The train jolts and immediately stops again. The sardines do a little reshuffling and the woman's body no longer needs to be folded into Joe's. She looks down at her feet, still smiling. Joe looks sideways as someone ruffles their broadsheet newspaper. There is a cartoon depicting the new Prime Minister as Walt Disney's Bambi. Joe closes his eyes. He hopes for an update on the Bounty girl on the beach, but she is nowhere to be found. Instead, a small ship sails into view. Joe's thoughts are drifting back to when he was on an all night booze cruise. *Oh, never again! Even this train is better than that...*

... Joe was with Archie and a group of Archie's media colleagues, on the election special all-night booze cruise on the River Thames. The voyage began at Kingston-upon-Thames and went all the way to Southend-on-Sea, before returning back to London. In the very early hours, Joe and Archie had stood on the prow of the barge looking across the fast flowing, black water. Large mobile phones, as big as bricks, had been ringing all night. Word got around ship that the election was a landslide. Joe drank a lot of beer that night but he still had his senses about him, unlike Archie who was totally wasted. As the ship chugged towards the Royal Festival Hall on London's South Bank, it was clear to Joe that something significant was going on. Lots of small vessels were appearing on the river. Police officers were lining the embankment. Two helicopters hovered noisily overhead. Then a police launch came alongside them, a police officer was shouting instructions to the crew. When they were almost opposite the Royal Festival Hall, Joe saw a crowd of people gathering around a stage. It was decorated with flashing disco lights. On the stage were a drum kit, other musical instruments and a rostrum.

A man in a suit climbed on stage with a woman. "That's the new Prime Minister!" someone yelled. "They've flown back to London already!"

The Prime Minister began speaking to the crowd through a microphone. It was very difficult for Joe to make out what he was saying. He just about heard the words, "A new dawn has broken..." and then the sun rose, immersing the river and the crowd in light. It was a never-to-be-forgotten sight. The ecstatic crowd roared and then the band, D:Ream, got on stage and played *Things can only get better!* They kept playing the song over and over as people celebrated.

Eventually, the little ship began chugging up the Thames again, with Joe feeling a renewed sense of vigour. Whilst Joe appreciated the historic moment, it all seemed to go over Archie's head. He'd had too much to drink, again. When Archie disembarked at Kingston, he missed his footing. He hit his head on the side of the barge and knocked himself out. There was a lot of blood. Joe tried to stem the flow with his shirt. He borrowed someone's mobile phone, the first time he'd used one, and dialled 999 for an ambulance. Joe travelled with Archie in the ambulance and they spent five hours waiting in casualty. *Never again!*

Joe finds London life intriguing, but he spent the first year looking like a rabbit caught in headlights. He would say "good morning" to complete strangers on the tube who would return a horrified look as if they were about to be mugged. When Joe first started work, the novelty of earning a good wage was wonderful. He used to put five pound notes into homeless people's sleeping bags. Now Joe is a more sophisticated man about town. He likes to wander around the museums and art galleries, examining the treasures of the world. He partakes in Soho's café society and enjoys meeting his cosmopolitan friends in Hoxton. He delights in London's architecture, its squares and parks. But Joe has also been feeling a bit tired of late. The pace of London life is so fast and it has been getting to him. The pavements are alive with people, and someone always wants the paving slab he is standing on.

Joe longs for peace and quiet, big skies, and wild places. His hopes for travel are dashed by insufficient funds or limited annual leave. He regularly pops into the travel agents on Kensington High Street, searching for glimmers of hope. On one visit, Joe asked if it was possible to visit the Sahara Desert for a long weekend. He explained he wanted to experience silence, to reconnect with his inner-self. The young lady behind the desk was intrigued. She asked if he'd considered Benidorm, out of season, as the pensioners are all in bed by nine. Joe surmised she must be on some kind of commission to sell Benidorm.

"That would be my idea of hell," he asserted.

The sales assistant returned to her theme.

"If you go to Benidorm there are coach trips to the mountains."

Joe slightly raised an eyebrow at the word *mountains,* but then he reiterated that his heart was really set on the desert. He wanted to see the wild flowers after the rains. The sales assistant concentrated hard and then to Joe's amazement she revealed a brochure showing a desert near Benidorm. He booked immediately. A few days later Joe was flagging down a car on a remote desert track, feeling disorientated and rather distressed. He had run out of water after traversing Spain's deepest gorge, but that is another story.

At last, the tube train jolts into action. This time, to the great relief of the passengers, it quickly picks up a reassuring speed. After a few minutes, they arrive at High Street Kensington. Through the windows, people look as if they are about to pounce on the train. The doors thunder open. A solid wall of cruel humanity elbows its way forward. A London Underground operative barks instructions like a lion tamer at the circus.

"Get back! Get back! Let the people off the train first!"

Joe feels his body being lifted involuntarily by the wave of smartly dressed commuters exiting the train. Before he takes one step of his own volition, he is halfway down the platform, clutching his brown leather briefcase to his chest. It is fortunate for Joe that this is his stop. He can allow himself to go with the flow. He has never quite got used to this morning ritual, even though he has been doing it for several years.

The wave of humanity crashes on to the steps amid a spray of human limbs. The steps lead up to an airy shopping arcade and the light of Kensington High Street, but down here it is the stampede of the wildebeest in the Serengeti. Joe is at the point where he needs to cross the river and climb the steep bank to be free from the snapping crocodiles. It is no place for the weak or the old. Joe approaches the first step and scowls as he is shoved in the back. He wants to turn around to remonstrate with whoever shoved him, but he might miss his purchase on the first step and be trampled to death.

Announcements are bleating out: "Move forward! Keep Moving!"

Joe must climb the steps. At last he reaches the summit and passes through a turnstile. He enters the vaulted shopping arcade. A little further on, there is a cool breeze, and then, at last, the real world. The sun is shining above the pleasantly proportioned canyon of Kensington High Street, and it feels warm on his face. Joe breathes deeply. After that long, hot tube journey, the spring air is fresh. For a moment, he rests, leaning back against a shop-front. He runs his fingers through his short-cropped hair and looks around. Rushing commuters are everywhere. Joe is often on Kensington High Street. He has been involved with the improvements that have been made to it. It looks smart.

Hordes of people are climbing up from the underground station, flowing out on to the street. These are the workers being ferried in, most are in their twenties or thirties. Many of them walk in pairs, chatting, and laughing, whilst others stride alone, more purposefully. These commuters form a tributary that merges into the main flow along the high street. Everyone is smart and dressed for action. The people coming in the opposite direction, flowing into the shopping arcade, are a different breed of commuter. They are Kensington's wealthy residents, heading down to their local underground station. They have a short journey to swanky offices in the City and West End. They are older, more varied, and exotic. A few younger women are scattered amongst them, and they are physically stunning. From his shop-front perch, Joe notes the quality of the gene pool.

Two heavily made-up elderly ladies chat to each other as they approach Joe. Their stooped bodies belie their perfectly sculpted faces. One of them wears a tartan mini-skirt and has a manicured bouffant hairdo in orange. The ladies walk past Joe, swinging tiny handbags. The one in the tartan skirt looks Joe up and down as she passes. An elderly gentleman follows in their wake, his wrinkled tortoise neck cranes out of an Armani suit. It seems that old age is just another little hurdle to jump over. This appetite for life is infectious. Joe pushes himself up from the shop window sill and walks over to the pedestrian crossing. His office is on the other side of the road, just around the corner.

Suddenly, Joe hears whistle-blowing. He turns around and through the crowd he sees flashing blue lights. There is a break in the traffic. Joe leans forward over the kerb to get a better view up the street. He can see police motorcycle outriders clearing the heavy rush hour traffic to the sides. A clear swathe of grey tarmac is revealed. Some car drivers are reluctant to move over. There is fierce whistle blowing from the police motorcyclists. One of them bashes his knuckles against the windscreen of a Mini Metro van. The poor driver, a florist, is confused about what she is supposed to be doing. The policeman screams at her. "Pull over! Pull over!"

Then, at the far end of the high street, a whole wall of police motorcycle outriders approaches, fast, with blue lights flashing. A wide, clear road stands before them. It is a strange sight.

"Lookz zerious mate, dun it?" says a youngish businessman in a sharp South African accent, turning to Joe.

"Yeah."

They stand together at the kerbside, watching. The line of police motorcycles and flashing blue lights get closer and closer. Other people on the pavement jockey for position, trying to get the best view of what is going on. For the younger commuters and tourists, this is a breaking news story, which they aren't going to miss, but Kensington's older residents continue bobbing up and down. They have seen it all before.

Kensington High Street is a scene of crowds and gleaming Art Deco department stores, and now this strange empty highway. Then, all of a sudden, it is whoosh... a long convoy of black limousines and vintage Rolls Royce's goes whizzing by. The spectacle is strangely timeless. Joe stands at the front of the crowd, beside the pedestrian crossing. He has to be careful as people are pushing from behind. The fleet of limousines is travelling too fast for Joe to see who the passengers are. He likes the colourful flags waving on the car's bonnets and roofs.

"Now zat's power!" says the South African, "You cin cross if you want to mate. Tha green manz flashing for ya."

The green man is indeed flashing to say it is safe to cross, but people are stuck on the pavement and precariously on the little island in the middle of the road. Nothing is going to stop this motorcade, certainly not a flashing green man. Joe marvels at the easy passage of the people in their limousines, straight through the cleared rush hour traffic. At the end of the motorcade is an ordinary black family saloon, a security car, which appears incongruously small behind a Phantom Rolls Royce. It has a neon sign in the rear window, flashing the words - *STAY BACK!*

"Zee yah mate," says the South African. Joe nods back and smiles. Within seconds of the convoy passing, the normal rush hour rhythm resumes. The green man flashes again and Joe crosses over the road. As he strolls into his place of employment, the Regeneration Company, he wonders if what just happened might have been a figment of his imagination.

The refurbished reception area gleams in white light. Joe

greets the glamorous fifty-something receptionist. She is wearing almost theatrical make-up, which doesn't seem to fit in with the minimalist surroundings. Her name is Natasha and she greets Joe in a forced posh accent. When she realises they are alone, Natasha's smile turns into a frown. She reverts to her native cockney and speaks out of the corner of her narrow mouth.

"I'm sorry lovey, there's trouble brewing around 'ere."

"What d'ya mean, Tash? What kind of trouble?"

"New rules and regs from Gaffer Flannel."

"Oh, no, what now?"

Natasha looks beyond Joe, she smiles graciously as a group of businessmen enter the reception area. One of the men speaks up.

"Good morning, we're here to see Mr Flannel."

"Ah, good morning," says Natasha, resuming her posh accent. "I think you mean Mr Flemel."

She invites them to take a seat. Natasha turns to Joe and whispers in her cockney accent.

"I don't like speaking about anyone behind their back, but somefing's got to be done about *Flannel*. I'll clobber him meself, if he ever speaks to me again the way he did earlier."

"Sorry, Tash, I've got to press on, I'm bursting for the loo," says Joe, anxious to avoid one of Natasha's long monologues.

But Natasha isn't ready to let him go yet. "Everyfing he does is designed to impress the board, he down't give a flying fig about the team."

"Yeah, I know, I know what you mean, but look…"

"Alright lovey, I can't natter on, I'd better get his nibs for this lot, tatta for now sweetie pie."

Vernon Flemel, alias *Flannel*, is a senior partner in the company; nobody likes him.

Joe walks through a doorway off the gleaming reception

area. He enters a slightly shabby open-plan office, where there are about fifty workstations. Over the last five years, Joe has received three promotions and each one has meant a new desk, closer to the coveted windows. Last week was his most recent promotion. He has finally achieved the heady accolade of a desk beside a window, with a beautiful view.

Joe yelps as his shoulders are forcibly grabbed from behind. He turns around. Two piercing Celtic blue eyes are fixed upon him. It's Jock, a large, boisterous, Scot, over six feet tall, sixty years of age, with long unkempt, grey hair.

"Ah, morning Jock, how are you?"

"Oh, I'm glad to be alive on such a fine morning!"

Jock is in the middle of showing Kylie, an attractive trainee from Australia, how to do a Scottish fling.

"We'll show you what we've learnt," he says, grabbing Joe's arm and swinging him around as he sings. Joe drops his brown leather briefcase to the floor and laughs as he is forced to do a couple of turns. Jock now grabs Kylie and he turns her around skilfully. Joe and Kylie step back, they watch with open mouths. Some tribal calling has taken hold of the old Scot. He is standing with his arms arced above his head, waiting, motionless. There is silence. Jock taps his right foot three times, as if in response to an imaginary piper. The atmosphere is charged. Jock begins to dance. His ungainly old body somehow leaps through the air like a deer. He embraces the space around him with his outstretched arms, like a ballerina. His bright eyes are dancing. He is back in the Scottish Highlands of his childhood. His dance lasts only a few seconds, but it is quite remarkable. He returns to earth with a thud and very heavy breathing. His face is as red as a beetroot. He is so breathless he can't speak. Joe and Kylie stare at each other, wide-eyed. Kylie pats Jock on the back, hard, to help his breathing.

"Are you okay, sport?"

"Could you give me a drop of mouth-to-mouth?"

"Nah!"

At last old Jock can mutter a few more words.

"I haven't done that for a long time!" he gasps.

He still looks a little shaky. Kylie says his dancing is brilliant and Joe agrees. Jock is still gasping for breath. Joe looks at him with some concern. After a while, Jock stands up straight and he addresses Joe and Kylie in a serious tone.

"Now, look you two, we've got to remain cheerful! Got it?"

Joe wonders what is going on. "Has this got something to do with Flannel?"

Jock looks worried. "I'm not saying anything more. I'm not getting into trouble with that man again. I nearly hit him last Friday."

Jock mutters something about a red email from Flannel that has been sent to everyone. He wants Joe to stay cheerful when he reads it. Joe is intrigued. Jock is still a little unsteady and he moves over to support himself against his drawing board. Joe follows him and puts a hand on his shoulder for support.

"Hey Jock, did you see that motorcade going down the high street earlier?"

Jock looks blank - he is still focused on breathing, but Kylie nods.

"Yeah, I saw it. It was the Emperor of Japan going to Windsor Castle, from Buck House."

"You Aussies seem to know everything. I don't think much of the Emperor's timing. He's caused havoc with the rush hour traffic."

Now Jock looks indignant. He places one hand on his hip and he wags a finger at Joe.

"It's Her Majesty's highway, she'll do with it as she pleases."

"I'm not sure the highways engineers would agree with that."

Jock concedes the point. "Yes, the highway engineers seem to be a higher power."

Jock is a good listener. He always lets Joe share his innermost thoughts, no matter how bizarre they seem to everyone else. Joe feels a thought welling up now and he decides to share it.

"Jock, you know they've got a neon sign at the back of police security cars saying *STAY BACK!* Just think, two thousand years ago, the same message was being shouted from the back of Roman chariots, travelling along the very same road, keeping the plebs back."

Jock looks stern and he wags his finger at Joe.

"You're very deep, young Joe, but just try to be cheerful, okay?"

Jock is the one who christened Vernon Flemel, *Flannel*. It happened during Vernon's first week at work, when he said, in front of Jock, that the Scots were tight-fisted. Everyone thought Vernon was joking at first, but then he backed up his statement with statistical evidence. He was serious. This upset Jock. If Vernon was going to make an enemy in the office, Jock was a bad choice. Jock has been with the company since it was set up in 1978 and he is still good friends with most of the Board members. Many of them played rugby together in their younger days. The Board would never get rid of Jock. Added to this, everyone else in the office loves the old Scot, not least because he keeps their spirits up. Jock always calls Vernon, *Flannel* and this makes Vernon's blood boil.

Poor Vernon. He spent last weekend visiting his indomitable mother. She says her home is in the foothills of the North Downs, but everyone else calls it Dorking. When Vernon revealed his troubles to his mother, including the fact that his work colleagues call him *Flannel*, she advised him not to let anyone see he was upset by it.

"Just brush it off darling," she said. "Remember, your father had to overcome great obstacles before he became the Deputy Chief Constable of Surrey. The name-calling will soon wear off."

"And if it doesn't, what then mother?" the forty seven year old Vernon asked in a shrill voice.

"Then evict the Pict!"

Raised voices are heard from the other end of the open plan offices. Jock, Joe and Kylie turn to see what is going on. They all look surprised.

"That's not really the point though, is it Muriel?" shrieks Vernon, "The very fact that a wasp's gained entry proves the sealed ventilation system has been violated!"

Muriel, a middle-aged administrative assistant, who has been a loyal employee for twenty-two years, looks very upset. Her problem is that she likes fresh air, but window opening is strictly forbidden because it supposedly renders the air conditioning ineffective. Everyone in the office knows the air conditioning system doesn't actually work, it never has. Muriel is a covert window opener. Vernon is stamping down on her belligerence. It is all too much for Muriel. As she stomps off she makes a sideways glance at old Jock, the only member of staff who has served in the company longer than her. Muriel shakes her head, she gives Jock a miserable look and then she marches through the door that leads into the gleaming white reception area. Muriel stands there for a moment facing the seated guests, and then she screams.

"I'M SO SORRY WE'RE NO LONGER LIVING IN A BLOODY SEALED POD. IT'S ALL MY BLOODY FAULT!

The shocked visitors in the reception area stare at Muriel aghast, but she quickly steps back into the private office area. Natasha, the receptionist, leaps up from her desk and rushes over as fast as her snakeskin stilettos allow, desperate to offer Muriel support. Muriel looks at Jock again.

"It's all my fault," she says, breathing heavily and her lower lip wobbling.

"Quite right, Muriel, but remember your blood pressure now, my darling." Jock looks petrified, he is turning beetroot again.

Muriel looks so grateful for this support, she gives a weak smile, and then she bursts into tears. She rushes off towards the ladies toilet with Natasha running after her. Jock scowls at Vernon.

Joe wanders over to his desk, baffled but not surprised by the antics of his dysfunctional office. At least he has got his new desk, and a view through the window. *What a view and it's all mine!*

Joe looks over leafy gardens, relishing the sight of fresh green leaves, luminous in the spring sunshine.

"We only need one prima donna in this office," shouts Jock from across the office, his voice still shaky.

Jock has not been promoted since he joined the company in 1978. He occupies the worst workstation in the office, but he never complains. Joe smiles and places his briefcase on his new desk. He sits down on his new blue swivel chair. He chose the chair himself, from the office furniture catalogue. It's got *executive* armrests. Joe turns his computer on. He is still getting to grips with the new machine. He has a message marked in red from Vernon. The content is, *"Very Important!"* It is a general circulation message sent to everyone in the company. The heading is, *Staff Privileges and Responsibilities*. Joe opens it. There is a long list of new rules. He is astounded to learn the company's annual sports afternoon is cancelled. Ever since Joe has been with the company they have enjoyed one afternoon off a year for a baseball game in the park, everyone joins in. They usually play against other companies and it is a useful networking event. The older employees watch, chat and provide the picnic. For some reason, this is now on a list of benefits that have been terminated. Joe scans the other edicts. Christmas cards are no longer to be displayed. Apparently, they are incompatible with the new decor.

Joe sighs heavily. In a way he is relieved. The writing is on the wall. He has been thinking about moving on for a while. This e-mail will speed the process up. He reflects for a moment upon the things he has done with the Regeneration Company. He has been involved with some exciting projects all over the country, and in Europe too. He is particularly pleased with the Kensington High Street project. The vision behind it grabbed his attention. There was something about the approach that struck a chord. The Royal Borough of Kensington and Chelsea took the view that public space should be well cared for, as the space in private homes and gardens is cared for. After all, public space provides the stage for public life. If you build better high streets and squares, people feel they belong and they participate. A stronger society is built. Joe seized the opportunity to work on the project because of this vision. Now the council is applying the lessons learnt across the rest of the borough. This means a lot more work for Joe's company.

Joe has published articles about his company's successful projects. A few weeks ago, a very prestigious client, the Features Editor of *The Times*, approached him. She wants Joe to write a piece about Kensington High Street. There is a tight deadline. Joe is excited about taking his ideas on to a much bigger stage. Now that he has decided to look for a new job, he will need to get his name better known.

More of Joe's colleagues arrive in the office. Joe is trying to work on his half-finished article, but there are too many distractions. Grunts of "Morning" are followed by expletives and cries of alarm as the workers discover their "red" message from Vernon. Angry words ricochet around the office. Joe is pulled between his article and joining a rebellion.

Suddenly, the office is still. A dark shadow descends. Joe is aware of a sinister presence. It is behind him. He swivels around on his chair, tightly clutching his executive armrests. Vernon is looming over him, running his fingers through a flop of greasy, dyed black hair. He produces a ticket out of a corduroy cap and waves it in front of Joe's nose. Joe's pulse quickens. One of the edicts in Vernon's email referred to attendance at corporate hospitality events. It stated that when an invite is received, it is to go into a hat and there will be a lottery to determine who attends.

Vernon stares at Joe.

"There you go Jake…oh, no, sorry, it's Joe isn't it? Well, you're the lucky winner! It's the invite to attend the preview of Stacey McCall's new exhibition in North Kensington! This is the best *jolly* of the year so far!" Vernon's loud voice is for the benefit of the whole office. Joe is silent, unsure of how to respond. Vernon does a strange movement, a bit like a curtsy, then he turns on his heels and walks back to his partitioned-off cubicle. No one is looking at their computer screens now, all faces switch between Joe and Vernon. The door to the cubicle clicks shut.

There follows the flight of a heavy, substantial item of office stationery. It is a hole-punch, accelerating at speed through the air towards the door of Vernon's office. Joe calculates the trajectory. It has been launched from Jock's desk. Jock feigns concentration on his drawing board, but he has thrown it. Thump! The hole-punch impacts the wall just above Vernon's door. There is a lesser thump when it hits the ground. The office is filled with gasps and shocked whispers. A large chunk of plaster falls off the wall. White debris covers the carpet. There is muffled laughter, across the office. Vernon must have heard the noise, but he doesn't appear. He has gone to ground.

Joe is unsure about what to do with his invitation. At one level, he is repulsed by the theatrical way Vernon gave it to him, but then Stacey McCall is the latest edition to the "Britpack", the young British artists causing such a stir in the media. Joe thinks her work is weird, but what does he know? It is still worth a look, isn't it? Jock walks over and places an arm on Joe's shoulder.

"You're not going to go are you, son?"

"Probably not," Joe lies. He has already decided he will go.

5 Archie's Waterloo

It is five thirty in the evening. It has been a busy day at the Regeneration Company. Jock makes his way out of the office, shouting over his shoulder to Joe.

"Don't stay too late young man, you can have too much of a good thing!"

Joe has been working late over the last week due to a demanding workload. Half an hour later, his eyes are so strained he can't concentrate anymore. It is time to go home. He arranges his papers into bundles, pauses and stares out of the window. Houses are lighting up. He can see into the kitchen of a town house. A couple are preparing their evening meal as their children sit at a table. Joe sighs, he is tired. He wants to see new things, to live more adventurously, to get a girlfriend. He picks up his brown leather briefcase and makes his way across the office floor. His shoulders are slumped like a hunchback because of the weight of his case. His heart lifts momentarily when he spots that Kylie is still working at her drawing board.

"Hey Kylie! Fancy a beer?" he asks hopefully.

"Ah, Joe, you're still here. I'd love to, but I've got to get something finished for my boyfriend. He's doing a gig. I'm making a poster to promote it."

"Oh, okay, no worries." Joe tries not to look

disappointed. Kylie returns to her extra-curricular activity. Vernon would do his nut if he found out what the office computers were really used for. As Joe walks out of the office he muses: *What is it with attractive Australian women and the name Kylie?*

There is still a glimmer of light in the sky over Kensington. Joe decides to take the bus home for a change. Even though he is in the middle of London, the evening air is fresh and pleasant. He wants to enjoy it. The journey home by bus will be a lot longer than by tube, but it doesn't matter. He doesn't feel like being underground.

After a couple of minutes of waiting a friendly old red London bus sails up the high street displaying the right number. It will take Joe all the way home. The bus pulls up and rattles like a tin can with an angry bee stuck in it. Joe jumps aboard. The elderly inspector grunts and the engine roars. The bus isn't quite full and Joe gets his favourite seat at the front of the upper deck. He has the best seat in the house. *This'll be a nice little tour.*

For a while, Kensington passes by like a citadel of sophistication, but then the bus passes into the encampment of the ordinary. It is a less-cherished environment with massive advertisement hoardings displaying messages about cat food and bleach.

The bus pulls over at a stop and people jostle to get on board. Joe is snug and warm. He looks out of the window at a confusing, unloved scene. There is a busy traffic junction with signs, redundant poles, rusting guardrail and lots of fly-posters. Millions of pounds have gone into creating this hideous junction. Joe is feeling the strain of big city life. He breathes out deeply. He has not been beyond the M25 for ages. He is incarcerated in its ring of carbon monoxide. Joe's attention is now drawn to a young couple, a man and a woman, wrapped up in sleeping bags in the entrance of a boarded-up shop. There is a Staffordshire bull terrier curled up beside them, on a dirty blanket. Joe sees similar scenes every day. When he first arrived in London, he couldn't pass homeless people without giving them a fiver and a reassuring smile, but now he hardly even registers them. And yet, seeing this couple huddled together in the doorway makes him feel sad.

Joe presses his nose against the bus window. He wipes away the condensation caused by his breath. Three men and two women, all about Joe's age, walk up to the homeless couple. One of the men squats down and starts talking to the homeless guy. The others carry plastic food containers and blankets. They set up a little food station. Joe's neck strains, he is trying to see what is going on. The window steams up again. He wants to get a better look at the guy squatting down, there is something familiar about him, but another man is in the way. The man steps aside. Joe realises why the guy is familiar. It is Luke. "Luke!" Joe shouts out loud. The engine of the bus is revved-up, there is no way Joe's going to be heard over it. He tries frantically to unwind the little window but the handle won't budge. The bus pulls off and gains speed quickly. Joe grabs his brown leather briefcase and flies down the steps. The elderly ticket inspector and several standing passengers are pushed out of the way.

"Stop the bus!" Joe shouts frantically and rings the bell repeatedly. The bus slows down. Joe jumps out from the open back.

Joe's feet land on the pavement. The rest of his body follows and topples over into the path of an elderly black lady in big glasses. She gasps. "Oh! Sweetheart, are you alright?" The lady tries to help Joe back to his feet. He sits for a moment on the pavement, dazed and disorientated. He is breathing heavily. The lady retrieves Joe's briefcase which has landed a few metres away. She hands it back to him.

"You okay darlin?"

"Yeah, I'm alright, thanks."

"You sure now?"

The woman keeps an eye on Joe as he walks off, shakily, towards Luke, who is still speaking to the homeless guy.

Luke retains his youthful good looks. He has got short, spikey hair and an out-of-doors glow. He is wearing a reddish-brown leather jacket and blue jeans. He looks like an off-duty pop star. When the five friends were teenagers and generally inseparable, Luke had a tendency to drift off, to be alone. He wouldn't be seen for days and then he would reappear in the middle of their social circle, without explanation. His independent spirit annoyed the others, who liked to be in daily contact with each other. This time Luke hasn't been in touch with any of the others for a very long time, and Joe had just about given up on him. Luke's attention is focused upon the homeless guy. It is an intense conversation and it is not an appropriate time for Joe to butt in. He waits, awkwardly, watching the slow-moving traffic go by. There is an attractive young woman with blonde hair beside Luke. She speaks to the homeless girl, who is still tucked up in her sleeping bag. The other helpers prepare food. One of them looks over to Joe with a curious smile. Joe nods back, clutching his briefcase defensively to his chest. He points at Luke.

"I know him," he says, exaggerating each syllable, hoping they can read his lips.

"Okay," the guy mouths back in similar fashion.

Joe feels very out of place, standing alone on the street in his business suit. The fact that Luke is talking so easily and for so long to a homeless person strikes Joe as bizarre. Luke and the homeless guy retain direct eye contact as they talk. Joe wonders if he looks into people's eyes like that. He is pretty sure he doesn't. He strains to hear what is being said, but it is impossible to hear over the noise of the traffic. Joe scratches his head. The only organisation he can imagine being on the streets, feeding the homeless, is the church. He feels a sinking feeling in the pit of his stomach. There is a gulf between him and anything to do with religion. The thought of Luke being on the other side of that gulf is appalling. Joe looks at the homeless guy again. He is so young, perhaps sixteen, and very unkempt. Joe can smell him from several metres away, and yet he looks quite content, smiling serenely. The Staffordshire bull terrier looks up at his master, as if to ask if everything is okay.

At last, Luke stops speaking, he stands up and turns around. Another man comes forward with a bowl of food for the homeless lad. For a split second, Joe thinks about walking off, but it is too late – Luke has recognised him. He is walking over and he looks overjoyed. Joe smiles back, all doubts are blown away. Joe offers Luke a handshake, but Luke hugs him. It is an awkward embrace. Joe's arm is pressed into Luke's chest and Luke's shoulder catches Joe in the jaw causing him to bite his tongue. Joe reveals none of the pain, but expects to see blood.

"It's so great to see you Joe!"

"It's good to see you too Luke," says Joe as best he can, through his numbed jaw.

"It's been too long. How's everything with you?"

"Okay. What about you? You're looking good."

"I'm alright mate. You're looking good too."

Joe finds it hard to believe the compliment, especially after he has fallen off the back of a bus and been elbowed in the jaw.

"Well, you know, I'm basically okay, just a bit knackered after a rough day at the office," he says, trying to regain some of his composure. He glances at the homeless couple and then looks back at Luke with a puzzled expression. He explains his surprise at seeing Luke with homeless people. He adopts a more concerned tone.

"Don't take this the wrong way, Luke, but you aren't getting a bit too serious are you? I mean, I'm not sure what you were saying there, but…"

"But what?"

"Well, you were always good fun you know, pretty wild too, you won't lose that will you? Old friends can be honest with each other, can't they?"

There is an awkward silence. Luke scratches the back of his head, unsure of how to respond. The homeless couple are enjoying their food. The lad passes morsels to his dog. The other helpers sit beside them. Joe, embarrassed by the silence, turns away. He looks up the road. There is a long line of glimmering red tail lights, commuters leaving the city for comfortable, suburban homes.

In his own mind, Joe tries to assess the situation. *Have I lost Luke? Has a chasm opened between us? Can I build a bridge to him?*

"Luke, look, I'm really sorry," says Joe. "I've had a long day. Like I say, I'm pretty knackered. I'm just a bit, you know, cautious about religion and that sort of thing. I thought you were too. I have enough trouble with Archie and the weird spiritual things he gets into!"

"What's Archie involved with now?" asks Luke, apprehensively.

"What, at the moment? Oh, it's something to do with Red Indians and peyote, but it seems to change every month."

"Peyote? That's a hallucinogenic drug isn't it? Is he alright? I don't even know where he's living. Is he in London?"

Joe takes a deep breath. "Surely you know he's living in London, don't you? Why don't you call him, then you'll know if he's alright?"

Luke looks scolded.

Joe quizzes him further. "Why haven't you been in touch?"

"I've been away a lot, working with a boatyard."

"You're not a lobster fisherman, are you? That's what you said you'd be. Do you remember that night in the forest?"

Luke doesn't have the faintest idea what Joe is talking about. Rather than fishing for lobsters, he explains he sells yachts to wealthy patrons from a Mayfair office, and he also spends time at the boatyard in Devon.

"The best thing about the job," adds Luke, "Is that I get to deliver some of the yachts around the world." He has just come back from Cannes, hence his suntan. Joe is impressed, but he still looks pensive. He reflects upon the fact that Luke spends a lot of time in London, and yet he never makes the effort to get in touch.

Luke tries to put Joe at ease. "I love sailing Joe, but I've probably learnt more from volunteering with the homeless. We do it with this church in Knightsbridge, you should come along."

Joe snorts. "Have you got a fish on the back of your car now?"

Luke laughs. "You're joking aren't you? With my driving, they'd never let me have one. Look, Joe, I'm really sorry for not keeping in touch."

Joe accepts the apology graciously, and then he continues. "Hannah's still working for an aid agency with refugee kids in Lebanon. I send her postcards, but I don't get replies."

"There's trouble again in Lebanon. It was on the news this morning, it's a dangerous place," replies Luke.

Joe winces. "Oh, no, don't say that. I'd better buy a newspaper."

Now Luke wants an update on Cathy. Joe looks thoughtful. "I saw her about a year ago, when I was last at home. She's working as an assistant for a government minister. Oh, and she's going out with a Frenchman."

"I know about the government minister, my dad gave her a reference. The French boyfriend's news though, you met him?"

"Nah."

"And how's Grandad?"

"Oh, alright, I think. Actually, I haven't spoken to him for ages, that's bad isn't it?"

"Oh, so I'm not the only one that's crap at communication!"

"Point taken." Joe looks away sheepishly.

Joe sees the homeless couple, wrapped up in their sleeping bags, eating a meal out of plastic dishes. A well-dressed couple, a man and a woman in their mid-thirties, walk by. The man shouts over to them.

"Losers!"

The homeless lad gives the man a wave and a smile. Joe is taken aback. The woman slaps her partner on the shoulder, admonishing him, but when they've gone a little further, they start laughing. The homeless couple finish off their food. The volunteers pack things away.

Luke pats Joe on the back.

"You're not going to rush off are you?"

"No, I'm not in a rush."

"Good, listen, we've been walking the streets for a few hours, we're going to get a coffee now. Will you join us? I want you to meet Serena, my girlfriend."

Before Joe can answer, the homeless lad walks up to him. He thanks Joe for everything he's done to help. Joe smiles back, feeling slightly embarrassed, and he explains he hasn't actually done anything. His smile suddenly drops when he sees that the boy's body is emaciated. Joe hadn't realised just how painfully thin and pale he is. Luke interrupts.

"Joe, come here a second, let me introduce you to the others."

Joe pulls himself together. Luke places his arm around the attractive girl who has been helping to serve the food. She has bright blue eyes, blonde hair, full lips, and her skin is tanned.

"This is Serena, my girlfriend." Now Luke turns to Serena. "And this is Joe, my best friend from home."

"Oh, Joe? I've heard all about you!" says Serena, which warms Joe's heart.

"All good I hope? Hey, you look really familiar, have we met before?"

Luke interjects. "Serena is an actress. You've probably seen her on the telly."

Joe is impressed with Serena. She is kind and beautiful, a perfect match for Luke. He feels a bit jealous and wonders if she might have any single friends he could meet.

The other volunteers are introduced to Joe with friendly handshakes. Joe is now feeling tired, awkward and uneasy. He is clutching his briefcase defensively close to his chest again. He is in two minds about joining Luke and his friends for a coffee. He would love to talk some more to Luke, and his friends seem nice enough, but he is anxious to get home, it is getting late.

"I'll tell you what Luke, how about if I give you my telephone number and we can meet up at the weekend, if you're free?"

"Yeah, okay, but are you sure you won't join us for a coffee now?"

"Go on, come with us," says Serena, but Joe shakes his head and smiles. Luke knows that when Joe has made up his mind he can be very stubborn, so he just gives Joe a card with his contact details on it.

"Blimey, that's one of the smartest streets in Kensington," says Joe staring at the card. Luke shrugs his shoulders.

Joe yawns and stares blankly into his computer screen. He is bored and his thoughts are drifting towards the Bounty advert. The working day is only half done. It is the private viewing of the Stacey McCall exhibition tonight, in North Kensington. Joe has the tickets in is wallet but has decided he will not go unless a friend goes with him. His new mobile phone rings out in a manic tone. It is Archie.

"Hi Joe, do you fancy meeting up for a pint tonight?"

Joe's face lights up. Archie is a good mate, maybe he will go to the exhibition. For the last couple of years, Archie has been riding a wave of excess, screaming, "*Look at me!*" He is enthralled by London life and all of its possibilities. He has a group of aficionados, actors and artists, all of whom are "filling-in-time" with more mundane jobs, such as being clerks in the civil service. Archie moved to London when Joe and Luke were still at university, he sussed the place out for them. Archie is telephoning at the expense of his employer, the Peckham Chronicle. He has worked for this free newspaper for six years, selling advertising space.

Archie continues. "I'm sooo bored Joe. I can't wait for the weekend! I'm on my park-where-you-want scooter today, so I can meet you anywhere you like. How about a beer in the West End?" Archie parks his scooter on any strip of private land that is available, secure in the knowledge that the traffic wardens cannot ticket him there.

"It's good to hear your dulcet tones Archie. Hey, do you fancy a bit of the high life tonight?"

"High life? What do you know about the high life? When I wanted to go to a lap dancing club, you said it was too seedy."

"Lap dancing isn't the high life, Archie, it's naff. Listen, you've said you want to see all sides of life, right?"

"Yep."

"Okay, listen."

"I'm listening Joe."

"I shall say this only once."

"I'm ready."

"I've got an invite to see Stacey McCall's exhibition, do you want to come?"

"Can you repeat the question please?"

"No."

"Stacey McCall, you mean the lanky Mancunian bird, who does the modern art?"

"The one and only."

"Look, I've got an out-of-work actress sitting next to me, d'you remember Sam?"

"Big baps?"

"That's the one, you got off with her."

"Oh, yeah."

"Anyway, she's Stacey's biggest fan. Can she come too?"

"I don't know if we'll all get in, it just says to bring a guest on the ticket. I suppose we could give it a go."

"Where is this gig?"

"North Kensington"

"Well, if we don't get in, we'll just go to one of the trendy bars around there."

"Okay, let's meet at half past seven at the corner of Notting Hill Square, okay?"

Archie's boss must have come in at this point.

"That's a half-page spread with your fifty percent loyalty discount."

"Eh?"

"Goodbye sir."

Joe passes through the turnstiles at the busy Notting Hill tube station, just before seven thirty. He is not in a rush because he knows that Archie is always late. There are people everywhere, criss-crossing the underground plaza, making their way to the various exit points. They seem to have an inbuilt device, enabling them to navigate their way at considerable speed without bumping into each other. Most of the people know exactly where they are going, but a few suddenly change their direction resulting in some near misses. One young man seems to be particularly confused. He is trying to get to a map on the wall to see which exit point he should take. He holds a guitar case in one hand and he is trying to manoeuvre a bicycle with his other hand. He keeps stumbling into people. He offers profuse apologies but nobody stops to listen. Joe weaves his way through the crowd. He gives the young man with the bicycle and guitar a wide berth. He wonders if he might have looked so out of place when he first arrived in London but, no, he'd never take a bike *and* a guitar on the tube. That is just daft.

Joe makes his way to the exit. He passes a beggar, a busker, and colourful stalls selling their wares to rushing commuters. Joe looks up the steps that lead to the street. The traffic is roaring and there is a fresh smell of rain. He runs up the steps, leaving the cramped underworld for the cosmopolitan commotion of Notting Hill Gate. Joe elbows his way through congested pavements and then he stops for a moment to peer through the window of a bookstore. It is late night opening. A middle-aged white couple stand beside him, interested in an esoteric book. They are both wearing embroidered turbans. Joe flashes a look at them: *Where do they think they are, Beverley Hills?*

After a short walk, Joe arrives at Notting Hill Square, eager to meet his friends. He looks around the street corner, there is no sign of Archie: *Why is he always so late?*

There is a light grey drizzle and it is quite cold and dark. Joe shelters under a tree, rubbing his hands for warmth.

Fifteen minutes of waiting and there is still no sign of Archie or Sam.

A group of workers leave their office converted from a Victorian town house fronting the square. They are off to meet friends at a nearby restaurant. Some of the buildings around the square are still houses, as originally intended, and are now worth millions of pounds. An elderly lady comes out from one of them and she does not return Joe's smile when she deposits a rubbish bag beside him. The middle of the square has a lush garden, enclosed by black railings. There is an incongruous line of recycling bins within it and the old lady reappears beside them, diligently sorting through bags, depositing various items with clangs and crashes.

Around the corner come two swaggering figures, walking arm in arm, under a large, green golfing umbrella. It is Archie and his friend Sam. As they draw nearer, Joe notices Archie isn't wearing his glasses. They greet each other with playful high fives.

"Late as usual," says Joe. "What's happened to your glasses?"

"Hello Joey boy. I've got contact lenses now. You know Samantha don't you?"

"Yeah, hello again, Sam," says Joe with a nod and a smile.

"Hello again, Joe. Have you recovered from your hangover?" asks Sam smoothly, blushing slightly.

"They've all rolled into one."

Sam is fairly plain, but she has got a marvellous, curvaceous figure, and spiky, bleached hair. Three earrings are worn in one ear. Archie still has his bright ginger hair, and he has put a bit of weight on, which doesn't escape Joe's attention.

"Archie, are you putting on weight intentionally?"

"Yeah, it's a sign of my wealth."

Sam is an arts buff and she knows all about Stacey McCall. Joe knows nothing about modern art, he is more interested in the fact that there will be free alcohol. The friends discuss where the art gallery is. None of them know that particular neighbourhood at all well. Sam rummages in her tiny bright green handbag and reveals a surprisingly large London street atlas.

"What else have you got in there?" asks Archie. After studying the invite and doing a little map reading, they realise the gallery is further away than they thought. Joe explains it is best to go up the Ladbroke Grove. Archie suggests a taxi.

"No," replies Joe. "There's a good little pub around the corner, let's have a drink, get warmed up, do some more map reading, then we'll *walk*. Come on, we'll soon be with the in-crowd up't north."

The three of them walk up the street arm in arm, under the umbrella, and then they disappear into a local pub.

It is a comely old tavern, with dark wood panelling and stained glass partitions. There is no music, just the murmur of conversation. The friends step through a hidden doorway set within the panelling. There is a sign above that reads, "*Residents Only*" which they ignore. They have entered a cosy, dimly-lit lounge. Joe has been in here many times before.

"The separate compartments were originally designed to segregate the different social classes," he says.

"Really? Oh, you're very knowledgeable aren't you, Joe?" says Sam admiringly.

"I am," replies Joe with a wry smile.

Archie takes their orders. He walks over to the bar, waving a ten pound note at a disinterested barmaid. She is preoccupied with her new mobile phone. There are sympathetic nods from three elderly, purple-faced men, propping up the bar.

"The service is terrible, but the beers worth the wait," one of them confides. Another one of them keeps looking over at Sam. Eventually, the young South African barmaid serves Archie.

Archie returns to Joe and Sam with hands full of drinks and pockets stuffed with packets of crisps. His pale face is flushed. Joe tastes the beer. "Very fruity."

"Hey, it's a shame Luke isn't here isn't it?" says Archie, out of the blue.

"Oh, I meant to tell you, I saw him the other day."

"What? You saw Luke?"

"Yeah."

"I haven't seen him for ages. You never told me you saw him. Why didn't you tell me?"

"I'm telling you now, aren't I?"

"Did you go for a drink together?"

"No, we just passed each other in the street."

"What? You just bumped into him in the street?"

Joe nods back. Archie continues to press.

"In a city of eight million people, you just bumped into each other?"

"Yeah. It's weird isn't it?"

"I can't believe you didn't call me?"

Sam interjects at this point. "If you two are going to have a *domestic*, I'm leaving."

The boys shut up and stare into their crisp packets.

A little brown terrier trots over and sits on the floor next to their table. It looks up at them longingly. Joe bites off half a crisp and feeds it to the dog. The terrier takes the morsel, very gently.

"Does he remind you of Deefor?" Joe asks Archie, but he doesn't get a reply. Archie looks very distant. There is another side to Archie that Joe doesn't know about. When he is alone in his tenth-floor council flat in Peckham,

Archie occasionally finds himself crying. He has not told his friends, but a few months ago his parents took old Deefor to the vets, and had him put down. Archie's parents didn't tell him what they had done until several days after the event. He hasn't spoken to his parents since, and he still hasn't come to terms with what they did. Seeing this little dog now, which looks just like Deefor, reminds him of his loss. He wants to tell Joe about it, but he's afraid he might cry. When Archie feels really let down, he finds it hard to forgive. He can remain offended for a very long time.

An hour later, the three friends emerge from the pub. There is a slight drizzle and it is colder.

"I've only had a packet of crisps to eat," says Joe. "There'd better be some big nibbles at this *do*. I'm feeling quite pissed and I'm starving."

"You're always going on about your stomach aren't you?" replies Archie, rather severely. Joe ignores the insult and huddles up beside Archie and Sam under the big green umbrella, which is pressed against the weather. They march forward purposefully, following the route planned in the pub.

They walk along residential streets and on every corner there is a pub, or a church, or an interesting shop to look at. They cross garden squares and take short cuts down cobbled mews. Feeling damp and cold they stop for a moment beside a parade of shops. At the end of the street stands a massive brooding tower block. The top of it thrusts forward, like the prow of a ship cutting into the sky, and it is all lit up. It is like a sentinel guarding the northern gateway into Kensington.

"That's Trellick Tower," says Joe, bracing himself against the weather.

"I like it," replies Sam.

"Bloody architects!" adds Archie.

Shielded behind the umbrella, the three friends continue their walk. Sam tries to look at the display in a designer boutique, but the boys drag her on towards the towering edifice. They reach the base of the tower. It is a gloomy space, beside a noisy, heavily-trafficked flyover. They walk on and cross over Kensington's northern frontier. It instantly feels gloomier. Joe feels as if he is being watched. This night will change the course of his life.

They walk through gloomy, confusing spaces, defined by warehouses and flyovers. With every step, they are being forced further underground. There is relief when a graffiti-covered street name matches the address on their invitation. It is a grey, cobbled street. This area is new to Joe, he hadn't realised how industrial it was on the other side of the flyover. The high walls flanking the narrow street belong to manufactories and the sense of enclosure is foreboding. There are no windows, just blind brick walls. There is a hump in the road in front of them. Archie looks over a low wall at a canal that is as black as tar.

"This makes Peckham look idyllic," he says wryly.

Joe spots promising activity in a converted railway arch and so they head for it.

Expensive cars line the street with chauffeurs sitting in them. One in a Mercedes is reading a newspaper, another in a Bentley is on a mobile phone, and yet another in a Daimler is fast asleep. These flash cars look conspicuously out of place in such an industrial scene.

Archie is getting excited. "At last, we're going to be where the action is." Joe is feeling a little nervous about getting three people in with one ticket. He turns to Sam.

"If there's any problem getting in, say you're my partner."

"Okay," replies Sam, looking really pleased.

"What about bloody me getting in if there's a problem?" says Archie. "Why can't I be your partner?"

"Pretend you're his personal assistant," replies Sam, firmly.

"Sod that, I'll be your art buying agent, okay?"

"Whatever," says Joe. For a moment he wonders if he should just give the ticket to Archie and Sam. He could go home, have a quiet beer and get a good night's sleep. But they have come so far, perhaps they should at least try to get in.

"Why are there so many bouncers, Joe?" asks Archie.

"I don't know, I've never been here before, have I?" replies Joe, curtly, and then he adds, "I suppose it's because it'll be packed with celebrities."

Brutal looking security men with fat heads are all around them, speaking into walky-talkies. One of the bouncers holds open the stainless steel entrance door. The friends enter.

"Good evening," says Joe to the doorman.

"Ello, alright?" growls the doorman.

"Top notch mate, top notch," says Archie with a flick of his wrist and a nod of his head.

They are standing in a dimly-lit, stark reception area. Two stunning young women, one blonde and one brunette, sit behind an antique desk. An older woman, with spikey blonde hair and orange trousers, walks up to the desk. It is Stacey McCall herself, the famous artist whose work they have come to see. Stacey looks Joe up and down, turns to Sam, and then looks at Joe again. She talks to Joe in a strong Manchester accent.

"Are ya comin in love? The party's beginning to rumble."

The blonde receptionist steps out from behind the desk.

"May I take your coat madam?"

"Oh, I've never been called madam before," says Sam giddily. Joe and Archie frown with embarrassment. The receptionist smiles coldly. She proceeds to take all their coats for which they are given paper receipts. Sam looks slightly distressed.

"You okay?" whispers Joe.

"Just feeling a bit overwhelmed, you know, meeting Stacey," she gasps.

Joe notices that Sam has exactly the same spiky hairstyle as Stacey.

The blonde receptionist ushers them through a set of double doors and the noise that greets them is shocking. It is a raucous party. They have entered a cavernous hall packed with people who are excited and drunk. Most of them are squealing and screaming with laughter. The walls of the hall are finished in rough brick. There is an impressive high vaulted ceiling with sparkling chandeliers hanging down from it. At the friend's feet is a floor of polished white concrete. Joe cups his mouth with his hand and places it against Archie's ear.

"Nobody's asked to see our invite!"

Archie winces at the shot of hot breath down his ear. He then answers Joe, using the same technique.

"I know! It's like a zoo! I love it!"

The last words are shouted so loudly into Joe's ear, they hurt. Joe clenches his fist as if he is going to hit his friend. A few curt words are exchanged, although it is impossible to hear exactly what is being said over the hullabaloo. Sam remonstrates for the boys to pull themselves together. Then she spots where Stacey McCall is standing encircled by a group of admirers.

Everyone looks like a supermodel except for Archie, Sam, and Joe, who look pale by comparison. The friends are in awe of their surroundings but they are also in need of a drink. Archie points out where the bar is. They wind their way through the roaring throng. It is so packed Joe finds it helpful to hold onto the back of Archie's shirt to ensure they don't get separated. Sam holds onto the back of Joe's shirt. As they wind their way through the crowd they notice familiar faces from television, including a couple of footballers from the England squad. They reach the bar where glasses of champagne are arranged in readiness for them. Joe, Archie and Sam each down a glass of free champagne with such undignified haste it is obvious they are neither glitterati nor art buyers.

Attractive waitresses float around topping up empty glasses. Archie notices a couple of women looking down their noses at him. He stares back at them and then he grabs hold of Joe.

"Mwah-mwah-mwah. Dahrling! Mwah-mwah," he says, speaking gibberish theatrically.

Joe looks worried.

A room off the main hall contains the art of Stacey McCall, and it is all for sale. It is getting late though, and most of the guests want to socialize now they have examined the exhibits. Sam, however, is determined to see her idol's work. She drags Joe and Archie away from the bar. Joe is quite interested to see why Stacey's work has created such a stir in the media. They walk under a brick archway and enter a large exhibition space.

"I'm glad there are less people in here," says Joe.

"Yeah, I can actually breathe now," replies Archie.

"And I can hear what you're saying," adds Sam.

The friends take a moment to stretch their limbs. Black screens are arranged all around them, upon which hang twenty paintings. A few serious art buyers are still examining the exhibits. These people are very stylish. A spotlight shines upon a woman's hand, her finger sparkles like a rainbow. She is wearing a big diamond. Sam marches up to the first exhibit. Archie and Joe follow like sheep. They all inspect a tall painting of three black dots in the middle of a white canvas. Suddenly, Stacey McCall, the artist herself, appears from nowhere and she pushes the friends out of the way, with no word of apology. Stacey converses with a middle-aged American with a goatee beard. All that Joe can now see is the back of this man's head. Joe takes a step sideways and he decides that observing the artist is more interesting than looking at her art. Stacey looks searchingly into her painting and the American strokes his beard.

"It's an ironic continuation of romanticism. Do you get it?" Stacey asks the American, but he just continues to stroke his beard. Then in a broad Texan accent, he drawls.

"So, argh, how much d'yah want for it Stacey?"

"Ya'wot?" Stacey is flabbergasted. She runs both of her hands through her spiky hair and grabs her scalp.

"Yer know what the price is, it's on ya list! Yer shouldn't be asking an artist about money anyhow, don't yer know that?"

The American is undeterred. "Yeah, but what the heck, what about if I was to give yah cash and right now? How much?"

Stacey is angry now. She throws her head back and stomps off. After a few paces she turns around. Her voice is shaking with rage.

"You ain't havin it!" She stamps her foot. "You just aint 'avin anything of mine, ever!"

Archie turns to Sam. "Oh, she's very Haute Couture".

Sam flashes a stern look at him. "Can't you show her a bit of respect? Can't you see she's upset?" Sam looks longingly towards Stacey as she disappears through the archway. The American buyer continues to look at the art, as if nothing untoward has happened. Stacey's agent comes rushing over to him. She is a very respectable looking middle-aged lady who is anxious to redeem the sale.

The friends take a moment to reflect upon Stacey's tantrum and then proceed to the second piece of work. It looks like a child's painting of a dinosaur but with a real kidney attached to it. Joe stands with his arms folded, grimacing. Archie is stroking his chin.

"What do you think of it Joe?"

"It's weird isn't it?"

"I wouldn't say it's weird, that's a bit judgemental."

"What would you say? You don't like it do you?"

"I don't have to like it to respect it."

Joe can't take much more of this.

"Let's split up, I'll meet you at the bar in twenty minutes, okay?"

The others agree.

Joe wanders off to the far corner of the room. He notices something unusual. There is a faint thumping beat, it seems to be coming through the concrete floor. He can feel a vibrating through his shoes. It is a curious sensation, like a very mild earthquake. Joe walks back through the archway and the general din makes it impossible to perceive the underground rumbles. Now Joe feels out of place because everyone else has someone to talk to. He stands alone, feeling a bit awkward. He nods and smiles at a pretty waitress, she comes over and speaks in faltering English.

"Can I 'elp sir?"

"Oh, yeah, listen!"

"I'm listening!"

Joe mouths each syllable clearly to ensure he is understood.

"What-is-go-ing-on-down-there?" He points to his feet. The waitress looks confused.

Joe points to the floor again.

"What-is–go-ing-on-down-there? What-is-the-rum-bling-sound?"

Understanding illuminates the waitress's face.

"Oh, yes! Yes, there iz a club under us, is owned by same man, okay? You can go to it if you want."

Joe looks curious. "How do I get there?"

The waitress gives him directions. He needs to go down a small staircase, descending from a corner of the hall. Joe can just make it out, behind a group of people. He thanks the waitress and departs to have a quick look. He traverses through the crowd and descends the steps, ignoring the "private" sign.

Joe finds himself in a small hallway. It is all painted black. There is just one door off it. The rumbling earthquake is much louder down here. Joe pushes the heavy door open. It is made from solid metal, like the door to a walk-in meat freezer. Wet, hot air smacks him in the face and a wall of music assaults his ears. Joe steps back, shocked. Then he goes through the doorway and dissapears into a cloud of sweat. The metal door closes behind him.

The air is humid and heavy. It is difficult to breathe or to see anything. The bass is so loud Joe's body is vibrating with it. He is standing on a very wide balcony, containing a lounge area with sofas and chairs. His eyes begin to adjust to the darkness. People are standing and sitting in groups. There is a bar at the far side of the balcony with three men sitting on stools. In front of Joe is a metal balustrade. He takes a few steps forward and tentatively peers over it. It is very dark, but he can see he is in a vast hanger and he is surprisingly high up. There is no telling exactly how high or long this place is because its dimensions disappear into blackness.

Joe is about thirty feet above the main floor level. Beneath him are literally thousands of scantily dressed revellers. They are dancing wildly, blowing whistles, embracing each other, and waving their arms in the air. It is a massive rave, a heady combination of heat, noise and flesh, one amorphous mass of humanity. Everyone is losing themselves in the music. Joe feels his heart beating violently. It may be the late 1990s but up to now the rave scene has somehow passed him by. These people are clinging on to the bitter end of that scene. It feels dangerous, but exciting.

A dark-skinned man carrying two fancy cocktails walks over to Joe from the bar area. He has a proprietorial air and is aged around forty.

"Av a drink? Enjoy!" he shouts into Joe's ear, as if he is an old friend.

Joe accepts the drink. He has got a strange wild look in his eye, like a racehorse in the starting pen. A vein in his temple is slightly throbbing through his skin. He is confounded by his surroundings, and he is still taking in the possibilities of the place. The man waves his hand in front of Joe's face to get his attention. Without thinking, Joe knocks back some of the drink. Then, as best he can, he indicates he wants to get to the dance floor. The man points towards the far end of the balcony, where two DJs control the music amongst a mass of electrical equipment. Next to them is a metal industrial staircase, leading down to the rave. Joe has forgotten about Archie and Sam. He just wants to indulge in the rave.

The dark man walks back to the bar and his friends greet him with cackles of laughter and a pat on the back. Joe makes his way to the dance floor, negotiating his way around sofas and huddles of people.

Joe clambers down the steep, metal steps. The back of an enormous security man blocks his way. Joe taps him on the shoulder, but he doesn't seem to notice. After an inordinate wait, the fat bouncer gets out of the way. Joe launches himself into the rave. Young men and women greet him with smiles and embraces, as if he is some long-awaited star. Joe is carried away by the swaying mass, drifting far from the staircase. The excitement is intoxicating, his heart is racing. People are dancing beside him, stroking him. Something strange is happening in Joe's head and chest.

Adrenalin is pumping through him. Now a warning bell rings in his head. His vision blurs. In his mind's eye he can see the cocktail he was given. His instincts are being pulled in two directions.

Let rip, be a part of the rave!

A quieter voice can also be heard.

Leave, immediately.

Now he is feeling queasy.

Joe is desperate to clear his head and to drink some water. He remembers his friends.

Where is Archie?

Joe notices a disturbing, vacant look in the eyes of the man dancing beside him. Now he spots a toilet sign. There will be water there. He pushes his way through the throbbing mass. Young people are lying lifeless on the floor alongside the dancers. One of them grabs Joe's foot. He is about the same age as Joe. There is a strange expression upon his face. He looks sick. Suddenly he goes into some kind of a convulsion. Joe is concerned. He squats down beside him.

"What's wrong with you mate?"

Out of nowhere, the dark man who gave Joe the cocktail reappears, right in front of his face. He glares angrily at Joe and starts shouting at him and pushing against his chest.

"Leave him alone!"

"Eh? What's it to you?" Joe doesn't wait for an answer. He turns back to the young guy on the floor, who is trying to say something. His pleading eyes meet Joe's, just for a second, then he convulses again, as if he's going to throw-up. Joe feels increasingly light headed, but he wants to help this guy who is totally wasted.

"Leave him alone!" shouts the dark man again, pushing against Joe's shoulder. He looks brutal. The young guy on the floor grabs Joe's shoe. He looks desperate. Joe wants to ask him what he has taken, he wants to help him, to tell him life doesn't have to be like this. It is impossible to talk properly and Joe's own head is getting cloudier. It is getting harder for him to think at all. Joe staggers to his feet. His legs are wobbly.

"Just piss off!" mouths the dark man savagely into Joe's face. Then he turns around and starts communicating with someone through a tiny microphone.

Now the fat bouncer is making his way over. Joe is in danger. He has got to get out of here. He tries to focus but his head is thumping. Now he starts moving, pushing his way through the sweating, dancing crowd. Joe is looking for a green exit sign. It will be his escape route. He staggers between bodies in the darkness.

"How-do-I-get-out?" Joe mouths the words to a ghostly figure, neither male nor female. The ghost doesn't answer, it just tries to dance with him. Joe asks someone else, who replies with a vacant smile. The fat bouncer is getting closer. He is throwing people out of his way.

"How do I get out?" Joe keeps asking the same desperate question. There is a guy who looks like Luke, but is it really him? He is pointing through the darkness. Joe heads in that direction. There is a green exit sign in the blackness. He rushes towards it, pushing away groping arms. Joe is standing in front of a "*NO ENTRY*" sign. He pushes the door open. An alarm bell rings out. He enters a dimly-lit, carpeted reception area. Several security men with enormous heads stand in front of him. Joe looks straight ahead. There is another line of doors beyond the bouncers, with a green emergency exit sign above them. It takes all of Joe's strength to march forwards. He squeezes between the bouncers, pushes down on the bars on the doors and lunges forward. Another alarm is triggered.

"Hey where's he come from?"

"Dunno"

"What's he up to?"

"Are you gonna stop that lad or what?"

"Dunno."

Joe staggers out. The cold night bites at his face and the fog remains in his head, but he keeps on walking. He has left his jacket but nothing could bother him less, they can burn it for all he cares. He staggers down a dark street, not knowing where he is, he stumbles and leans against a wall. There is the canal. He doesn't want to go down there. Somehow he keeps going, fighting off sleep.

At last Joe finds the sanctuary of a bus stop. A red blur emerges out of the darkness. He wants to wave it down but first he must rest on that lovely plastic seat. Sleep consumes him…

Far below the high vault of Waterloo train station, directly beneath the large clock that hangs in that vast concourse, Archie stands swaying in front of the customer information screen. Standing unusually close to him is a family group. The mother wears a headscarf, the father and their young sons wear ill fitting suits. Four battered suitcases stand beside them. The minute hand of the clock moves to the vertical. It is half past eleven.

The smallest boy looks up at Archie with big brown eyes. The father holds up a piece of paper. Written upon it is the address of his brother who left Pakistan ten years ago. Two drunks in dishevelled business suits join them at the screen before running off to catch the last train to Woking.

The brown-eyed boy turns and stares at a noisy group of revellers swigging from bottles of beer. They are headed for the taxis and then a club in Hoxton. The glass doors open automatically, and as the clubbers leave a very smart couple enter pulling their suitcases on wheels. There is some banter between them and the clubbers but it appears to be good-natured.

Archie is almost comatose. He has been standing in front of the information screen for about ten minutes. He has given up trying to focus his eyes upon the floating words. The smart lady is approaching him with her suitcase wheels rattling loudly.

"Archie! Archie! Is that you?"

Archie's heavy eyelids open and Cathy's face slowly comes into focus.

"It is you!' Cathy embraces him in a swift hug. "How are you, Archie?"

"Pissed, solo, can't focus. I've lost Joe and Sam, and Deefor's gone," he is becoming tearful.

It is obvious that Archie is very drunk but Cathy's main concern is to get to Bayswater to meet up with Hannah, who is going to stay with her for two nights. Cathy and her boyfriend, Jean-Paul, have just disembarked from the Eurostar after a trip to Paris. They recently got engaged and they have been to visit Jean-Paul's parents. Their train got stuck in the Channel Tunnel, that is why they are so late.

Cathy whispers something into Jean-Paul's ear and then she turns to Archie again. "Do you know what your address is Archie?"

Archie tries hard to remember where he lives.

"I think it begins with the letter *c*. It's on the tip of my tongue..." He belches loudly. He is losing bodily control. "No, hang on, I used to live there, now it's a *p*. I've lived in so many places. I'll be alright in a minute. It's just that my legs don't work. I might have a nap. I could get the first morning train... I feel a bit sick..."

Cathy resolves to take Archie home with her. He cannot be left in this state.

Jean-Paul reminds his betrothed of an important fact. "There's only one spare bed and it's a single. Hannah's been promised it."

Archie revives a little. "It won't be a problem, we can

sleep head to toe."

Jean-Paul and Cathy grab hold of Archie's arms. They escort him through the glass doors and into the back of a taxicab.

The red tail lights of the taxi disappear under a railway bridge. The glass doors leading into the station fling open and the family who earlier stood beside Archie come trundling through. The brown-eyed boy struggles with a battered suitcase. They all stand still for a moment, breathing the chill London air. The boy looks up at his father who smiles back reassuringly.

"You have to change! All change! It's the end of the line!"

The voice bellows in the dark. Joe passes from one level of consciousness to another. A slit opens in a puffy eyelid and light streams in. He focuses on a dirty window. Above it is an intrusive, glaring light. It is making his head throb.

Joe is on the upper deck of a modern London bus. An old, brown wrinkled face appears in front of the blinding light, which forms a halo. It speaks.

"Are you alright, son?"

Joe lowers his head and closes his eyes. After a while he looks again, squinting, with narrow eyes. The face is still there.

Joe groans. "Where am I?".

"Croydon," replies the bus driver. There is a murmur from the back of the bus. "Ah, there's another one who thinks we do bed and breakfast."

Joe turns and his heavy head thumps. A lad is stirring on the back seat of the bus. The driver walks over to him and gives him a gentle shake.

"Come on, rise and shine!"

The lad looks alarmed.

"Where am I?"

"You're in Croydon too!"

"Where's Croydon?"

"It's here!"

The driver scratches the back of his head and then he walks back to Joe.

"Where do you need to get to, son?"

"Clapham."

The driver nods and then he turns to the other lad.

"How about you, where do you live?"

"Balham."

"Okay, I'll take you both home."

Joe looks confused. "Will you really take me all the way home?"

The driver nods.

London's streets are empty and the bus tears through the emerging grey dawn at speed.

The other lad is dropped off in Balham and Joe now stands beside the driver's cabin, giving directions. They navigate their way around tight back streets, packed with parked cars. The bus pulls up in front of a Victorian terrace. This is where Joe lives, in a shared basement flat. Joe turns to face the driver.

"I'm so grateful for the lift, what's your name, you didn't tell me?"

The driver's wrinkly brown face crumples into a smile and he gives a wink.

"Take good care of yourself, Joe!"

Joe disembarks. He watches the bus speed off. It misses a parked car by two centimetres.

Joe finds his keys in his trouser pocket. It is a relief he didn't leave them in his lost jacket. Now he treads carefully down the little flight of steps that lead to his front door. He enters the flat quietly, drinks some water out of the tap, and then he collapses onto his bed.

6 Luke's Light

Joe's eyes flash open and he bolts up in bed. He has experienced a very vivid dream in which he was crossing a river towards a light. On the other side of the river was the Gothic gatehouse that stands at the entrance to Grandad's council estate. He cannot remember if he made it to the other side of the river. He needs to know.

In his mind's eye, Joe sees a picture of Luke talking to the skinny homeless lad on the street. Joe gets out of bed and stumbles across his bedroom. His head still hurts. He finds his wallet lying amongst clothes and other debris. He recalls the kindness of the bus driver and wonders what happened to Archie and Sam. He finds Luke's card with the telephone number and address written on it. He takes a deep breath and dials Luke's number. There is a very long wait. A sleepy-sounding Luke eventually answers the call.

"Hello?"

"It's Joe here."

"What's happened?"

"Nothing. You sound as if you've just woken up."

"Do you know what time it is?"

Joe glances at his watch. It is half past five in the morning. He has been asleep for twenty-three hours.

"I'm really sorry for calling so early, it's just that I'd like to talk to you about something."

"What about?"

"It's to do with all that stuff on the street, with the homeless people."

Luke yawns loudly down the phone. "Come around then."

"What, now?"

"Might as well."

"I'll be there in about forty minutes. You're sure that's okay?"

"Yes, I'm wide awake now."

Joe washes his face. He then puts on a strange combination of clothes, jogging bottoms, a sweat shirt, a suit jacket, and trainers. He steps out into the remains of a cold night.

Joe walks quickly with his jacket collar turned up against the cold. His breath is visible in the air. A solitary star shimmers defiantly above the toxic orange glow of the streetlights. At the end of the street, a fox runs out. It stares at Joe fearlessly and then it scrambles noisily over a wooden fence.

Joe turns a corner and he looks along a straight street. It is tightly packed with parked cars. He spots a yellow Triumph Stag with a black hood. He checks the registration number. It isn't the car he thought it might be. He continues walking. A distant memory swims to the surface and he hears Grandad's voice.

"Don't worry it's just the traffic that's keeping them."

Joe tries to focus on the pavement in front of him. He passes under a neon red and blue London Underground sign and enters the station. The escalators don't work so he runs down the steep, shiny metal steps. The platform is empty. It is utterly silent with not a soul to be seen. Joe sits on a wooden bench.

Grandad's voice comes again. *"It'll just be your Aunty Rosie keeping them, that's all… no point worrying."*

Joe's head is feeling heavy. His dreamlike thoughts are drifting back to when he was eleven years old. His parents said they would collect him at five o'clock. At five thirty he put a chair beside Grandad's lounge window and there he sat, watching, waiting, and willing their blue Morris Marina to appear.

There is a distant rumbling in the black tunnel. Joe gets to his feet, unsteadily. The first train of the day approaches, the tunnel roars, lights are bright, the train is upon him.

Joe looks into the next carriage where there is laughter from an army of cleaners heading into the City. Older West Indian women are with their daughters, and some are with their granddaughters too. London is all theirs before the dawn.

Joe slouches into in his orange seat and his thoughts drift back in time.

He is a little boy staring out of the window. The clock ticks louder. Scenes are imagined of a happy reunion. His parents are like royalty and movie stars rolled into one, but where are they? Why don't they pick him up? He is feeling angry, he wants an explanation, he longs to hold them. They never arrive. Instead, at six thirty, a policeman comes to the door. Grandad starts wailing and thumping the wall. Grandad's grief was the most frightening thing Joe had ever experienced. Nan had been very poorly too. She died a few months later.

The train has arrived at High Street Kensington station. Joe steps out. He is the only person on the platform. The train pulls off. He jogs up the steps, smiling at the novelty of having the place to himself. He has never been the only person here before. The pale light of morning creates long shadows in the vaulted shopping arcade. It is all strangely quiet on the high street. A blackbird sings. Joe has never noticed birdsong on Kensington High Street before. The chill air holds the fragrance of spring gardens. Joe's hands are warm in his pockets. He crosses over the empty road and snatches a glance at the ugly office building that houses the Regeneration Company. He continues along a residential street, fronted by white stucco Victorian terraces climbing up the hill. The terraces have portico entrances, tall sash windows and small manicured front gardens. There are fruit trees on the pavement with a profusion of pink and white blossoms and a heady perfume. Petals fall like confetti, covering expensive cars.

Joe stops for a moment and breathes deeply. He is reminded of the cherry tree his nan planted when they moved into their new council home. Joe still can't get that yellow Triumph Stag out of his mind. It was a beautiful car, but there are painful memories too.

After the death of his parents, Joe had to move in with his Aunty Rosie and her boyfriend Trevor. Their Edwardian terraced house near the town centre had beautiful stained glass windows. Joe would sit for hours in quiet contemplation of the colours and patterns reflected upon the walls.

To begin with, Trevor welcomed Joe's arrival but he would later belittle him. It was Trevor who had owned a bright yellow convertible Triumph Stag. He was a mercurial character. He was like a Jacobean manor house that looks wonderful from a distance, but when you look through the windows, you see the interior has been gutted. He was a façade. Rosie thought he would make a great restoration project, but Trevor didn't want to be renovated just yet. He didn't want to give up his drinking or his drinking pals. It would be many years before Trevor underwent his restoration. In the meantime, fortunately for Joe, he was away a lot on business.

Joe walks briskly, past the long line of stepped, terraced

houses, climbing up the hill. These give way to mansion blocks with manicured gardens and black railings under tall rustling London plane trees. Joe smiles at the antics of squirrels jumping on a dewy lawn. The cold sky fills with crimson light. The bird song is loudening. It is a perfect early spring dawn.

As a child Joe harboured pangs of guilt about his troubled time with Rosie and Trevor. He wondered if his untimely arrival made things worse for them. He wanted to move out, but felt a sense of duty to stay with Rosie. He lived with them for two years. When he turned thirteen, he suffered a few anxiety attacks. He didn't really have any friends and spent a lot of time alone, riding his bike. His life was slowly overtaken by a fear of people. One day, home alone, he looked in the mirror and was troubled by his own reflection. He had a consuming realisation that one-day he would die. The sense of nothingness was terrifying. He ran out of the house.

An anchor for Joe during that time was his grandad, who regularly popped in to see him. He would do the gardening for Rosie, as an excuse to spend time with his grandson. The back garden was long and thin. At the end of it was an area of slabs where they would have their bonfires. Joe and his grandad spent ages out there, from dusk into the night, in their private world, delighting in dancing flames, staring into glowing embers. Rosie made them flasks of tea and potatoes were wrapped in foil to bake in the fire. They also made toast on the fire, then added butter and marmite. At a sombre time, these were comforting feasts.

After a massive drinking session, Trevor drove his Triumph Stag straight through the front bay window of the house. It was the middle of the night when Rosie and Joe were asleep. When Joe opened his eyes, Rosie was standing over him. She grabbed hold of him and they fled, through the kitchen and out of the back gate, still in their nightclothes. They ran all the way to Grandad's home. That was where Joe spent the rest of his adolescence, living in a much happier environment. A little later on, Joe befriended Luke and Archie in the technology class at school. Luke knew girls, including Hannah and Cathy. That was when Joe's social life began its upward spiral.

Joe arrives at the mansion block where Luke lives. He knows this area well. He passes it frequently on his way to the nearby pub, the Windsor Castle. Joe steps under a cast iron gateway and looks up at the building. It is in the Arts and Crafts style with fancy Dutch gables, ornate balconies, and terracotta tiling. Joe has been Luke's friend for fifteen years, but he has never been invited inside this building before. He thinks about the massive contrast between it and the council block he grew up in.

Shortly after Joe moved in with his grandad, the local authority housing policy changed and they got rid of resident caretakers. Grandad was forced to retire. At the same time, the better off council tenants were encouraged to move off the estate into private housing or accommodation provided by housing associations. As soon as their homes were vacated, the council moved problem families into them, those with a history of rent arrears and antisocial behaviour. The new tenants screamed at their kids and threw rubbish out of their windows. The remaining tenants were given the option to buy their homes from the council with significant discounts, but the estate was falling apart. The only person who used their *right-to-buy* was Grandad, who had no intention of moving. The estate became increasingly unpleasant.

Joe shakes blossom off his jacket. He walks up to the

entrance and presses the bell. Luke's voice sounds bright and breezy through the intercom.

"Hi Joe, come on up, it's the top floor, there's a lift."

The glossy black painted front door buzzes open. Joe wipes his feet, then steps into a carpeted lobby. He passes an empty porter's desk and decides not to take the lift, instead he jogs up the elegant staircase, two steps at a time. He arrives on the sixth floor upon a bright, wide landing. He is breathless and needs a moment to recover. Luke stands in a doorway, hands on hips. The smell of bacon wafts through the air.

"Something smells good," gasps Joe.

"You're wearing interesting clothes. Come on in, breakfast's nearly ready."

Joe enters the apartment. It is light and very spacious.

"So all of this is just for you?"

"You know my dad," replies Luke. "It's an investment. I'm just the caretaker. The view's cracking, quick, come and have a look."

They enter a bright lounge with a large bay window. French doors lead onto a small balcony, with a table and chairs. Joe follows Luke outside. They lean against the stone coping with both hands. The apartment stands upon the highest hill in Kensington. Stretched out for miles are thousands of roofs; pitched roofs, hipped roofs, gables, spires, bell towers, cupolas, a distant power station, and countless chimney pots upon ranks of terraced houses.

"Wow! What is it with your family and great views?" asks Joe.

Luke shrugs his shoulders.

"The roofs look like a massive beehive," adds Joe. "London's so old."

The sun breaks through the cloud. Slate tiles shimmer and steam as the morning dew evaporates.

Luke brings out the cooked breakfast, which is quickly

97

devoured. After breakfast they remain sitting on the balcony for a while, observing London's landmarks.

"I can see Big Ben!" remarks Joe excitedly. "I can actually see the Union Jack on the Houses of Parliament." Then he spots the Victoria and Albert Museum, the Science Museum, the Natural History Museum. Luke has a good understanding of the topography of London and the surrounding area. He explains the shape of the city to Joe, pointing out Primrose Hill.

"Do you see the green haze over there, in the distance?" he asks.

"Yeah."

"That's Wimbledon. The faint purple rise on the horizon is the Surrey Hills." Luke turns around and points up to the sky, where there are four aeroplanes circling.

"They're waiting for their landing slots at Heathrow." Luke leans over the balcony and points to the west. "You can see where they land, well, almost."

Joe leans over the balcony to look, he is awestruck all over again.

"It's so green, you've even got a forest, like at Lullingdon."

"Oh, that's Holland Park, it's where I go jogging." The canopy of Horse Chestnuts undulates close to the balcony with large wet leaves interspersed with conical shaped white blossoms.

The cooked breakfast helps to relieve Joe's headache. He continues to drink in the view and it lifts his spirit, but he cannot ignore the gnawing feeling that brought him to see Luke.

"So what's been going on with you then?" asks Luke, as if reading Joe's mind.

Joe takes a moment to structure his words.

"Well, London looks beautiful from up here, but it's got

a dark side too, you know? I've seen it."

"How'd you mean?"

"I was out with Archie last night, or was it two nights ago? Anyway, we weren't far from here, we got separated, I ended up at a rave."

"Do people still go to raves?"

"Apparently, yeah, people were having a great time, at least on the surface, but then…"

"What?"

"It was like looking into the abyss, people were desperate. I could see it in their eyes. This one lad in particular was totally wasted, he kept grabbing my feet. He needed help, but there was nothing I could do. What would happen if he couldn't get home? I think someone spiked my drink. What if I didn't make it home? The people you feed on the streets, are they the ones that never make it back?"

"I guess so. You've seen the dark-side but there's light too, Joe. "

"I'd like to help those homeless people. Could I give some money?" Joe's voice begins to shake. "If I'm honest Luke, I just feel very lonely."

Luke looks Joe in the eye. "I've felt lonely too before, you know?"

"Really?"

"Yeah, of course, but now I'm doing stuff that I'd never have imagined doing. These homeless people, they've all got a story to tell. Don't just give them money, why not come with me, take the time to listen to their stories."

Joe looks hesitant. "I'm not sure…"

Luke continues. "What have you got to lose? Meeting Serena really changed my life. It's through her that I'm part of a community. She knows lots of good-looking girls, we could do some introductions for you."

Joe looks more interested. "Really?"

"Yeah, look, I'm doing my voluntary work today, you're

more than welcome to come with me."

Joe stands up, scratches his head, leans against the balustrade, sits down again, pulls his chair towards the table, leans forward, and holds his head in his hands. He mumbles that he doesn't feel great.

"Perhaps another time then," says Luke.

"No, I need to get my head sorted out. You seem to have found something. I'll go with you today."

"That's great."

Joe looks out across London. What will this day have in store for him?

Half an hour later, Joe and Luke walk briskly towards a gatehouse that guards a very distinguished street. The air is fresh and the sky is blue, it is a glorious morning. Imposing Victorian mansions stand in large gardens along an avenue of London plane trees. This is the most expensive street in London. Most of the houses are ambassadorial residences. It is a street of the nations.

Distracted by a couple of female joggers, the uniformed guards don't give Luke or Joe a second glance. They walk on in silence, not noticing a black taxicab pulling up beside the security lodge. A guard exchanges a few words with the driver. There is a young woman sitting in the back of the cab, engrossed in paperwork. It is Hannah, on her way to a meeting at the Lebanese embassy. She woke up an hour ago in Cathy's Bayswater flat. She tiptoed around a heavily snoring Archie who was on the floor with a duvet thrown over him.

Joe and Luke approach Kensington Palace. It is a red brick edifice behind an extensive green lawn. A clock tower chimes like a monastic call to prayer. They could be walking in a medieval Tuscan cloister rather than twentieth century London. Luke nudges Joe and points to a large, chauffer driven, black BMW, pulling out from the palace.

"That's Princess Margaret."

They stop for a moment. The BMW approaches them. At the last moment the single, elderly female passenger turns to face them and she smiles briefly. It is clearly the Queen's sister, Princess Margaret. She is wearing glamorous make-up and has manicured black hair, but looks frail as she heads to Heathrow for her last trip to Mustique. The guards at the lodge stand to attention and give a formal salute.

Joe and Luke walk on through a narrow archway in an ancient garden wall, into Kensington Gardens. These are the historic grounds of the palace, now a public park. A few months earlier they were filled with flowers for Princess Diana. They walk across lawns and meadows, under mighty oak trees. Their trainers are soon drenched but it doesn't bother them. They approach a round body of water in the middle of the park. There are lots of swans, ducks, and a few toy sailing boats. They follow a path alongside the edge of the pool. An old man with a red face and bushy side-burns is ensconced in a deck chair. He holds a joystick and is diligently sailing a remote control boat. When he is not sailing he is a porter in Luke's mansion block. He breaks off from his nautical manoeuvrings and bids Luke good morning.

Luke and Joe continue their walk. After circumnavigating the pool they admire a spectacular equestrian statue. A young black woman walks towards them, dressed in designer clothes and rectangular spectacles. She holds hands with a small boy and a girl. Luke greets them and then he turns to Joe.

"This is Sonya, she's also a volunteer with the homeless people."

"Hi Luke! I'm in a rush. I've got to drop the children off at their grandmother's. I'll see you shortly."

Luke nods. "Okay! I'll introduce you to Joe later." Luke turns to the little boy. "Respect!"

They touch knuckles.

"Respect!" replies the boy before he is dragged off.

As they walk off Joe turns to Luke.

"It's bizarre how you know so many people. I thought rich people were supposed to keep themselves to themselves."

"I'm not rich," replies Luke.

Joe is puzzled. *Is he being serious?*

The illusion of their rural idyll is now interrupted rudely by the sound of roaring traffic. After a few more minutes, they are at the end of the park. They cross over a busy main road. After following shortcuts down alleyways and across cobbled mews, they arrive at a little churchyard. The ancient church looks as if it belongs in rural Hampshire rather than central London. People of varying sorts mill around the place, but most of them look well off. Luke points to a single-storey modern annex.

"That's where the team meets, in there."

"Oh, right." Joe looks apprehensive.

A middle-aged couple come up to Luke, they need to speak to him about something.

Joe's attention is drawn to the sound of singing coming from within the church. His curiosity gets the better of him. He walks over to the entrance and steps inside. He is surprised to find a plush carpeted interior. There are no pews, just comfy chairs. He stands alone at the back, sensing something different about the atmosphere.

Joe looks rather forlorn sitting in a plastic orange chair at a Formica table in the church annex. Volunteers are busy all around him.

"It is smashing to see a rough sleeper helping on the team," says a posh lady with a smile after observing Joe's eccentric clothing.

Joe is relieved when Serena, Luke's girlfriend, comes

over to him and squeezes his arm. She has a lovely smile. Luke is very busy but every now and then he manages to introduce someone to Joe. Sonya, from the park, reappears, without her children. There is a young man called Paul, originally from Oxford, who is something big in the City. Mike and Brenda are an older couple from Brixton. Joe is curious to meet them all and to see this other side to Luke's life. It is a world he knows nothing about. A nagging thought keeps arising though: *What am I doing here?*

"Okay, it's time to go!" shouts Luke.

Joe gets up from his orange chair and he tries to look occupied. Bags of clothes, boxes, and large containers of food are packed into the back of a white minibus. They are a jolly group but Joe still has concerns. He still cannot believe he has actually volunteered to feed homeless people at Waterloo Bridge. Luke comes alongside him, puts a hand on his shoulder.

"We're going to feed a lot of people today, Joe."

"How many?"

"At least a hundred."

"Really?" Joe is staggered.

"The sun's out, it could be a lot more. Come on, sit up front in the minibus with me."

Everyone gets aboard and the sliding door is slammed shut. Luke starts the engine and the minibus rattles into life. They pull out onto the main road and disappear into the London traffic. They are in high spirits, as if heading off on holiday.

"Are we nearly there yet?" someone jokes from the back.

Luke takes Joe through the procedures and it is soon clear that they are not on a holiday.

Luke continues. "Not everyone we feed is homeless. Some of them used to be, but now they live in hostels, some even have their own homes."

"Why do you feed them is they're not homeless?"

"They still need a good meal and a bit of support. Everyone needs someone to talk to now again."

"I know what you mean."

"We don't turn anyone away. There aren't too many rules, just stick together with the team, that's the main thing."

Joe goes quiet, mulling things over, mentally preparing himself. He resolves that he can serve others, at least for a couple of hours.

"You okay?" asks Luke.

"Yep."

"Cool. Will you serve the stew for us?"

"What does that involve?"

"Well, you stand behind the serving table, greet people, then serve stew into the beakers. Serena will be next to you, serving the spuds. She'll look after you."

Joe turns to face Serena who is sitting directly behind him.

"Is that okay with you?" He adds a smile, trying to cover his last-minute nerves.

"Perfect," she replies, returning his smile.

Luke shouts various requests to the others sitting at the back of the minibus. It is agreed that Mike and Brenda from Brixton will serve tea and coffee. Paul from Oxford will serve the sugar. Sonya will serve the bread.

"Can you give out the chocolate too please, Sonya?" shouts Luke.

Paul interjects. "She always eats half of it!"

"Tell you what Sonya, keep some of it back for all of us, we'll need it at the end of the day," adds Luke.

"We've got apples too, shall I keep some back for the team?" asks Sonya, but they all agree they should all be given out. The team is only interested in chocolate.

"What will you be doing Luke, while all of this is going on?" asks Joe.

"I'll try to make sure everything runs smoothly. I'll talk to the guys too. After the food's served we'll all chat with them, you should join in too. Just stick together though, don't go wandering off."

Joe nods intently. Now he stares through the windscreen of the minibus. It is like a wide-screen cinema showcasing the landmarks of London. Harrods, Buckingham Palace, Trafalgar Square, the Palace of Westminster, they have all featured.

"Are you enjoying the tour Joe?" shouts Mike from the back of the minibus.

"Yes, it's very impressive. I'm glad we took the scenic route!"

At last they approach Waterloo Bridge.

"Okay, everyone get ready, windows up!" Luke speaks with an air of authority. He turns to Joe and smiles. "Stick close together, okay?"

This insistence to stick together is making Joe feel more nervous. What would happen if they didn't stick together? He nods loyally and turns the handle to close his window. He can see a long line of homeless people waiting in an orderly queue. There are so many of them, more than a hundred, mostly young men. It is an apocalyptic scene.

Joe is thinking that these are the ones that never made it home.

The queue stretches for about fifty metres along the pavement beside Waterloo Bridge, and then it disappears down a ramp leading to a subway. A scruffy, bearded man waves in front of the windscreen. He is clutching an orange traffic cone in his other arm. Luke gives him the thumbs up sign as he parks the minibus. The bearded man runs around to the back of the bus and the cone is positioned as a warning to other motorists.

The volunteers clamber out of the minibus and everyone gets on with setting things up. Joe isn't sure what he should be doing so he stands beside the bus, bracing himself against the stiff river breeze. A few metres away is a dark, brooding subway. Joe shudders. *What's down there?* He would like to know. *Stick together!* The words echo in his mind. He turns away and forces a smile up at the bright blue sky.

A fifty-metre run of dented guardrail separates the minibus from the queue of homeless people. The volunteers pass the gear over the rail to the people in the queue, who then position it on the pavement. Luke is busy supervising events on both sides of the guardrail, which he frequently vaults over.

Mike turns to Joe. "Do us a favour Joe, pass up the food containers would you? They're in the back of the bus." Joe is pleased to have something to do. He lugs the first one out and rests it on top of the guardrail. A skinny, pale man on the other side of the rail calls for Joe to pass him the container.

"It's very heavy," says Joe. "Are you sure you'll be okay?"

"It's a free workout init? It saves on me gym bills."

Joe hands the man the container and it is then that the smell really hits him. It is a sickly mix of sweat, alcohol and urine. It almost overwhelms him. Joe quickly gets a grip of himself and resolves it isn't going to bother him: *Just serve these people, it's only for one afternoon.*

Joe attempts to vault over the guardrail as Luke did. He can do it surprisingly well. Paul also manages to do it. Serena, Mike, Brenda and Sonya, however, all walk the long way around. After a few minutes, the serving tables are set up and they are ready to begin. Joe stands beside Serena at the first table. In front of them are two enormous steaming tubs, one full of boiled potatoes and the other full of stew. Additional tubs are stashed under the table. Joe fidgets with a large serving spoon. He is feeling apprehensive. A young man, second in the queue, stares at him intently.

He speaks in a strong Liverpudlian accent. "What's fer dinna, eh?"

"Beef stew and potatoes."

"D'ya make it yerself?"

"No, some nice ladies in the church made it."

"Ah, tought so, give 'em our compliments will ya? We likes the ladies." This is followed by a coarse *Carry On!* style laugh.

"You aint even tasted it yet av ya Scalley?" says an old man, first in the queue.

"Ah, Paddy! It's always great stuff!"

Mumbles of agreement are heard echoing down the line, but people at the far end of the queue are getting restless. A rebellion seems to be stirring.

"Hurry up!" someone shouts.

Joe is relieved to have the serving table between him and them.

Paddy, at the front of the queue, has a face that is almost purple. A large squat nose and missing teeth give him a medieval appearance. There is a strong smell of alcohol about him and he has kind eyes.

"Would I give tanks for what we are about to receive?" he asks.

Joe is unsure how to respond. "Er, okay."

The old man makes the sign of the cross and with hands visibly shaking he mumbles an Amen. Serena nods and smiles at the old man, and then she presents him with a plastic cup full of potatoes. His old watery eyes dazzle bright blue as he concentrates hard on handling the container, as if it is full of precious gems. His eyes continue to sparkle as he speaks to Serena.

"So, how are ya m' Darlin?"

"I'm fine thanks Paddy. How are you?"

"I mustn't grumble luv. And how're they treating ya in that theatre of yar's?"

"Okay."

"And who's this fine young fella you've bought with ya today?" he winks at Joe.

Then the Liverpudlian butts in. "Will you get a move on Paddy. You've got all day to chat up women!"

"Alright, alright, Scally, can I not have a moment's civilized conversation now?"

Joe soon gets the knack of serving the food. The people seem to warm to him, as if he is one of their own. He keeps being asked the same question.

When's the chocolate coming out?

Joe mentions the apples but they are frowned upon. When one man demands chocolate and adamantly rejects an apple, Joe asks; "Why not an apple?"

"I aint got no teef, has I?" replies the man with a gummy smile.

"How can you eat chocolate if you haven't got teeth?"

"I suck it," he replies, grinning inanely.

An hour or so passes and all of the food is served. About half of the people who have been fed hang around, not wanting to leave. The volunteers chat with them. People lean against the guardrail or sit on the pavement in small sociable groups. A few solitary figures loiter nearby. It is like a social club and there is a lot of banter going on.

Joe is the only person looking slightly awkward as he stands alone and wonders what to do. He reflects that many of the people he served look like rough sleepers, but some of them are relatively smart and well spoken. He notices a woman leaning against the guardrail, not very far away, looking out over the River Thames. There was only a dozen or so women in the queue today. This lady really stands out because she has style. She is middle aged with long black hair, streaked with grey, partly tied up in a bun. She is wearing lots of junk jewellery. The river breeze ruffles her loose clothes. The woman turns away from the river. She is about to speak to an old man standing beside her, but then she notices Joe. He is still staring at her. The woman takes a drag from her cigarette and slowly exhales… and then she calls over to Joe.

"So how did they rope you into helping us vagabonds today?"

Joe is taken aback, she is so well spoken.

"I wanted to see how the other half live," he replies, instantly regretting his choice of words.

The woman laughs loudly.

"Oh! So, do you think you'll move in?"

"It's a bit draughty," Joe is now surprised by his own bravado.

The woman laughs even more loudly.

"Why don't you join us over here in the sun lounge?"

Joe walks over to the woman and they both lean against the guardrail. The sun is shining and it is a warm, pleasant afternoon. Joe feels light-hearted now the hard work is done. This strange parallel universe he has stumbled into intrigues him. He is interested to know why this well spoken, stylish woman, is living amongst the homeless.

"I'm Joe, what's your name?"

"Amanda."

Amanda offers her hand, which Joe shakes, and then she introduces the old man next to her.

"This is Clive, he used to have his own business, doing scaffolding up north, didn't you darling?"

Clive grins.

"What happened to your business, Clive," asks Joe.

Clive stops grinning. "Wife left me. Lost me business. Me mam died. Couldn't pay bills, got horrible, threatening letters. Council took me to court over Council Tax, ended up spending a fookin night in prison. I got on a train, ended up down 'ere. London was end of the line." Clive shakes his head, he doesn't want to speak anymore. He crouches down and rummages through his collection of plastic bags.

There is a brief silence. Joe turns to Amanda.

"I hope you don't mind me asking, but do you actually live on the streets?"

"Yah, I do, but I've also got a flat, in Chelsea."

"Why do you live on the streets, if you've got a flat in Chelsea?" It is the obvious question to ask.

Amanda turns away and looks towards the river again. After a moment she turns back to Joe. Her voice is softer and sounds more vulnerable.

"I used to be a researcher in the House of Commons. One day I was given an assignment to do research on homelessness. Then I met darling Jake, a rough sleeper. He's bloody charming! He helped me with my research. He dared me to do a swop, just for one night, my flat for his street. He said toffs like me were always doing research on him, then buggering off to their nice warm homes. So, I rose to his challenge. I haven't slept in my flat since."

Joe is perplexed. "So, how long have you been rough sleeping?"

"For about five years."

"And what about Jake?"

Amanda looks embarrassed, her face is flushed.

"The little shit's been living in my flat! Some of the boys are going to sort him out though, isn't that right Clive?"

Clive, startled to hear his name, stops rummaging in his collection of plastic bags. He looks up, grinning again. Amanda looks down at him, benevolently.

"Oh, well, perhaps not, you wouldn't be much help would you, darling?"

Joe interjects. "Amanda, what about your job, what about your life?"

"I never liked that world very much," she replies aloofly. Then she seems to remember something, but shrugs it off. Joe is dumbfounded. He sits down on the filthy pavement. With one arm folded defensively across his chest, and one hand holding his chin, he ponders the situation. Amanda sits down beside him.

Joe turns to her. "What's happened to you isn't right, it's totally unjust. You can see that can't you?" There is no reply. Joe wonders if he has fallen for a made-up story, but it could be true, couldn't it? He decides to ask another question.

"I can see with Clive there's been a series of events that could have toppled anyone. Was it like that for you? Was it one thing after another?"

Amanda looks deep into Joe's eyes. Joe holds her gaze. He isn't going to look away. At some level, they have connected. Through all of Amanda's coolness, he can see a vulnerable child. Her lower lip starts to wobble. Tears flow down her cheeks. She doesn't wipe them away, they just fall onto the dirty pavement. Her shoulders are drooped. She starts sobbing and shaking like a distraught child. Joe opens his arms and Amanda falls into them. They hold each other tightly. She continues to sob and shake. Joe knows he must not let go of her. Eventually, Amanda lets go of him. She finds a tissue and wipes the running mascara from her puffy eyes.

"I wasn't expecting this when I called you over," she says in a broken voice.

"Me neither, are you okay?"

"Not really, no. What an unsightly mess I must be. That's the first time I've cried... for as long as I can remember. It's probably some kind of psychological breakthrough!" She wipes her face with the tissue and continues.

"Something did happen to me when I was too weak to

defend myself. I don't really want to talk about it. I've never really been normal."

"Normal? You're better than normal. But we all need help sometimes, someone to talk to, don't we?"

"I suppose we do." Amanda pulls herself together. She smiles at Joe. "By coming here today and feeding us vagabonds you've really helped me."

"I haven't done anything."

"Yes you have, you've made me feel human again."

For a while they continue to sit on the pavement, and then Amanda struggles to her feet.

"Have you ever hugged a homeless person before me, Joe?"

"No, you're my first."

Amanda laughs.

Joe continues. "I'm going to ask Luke if there's anything they can do to help you get your flat back."

Amanda nods with appreciation and then she gathers up her plastic bags. Without another word she hurries off over Waterloo Bridge. Joe watches her. When she is some distance away she looks back and blows him a kiss. Her hair and clothes are buffeted by the wind. Then she crosses the road and disappears behind the traffic. Joe sighs and turns away. He takes in his surroundings. Everything is just as it was, with people chatting and joking. Joe feels as if he has been in a car crash.

The other volunteers are all busy packing tables and other items into the minibus. Joe decides to help them. Before he can do so, a young man with a bright cheery face approaches him, hand outstretched.

"Ello, I'm Phil. Just wanted to say fanks and good bye." He is about twenty years old, very tall, and as thin as a whippet with a pointy face. His blue anorak is several sizes too small for him. He is carrying a bulging black bin bag over his shoulder.

"Hello, I'm Joe. Where you off to Phil?"

"I'm off to Cornwall this afternoon." Phil searches in his anorak pockets and reveals a ticket. He holds it up to the sun, triumphantly, as if it is a winning lottery ticket. "I'll be departing Victoria coach station at four o'clock, for Truro. Amazin in it?"

Joe smiles. "Yeah, that's pretty amazing, Phil. What'll you be doing in Cornwall?"

"Oh, a whole new life, Joe. I'll be going from village to village, 'elping people out with odd jobs."

As Phil continues to speak, Joe pictures the road opening up before him, the open road of freedom. He recalls camping in Cornwall and the invigorating freshness of the rain-washed air. He repents of allowing his life to become too small. Could he go to Cornwall too?

Phil's voice brings him back to reality. "I've bin homeless for four years, ever since me step-dad kicked me out. I need a new start. I've gotta leave London. Luke's dun a lot to elp me, got me confidence back, even given me the dosh for me ticket, you aint to tell nobody that. I know you aint allowed to give us money." Phil touches the side of his nose with his finger to emphasise confidentiality.

"Anyway Joe, you dun a proper job serving the stew. Much appreciated! I'd luv to talk to ya more mate but I gotta go. I don't want to miss me coach do I?"

"Okay mate," replies Joe. "All the best in Cornwall. I hope your new life goes well."

"You bruvers av been a great help to me. See ya pal!"

Luke and Serena suddenly appear beside Phil. They are delighted to see him. It is all handshakes and hugs. Phil says goodbye to everyone again. He turns on his heels and walks off over Waterloo Bridge, in the same direction that Amanda went. He turns around and waves his coach ticket in the air.

"Come and visit me!"

Joe turns to Luke. "He's off to a new life, exciting, isn't it?"

Luke nods. "I'm pleased he's leaving London."

Serena looks concerned. "All the support networks are in the big cities."

"I know, but I've just got a good feeling about what Phil's doing, he's following his heart." Luke turns back to Joe. "Come on, it's nearly time to go."

"Is there time for me to take a quick look at the river?"

Luke looks at him quizzically. "You won't jump will you?"

"No, I just need a minute to gather my thoughts."

Luke glances at his flashy silver watch. "Okay, we've got ten minutes."

Joe walks over to the middle of Waterloo Bridge. He leans against a parapet and admires the panorama. The great bastion of the City of London, the keeper of Britain's treasure, is being rebuilt. Its skyline is dotted with enormous tower cranes, which look like alien lookouts. The fast flowing, murky River Thames cuts a great swathe opening everything to the sun and air.

Luke joins Joe and together they lean against the parapet, shoulders touching but not speaking. They are both staring at St Paul's Cathedral, the enduring survivor of booms, depressions, and wars. The golden cross on top of the dome is shimmering against the blue sky. Distant clouds are a reminder of the sea.

Joe turns to Luke and breaks their silence.

"Why is Amanda living rough? Is it to do with some issue in her past, maybe abuse? Do you think she's sleeping rough because she's looking for love?"

"That's deep. I don't know. It's good you spoke to her though. I've never seen anyone speak to her for so long before. I guess everyone's looking for love. You showed her some of that today."

"Some people would criticise us for what we've done."

"How'd you mean?"

"It could encourage people to stay on the street."

"Maybe they've got a point?"

"Maybe. It's good that people get a proper dinner though, and someone to talk to.

Remind me, how did you get into this again?"

"I fancied Serena. I did it to get close to her, at least to begin with. I was apprehensive the first time, especially when I saw all the guys queuing up. You've done a good job today. How'd you feel?"

"Absolutely knackered."

"We've got the washing up to do yet."

Joe's face drops. Then he remembers his promise to Amanda.

"Luke, is there anything that can be done to get Amanda's flat back for her?"

"I don't know. I'll talk it over with the others."

Serena is calling them from the minibus. Her voice is competing with the traffic and the river wind. Her words are blown away.

"Come on! We've got to go! There's one chocolate bar left!"

"I'll race you for it!" Joe pushes Luke aside and runs to the bus. Luke is still the holder of their school 100 metres sprint record and he soon catches up. Joe grabs Luke's shoulders and holds onto his neck in a conquering embrace. Luke punches himself free and wins the race and the chocolate.

Joe goes to bed at nine o'clock that evening totally exhausted. He falls asleep as soon as his head touches the pillow. The following morning he tries to ignore the ringing alarm clock. He reluctantly regains consciousness. The dream he is leaving behind is another vivid one. He was watching a magnificent white horse that was waiting for him on the other side of a river. Joe had begun to cross the river along a causeway lined with crocodiles, which slid away when he shouted at them. Again, he saw the Gothic gatehouse shimmering on the other side of the river. The horse was standing beside it. Now Joe sits bolt upright in his bed. Another dream about a river and the Gothic gatehouse. *What does it mean?*

Joe gets out of bed and prepares himself for the day. As he cleans his teeth he feels unusually eager to get to work.

As Joe travels into Kensington by tube he is thinking about his newspaper article. Noon is the deadline for submitting it to the Features Editor at *The Times*. When Joe arrives at his desk at the Regeneration Company, he gets his article on screen. He polishes the text and reads back a sentence to himself:

The de-cluttered Kensington High Street promotes pedestrian freedom and the new white-light ambience makes it glitter like a jewel at night.

At eleven o'clock Joe sends an email to Sarah Parker, the Features Editor, with his article attached.

An hour later Joe is strolling through Holland Park, making the most of the unexpected spring sunshine. It is his lunch break. He takes a seat on a bench surrounded by half open yellow rose buds in the ornamental rose garden. It is beside the remains of Holland House, originally built in the Jacobean period, it was at the heart of political society in the nineteenth century. Joe imagines what the dinners must have been like there, attended by prime ministers and royalty.

In front of Joe is a large ornamental Japanese-style pond. A few people sit on the lawn surrounding it, sunbathing, oblivious to the *"Keep off the Grass"* signs. On the far side of the pond the bright sun glows white on the bark of silver birches. The trees look as if they are bursting with energy. Behind them, tall, elegant Scots Pines pose in the sunshine. Joe lets his eyes rest upon the glittering water. Plop! A fish. His mobile phone rings.

"Hello," Joe speaks in his usual chirpy tone.

It is Sarah Parker, the Features Editor. "I'd like to run with your article, Joe. All being well, it'll feature in Wednesday's edition."

A relatively modest fee is agreed. Joe is delighted.

It is seven o'clock in the morning on the last Wednesday of April. Dappled light shines through the kitchen windows at Lullingdon Manor. The light flickers upon David Rogers' newspaper. He sits at a large refectory style table. He is dressed in a dark navy suit which contrasts with his thick mop of white hair. He is still fit and strong at seventy years of age. His reputation has grown since he purchased the city's struggling football club and took it into the Premier League. He has become something of a local hero. His family have ensured this new celebrity status hasn't gone to his head. He enjoys his cup of strong, freshly filtered coffee, scanning the newspaper for morsels about himself and people he knows.

Annie Rogers, Luke's mother, bursts into the kitchen from a garden door. She carries a large tray of seedlings. She looks flustered. The only make-up she wears is bright pink lipstick. Her face and neck are wrinkled, she is only two years younger than her husband, but she is still pretty. The colourful scarf tied around her hair gives her a slightly bohemian appearance. Annie is an early riser, cramming in reading the paper, gardening and estate maintenance before her charity work. She catches her breath and speaks to her husband with an air of urgency.

"Oh! David, you've got a dead badger on the drive. You should see the size of it! The poor thing must have been run over." Breathes again. "And you've got to read *The Times*. It's Luke's old school friend, Joe, he's got an article in it, about Kensington High Street." Another breath. "Oh, and there's an editorial in the *Post*, saying you should stand as mayor. Absurd! At our age?"

David looks straight ahead as still as the Sphinx. After digesting Annie's words, he takes another sip of his coffee. Annie stares at him expectantly.

"Well?" She requires a response.

David looks as if each word he says is being delivered with some discomfort. "Thank you Annie for sharing your stream of consciousness with me. Let me try to bring some order to the topics you've raised. Firstly, why is it *my* badger? Secondly, why is it an absurd idea for me to be mayor? Thirdly…"

There is silence, he's forgotten what came third. Annie readjusts her headscarf and she issues her rebuff, sounding very cross.

"It's *your* badger because it's your job to clean it up. I can't do everything!" She is in no mood for playing games. "The badger has got to be cleaned up straight away. I've got my Civic Trust ladies coming around. I don't want them to be upset by it."

"Oh, they'll probably appreciate a bit of zoology."

Annie stands there with her hands on her hips, she is tiny but formidable.

"Please put it in a black bin bag for the dustmen to collect. They'll be here any minute."

"If I put grass cuttings in a bin bag they refuse to take it. How do you think they'll respond to a corpse? Fred's coming to mow the lawns this morning, I'm sure he'll take care of *your* badger."

David looks forlorn. He continues. "Annie, have you

forgotten it's my important meeting with the leader of the council this morning. Aren't you bothered?"

Annie shifts her hands from her hips to her face which is contorted like the painting, *"The Scream"*.

"Do you mean it's your meeting to buy the housing estates?"

"You've remembered!"

"David, dear, this is so important. Those poor people have been suffering for too long. You know you're doing the right thing." Annie's tone of voice has completely changed, it is now gentle.

"I completely support what you're doing love, you know that. It's a coincidence that Joe's in *The Times* today. Is his council estate in your deal?"

"Yes, it's the first on the list."

"Thank goodness for that. It's become a terrible place. I didn't feel safe when I went there recently."

"Why did you go there?"

"I just went to have a look."

"When?"

"A few months ago."

"You mustn't go there again, not on your own!"

"Do you remember the opening, when the Broadway estate was first built? I'm sure it was 1969."

David sighs, with a far away look. "I remember. You were by far the most beautiful woman there."

Annie blushes like a teenager and giggles.

David continues. "That was the first estate we built for the council. The profit paid for this house."

Their conversation becomes nostalgic.

"How hopeful we all were back then," says Annie. "Do you remember our first house, the one in town?"

"Of course I do."

"I loved that little house. It was so easy to clean." Annie turns and stares through the sash windows that overlook her impressive herb garden. She notes the windows need cleaning again. She turns back to her husband and returns to the theme of the Broadway estate.

"I suppose it was the happy memory of the opening day, that's why I went back to have a look at the estate. I just wanted to see what it's like now."

"Okay Annie, just please don't go there again, not without me."

Annie chuckles.

"What are you laughing at?"

"Do you remember Beryl, Bill Robinson's wife, telling us off when we arrived in the Bentley. She said we upstaged the Mayor."

"Oh, yes. Bill Robinson was the chairman of the housing committee back then."

"We're fortunate to know Bill. He's come a long way hasn't he?"

"Yes, he's done well. Son of a milkman becomes Secretary of State for Regeneration."

"Poor Beryl," sighs Annie.

"Bill did the biggest council housing deal in the country. He wanted to build 365 tower blocks across Birmingham, one for every day of the year. With state funding, and my help, he got more than that."

"It's not such a great legacy though, is it love? The tower blocks have so many social problems."

David looks hurt. "They've put a roof over the head of thousands of people. You can't blame me for bad management."

Annie looks serious. "I don't blame you for bad management, but the evidence is clear for all to see. Horrible tower blocks aren't what you want to be remembered for are they?"

"No! That's why I'm meeting the leader of the council this morning."

"Of course you are, darling, and you're doing the right thing. Perhaps you should speak to Bill Robinson too, about the government's regeneration plans. Invite him around for dinner. Bill never did remarry did he, love?"

David shakes his head. "No, he never did. He never will. He almost left politics when Beryl died. I think he's alright now though."

Annie looks sad. "Poor Beryl." But she isn't distracted for long. She returns to her point and hammers it home like a barrister. "We're not in the summer of our lives. We mustn't leave children growing up in those terrible estates."

"I've told you, that's why I'm meeting the council leader this morning!"

Now Annie has presented her case, she puts her arm around David's shoulder and kisses him on the cheek.

David smiles warmly and squeezes his wife's hand. "Don't you worry Annie, when we're finally finished here, there'll be no shame."

He places his reading glasses on the end of his large, hooked nose.

"Now darling, let me read Joe's article."

Annie smiles. "I'll cook you some breakfast, you'll need a good start today."

Annie clangs around in her kitchen, with her husband flinching at the crash of a pan and the slam of a drawer.

Annie finishes off the breakfast preparations and David looks up from his newspaper.

"Joe's article is excellent!" he says. "I will give Bill Robinson a call. This article could help him with his urban renaissance policy. I'll give Joe a plug too." Under his breath, he continues. "With all the money I've donated to the Party, they owe me a few favours."

Annie looks pleased. "That's good dear!" she replies with a radiant smile and the slam of a cupboard door.

Just as David takes his first mouthful of sausage, the

telephone rings. Annie answers it, cheerfully. David's ears prick up when the words "Foreign Office" are mentioned.

Annie turns to David and she pulls a face. "It's Tristram Fortesque, he's from the Foreign Office. He needs to speak to you."

"Are you joking?"

"Of course I'm not. Perhaps it's something to do with Jamie, here take it." Annie passes over the phone.

"Hello, David Rogers speaking."

Annie sits beside her husband, listening in as best she can. She finds the long silences agonising. At last David says something.

"Half an hour you say?" He looks alarmed. "Well, I've got another rather important meeting to attend this morning." He looks at his watch. "Oh, I can fit it in, yes, it'll be okay." Another long silence follows. "My garden?"

Annie looks perplexed, why is he talking to this important person about their garden?

"Yes, we've got acres of lawn. No, there won't be a problem." David places the phone down.

"What on earth were you talking about? Come on, quickly, I can't stand the suspense."

David continues to stare down at his feet, deep in thought. Annie grabs hold of him.

"What's going on?" she demands to know.

"Right! Look sharp, Annie. Young Jamie's dropping in for a cup of tea!"

"What for?"

"He wants to have a chat with me. He'll be arriving in a helicopter in half an hour, en-route to Ireland."

Jamie, or rather James Montgomery, is Annie's nephew. He also happens to be Britain's Foreign Secretary. Annie is very pleased that he will be visiting.

"Jamie hasn't been here for so long. We saw him last year of course, at his wedding, but I don't think he's been to Lullingdon since Luke's eighteenth birthday party. I wonder why he didn't telephone himself? It's a bit strange to get a civil servant to call us isn't it?"

"No, it's okay, he's a busy man."

"So, this isn't a social call?"

"No darling, it won't be anything to do with the family, it's business, that's why the civil servant called me."

"But why would Jamie need to speak to you about business? What possible business could you have with the Foreign Secretary?"

"I don't have the faintest idea."

"It must be serious," says Annie, trying to makes sense of the situation.

"I expect so."

"Something to do with national security?"

"Possibly, more likely something foreign."

"But you're not very important, are you?"

"Not really."

"Ah, I know!"

"What?"

"Is Jamie a fan of your football club?"

David shakes his head. "He's a Spurs fan."

"My Civic Trust ladies will be here in an hour. A Foreign Secretary's bound to impress them."

David looks thoughtful. "Do you think we should still call him *Jamie*?"

"Why ever not?"

"Well, it was okay when he was a little boy, but now he's the Foreign Secretary. Perhaps he'd prefer to be called James, what do you think?"

"Oh, I hadn't thought of that. I could call Rosalind, see what she thinks?"

"Oh, no, there isn't time for you to call your sister. Let's call him James, so we don't embarrass him."

"Okay."

Twenty minutes later, Annie rushes back into the kitchen, dressed in a smart outfit. She yells at David.

"There's a policeman in our garden, with a machine gun! I hope he doesn't scare my Civic ladies. Have you got rid of the badger?"

David opens his mouth to answer but nothing comes out. He tilts his head to one side and listens intently. There is the faint sound of a helicopter. It is getting closer.

"I can hear him coming Annie! Come on love. I bet he'll land at the back of the house."

David and Annie can feel the helicopter vibrating in their bodies as it cuts through the air, but they can't see it yet. They place their hands over their ears, protecting them from the thundering, chopping noise. David looks up anxiously at the stone roof tiles covering his manor house.

"There it is!"

An enormous, purple helicopter casts a shadow over them. It drops down to earth quickly upon the manicured lawn, a hundred metres away from the house. Two men sit in the front seats of the helicopter and there is a huddle of passengers in the rear. The new youthful Foreign Secretary takes off his large headphones and jumps down from the helicopter, his hair is blown wildly. Another man follows him. Heads are kept down even though the rotating blades are far above them.

David and Annie hold hands like two small children, overwhelmed by the spectacle before them. James Montgomery and his colleague jog over to them. James looks like his cousin Luke but is taller, bulkier, and not quite so good looking. He kisses his aunt Annie on both cheeks, and then shakes hands with his uncle David and places a firm hand upon his shoulder.

"It's so lovely to see you, Jamie," says Annie. "How's Hilary? We haven't seen you since the wedding. Wasn't it a wonderful day?"

James smiles at being called *Jamie*, he hasn't been called that name for years. It brings back happy memories of playing with his cousins in the forest.

"We're all fine thanks Aunty Annie, everyone sends their love." James introduces the other man. "This is George. Can he use your toilet?"

George looks at them apologetically.

"I'm sorry, it's since I turned fifty, I seem to need the loo every hour. James said you wouldn't mind?"

David looks sympathetic. "You should try turning seventy, I need to go every twenty minutes."

They make their way into the house. George is shown where the lavatory is and then he makes his own way back to the helicopter. As the others walk up to the drawing room, James looks around.

"I haven't been here for such a long time, not since Luke's party. He'll be having his thirtieth soon won't he? How is he?

"Oh, gosh, yes, he'll be thirty soon. That makes me feel so old!" says Annie, "He's fine, enjoying life in London."

"Good. By the way, you haven't aged a day."

"Oh, thank you, dear, neither have you, we've got good genes."

James really does look ten years younger than his thirty-seven years. Annie makes her excuses as she has to get ready for her Civic ladies.

David and James enter the drawing room.

"That's an effective way of missing the rush-hour traffic," says David pointing out of the window towards the helicopter. James laughs and pretends he hasn't heard the line before.

"I'm very fortunate. It's from the Queen's Flight." He looks out of the windows. "Wow! I'd forgotten how impressive the view is. The forest looks magnificent. It looked wonderful from the air, it's so big."

David smiles. "Well, we have the Queen's ancestor Henry VIII to thank for it."

"That's right it was a royal forest wasn't it?"

"It was until Bishop Vesey convinced Henry to bequeath it to the people."

"Yes, the local benefactor who became the king's friend."

David smiles. "That's right. So, Jamie, are you the youngest Foreign Secretary ever?"

"No, Canning just beats me. Look, thanks for agreeing to see me Uncle David." He is clearly anxious to get down to business.

David lowers himself into his favourite leather armchair and he gestures for James to sit on the green settee. David looks intrigued.

"It's smashing to see you, err, James, it's not every day we get a visit from the Foreign Secretary. What do you need to talk about? I know it isn't football because you're a Spurs fan."

James snatches one more glimpse at the view and then he perches on the edge of the settee.

"I'm impressed with your club, congratulations on getting promoted. I like your new acquisitions."

David winces. "Please don't go there, my eyes still water when I think about the price of those players."

James glances at his watch, his countenance changes, he looks serious. "There are two reasons for my visit. Firstly, the Prime Minister says thank you. He's very grateful for your generous donations to the Party."

David fidgets with his fingernails.

James continues. "Secondly, I'm here on a matter of sensitive Foreign Office business. Will you treat it in strictest confidence?"

David shifts uneasily in his chair. "Of course."

"You won't even tell Aunty Annie?"

"Okay. What's it about, what can I do for you?"

"It might be a case of what cousin Luke can do."

"Shouldn't you be speaking to your cousin then?"

David's heart beats a little faster. "Luke's not in trouble is he?"

"No. This is to do with one of his old school friends. I'd appreciate your advice. The Westminster bubble is very small. My ex-diary assistant is friends with Luke. You know Cathy Baker, don't you?"

"Yes, I gave her a reference."

"She's gone to work for Bill Robinson now, our mutual friend, Secretary of State for Regeneration. He is a character!"

"Indeed, and the son of a milkman. Do go on. I hate to be rude Jamie, but I've only got twenty minutes. I've got a meeting with the leader of the city council this morning."

"Sorry, yes, I've got a meeting too, with the President of Ireland. The point is, Cathy told me about her friend Hannah, who works in a refugee camp in Beirut. There's a boy in that camp we need to get out, as quickly as possible."

"Why?"

"It's about keeping the Middle East Peace Process on track."

"Now you're frightening me. What on earth has Luke, or Hannah, got to do with the Middle East Peace Process?"

James leans forward and looks directly into his uncle's eyes.

"Several options are being considered. The best way to get the lad out is to do it quietly. This requires intervention by someone he trusts. I want to offer him a scholarship to study here in England."

James strokes his chin as he considers how much to say. He decides to share more.

"The lad's a virtuoso violinist. He plays in a symphony orchestra but he lives in a refugee camp. My wife, Hilary, has heard him play in Beirut. He's brilliant but he's in grave danger. Luke's friend, Hannah, knows him. I wonder if she'd help us to get him out?"

There is a long pause. "I'm sorry to hear about the boy's predicament, and you know I love classical music, but I still don't see where Luke fits in, or why the lad needs to come to England."

"Did you hear in the news about the assassination of Lebanon's Prime Minister?"

"Yes, it's a very nasty business. It reminded me of the hostages, what a distressing time that was."

"We know who the assassins are. They're a Syrian terrorist group, operating with relative impunity. They plan to use the boy to assassinate Lebanon's Deputy Prime Minister. He's someone we can't afford to lose."

"How will they use the boy?"

James stands up, full of nervous energy, his arms are outstretched. "The assassins are planning to put a device in his violin case. He'll be playing in front of the Deputy Prime Minister at a cathedral concert, very soon. It will be a massacre."

"Surely the boy will know if they put a device in his violin case."

"Oh, they have ways of making him cooperate."

David looks at his watch again. "But how can Luke help?"

James sits down. "Luke could ask Hannah to help the boy. We need her to put him on a yacht. It'll take him to Cyprus. From there, he'll be flown to London."

David doesn't look happy. "That sounds very dangerous for Hannah and I don't understand why Luke needs to be involved. Why don't you just get in touch with Hannah directly?"

"Would Hannah be more likely to trust Luke, or some secret service agent who might pay her a visit?"

"I'm not convinced Luke's the right person to talk to Hannah. They have an old group of five friends. There's another lad, Joe, he was always closer to Hannah, or there's Cathy?"

James glances at his watch. "Whether it's Luke, Joe, or Cathy, I need to act fast. If we don't act by the end of the week, there could be a bloodbath. I'd rather keep it in the family, with people I trust. I couldn't ask Cathy."

David looks anxious. "Can't you just send the lad a plane ticket, with some written instructions?"

"Afraid not."

"What about his parents, don't you need to talk to them?"

James shakes his head again. "He's an orphan, a refugee. He doesn't have parents or a passport. We need someone the lad trusts, to ask him if he wants a scholarship to study music in London, someone who'll put him on a boat. Is that too much to ask?"

"Jamie, there's no way I'd put Luke's life at risk, or the lives of his friends. I have the utmost respect for you and the high office you hold, but you're still new in post, and you're very young." David immediately regrets saying that. Scrambling for a more convincing argument, he continues. "Why aren't MI6 involved with such a sensitive issue?"

"They are. I'm here at their request. They've been liaising with Beirut too. This is the preferred way forward. The military option remains open, of course. It's just far more likely to result in the boy and others being killed. I don't deny the stakes are high. I felt I had to ask you though. I thought it right to speak to you first, rather than go to Luke. I hope I did the right thing."

David's voice is high pitched. "I'll go myself, instead of Luke or Hannah."

James smiles. "That wouldn't work Uncle David, the boy doesn't know you."

"Well, as I say, it's Joe that knows Hannah best. I haven't heard Luke mention her for a long time."

James looks stern. "But as I say, I don't know Joe. I can't just talk to anyone about this."

"I trust him implicitly. He's a fine young man. You met him at Luke's party."

There follows a brief discussion about Joe, what he does for a living, where he lives, and how best to contact him. They hatch a plan to get Joe into the House of Commons, so James can meet him.

David continues. "I'm concerned about Hannah's safety. Her life could be in danger if she does what you want."

"Beirut's dangerous again, we'll be bringing her back whatever happens. I've got to go now Uncle David, and you've got an important meeting too. I'm so sorry about the circumstances of our meeting."

David nods. "I hope for everyone's sake this matter gets properly resolved. What's the boy's name."

"Elias, but please don't repeat a word of our talk."

The Foreign Secretary's helicopter takes off. David and Annie stand together on the lawn, watching it disappear into the blue sky. They walk back into the house.

"How old do you think Jamie looks?" asks Annie.

"About sixteen," replies David and then he embraces his wife. He presses his face against hers. "I'm afraid I can't tell you anything, darling. I had to promise."

"Oh, Jamie's naughty, I don't think that's appropriate. You're not in any trouble are you?"

"No."

"Nor Luke?"

Before David can answer, the doorbell chimes. David releases his wife and wipes his brow.

"Well?" asks Annie.

"I promise you, we're all okay."

"Good. Now then, that'll either be a Civic lady or William for you. I don't want you to be late for the leader of the council."

"What a morning, eh? It's not even nine o' clock yet."

Annie takes David by the hand. They make their way through the panelled grand reception hall. Annie opens the front door and there in front of them, bathed in the morning sunshine, stands a middle-aged motorcyclist. He is dressed in leathers and has a short grey beard. He is David's chauffeur. He hands David a crash helmet and a leather jacket.

"Ride carefully please William, he's not as young as he looks," says Annie.

William straddles the BMW motorbike and gives Annie a salute. David mounts the bike and clings on tightly, the engine growls. They are off, down the crunchy gravel drive. They cross over the moat and approach the lodge cottage and the lichen-covered gateposts. David glimpses side ways and sees an enormous dead badger, feet sticking skywards.

7 Westminster

It is just after one o'clock, Joe's mobile phone rings out with a merry tune. He is sitting on a bench in Holland Park with a mouth full of chicken sandwich.

"Ello," he muffles inaudibly.

"Oh, is Joe there please?" says a refined female voice.

Joe immediately recognises Cathy's voice but she doesn't recognise his, it has been a long time. Joe establishes his identity.

"Oh, sorry Joe, you sound different," says Cathy. "How are you?"

"Fine, just eating a sandwich, and you?"

"Fine, did you know I was engaged to Jean-Paul?"

"Yes, I heard. Congratulations!"

"Thank you. I want you to meet him as soon as possible, everybody likes him. Now, it's great to catch up, but this isn't actually a social call. You need to listen carefully."

"I'm listening."

"Right, you know I'm the personal assistant to Bill Robinson, the Secretary of State?"

"Your status is well known."

"Don't be silly."

"Sorry."

"Listen! Bill's just called me. He's read your article in

The Times. He wants to talk to you. He's giving a speech in the House of Commons tomorrow morning, about his urban renaissance policy. We'd like some bullet points from you on the design of Kensington High Street. This could be a big break for you, are you up for it?"

Joe gulps, he is gob-smacked.

"Are you still there, Joe?"

"Err, yeah, when does he want these bullet points for?"

"We need the briefing note tomorrow morning, shall we meet at eight o'clock?"

"It's very short notice."

"You've got a day and a night, that's plenty of time. You'll do it then?"

"Yes, I'll do it for you, Cathy."

"Thanks honey. Be very concise, just a few bullets, no jargon. Bill acts like an imbecile, but he's actually very intelligent, he demands excellence."

Joe gulps again.

"Do you still work in Kensington?"

"Yeah."

"Good. Bill's got a flat around the corner. Let's meet in that new trendy glass building, with the coffee shop in it, it's on the high street, not far from the tube station, at eight, okay?"

"Yes, okay."

"Thanks so much sweetie, can't wait!"

"Me neither," replies Joe, but Cathy has already hung up.

The following morning, Thursday, Joe scrambles up the steps from High Street Kensington tube station. He is wearing his best suit, shirt and tie. There is a spring in his step. He is invigorated with purpose. He likes the idea of working for the Secretary of State and being a high-level influencer. He worked very late last night, but he doesn't feel at all tired. He is excited. However, his enthusiasm has been tested by a particularly long, frustrating delay on the tube, in the Earl's Court tunnel, again. Now he walks through the arcade's throng of commuters, heading for the high street. He stands still for a moment and adjusts his tie. He readies himself and snatches a glimpse at his watch. *It's 7.59 A.M. Drat!*

He has got one minute to meet Cathy. He rushes out of the arcade and emerges into the bright morning sunshine. He briefly looks up the high street. A tall woman suddenly appears, standing directly in front of him. She is clutching a market research clipboard and is wearing a bright red coat. She is demanding Joe's attention.

"Just one second, please Sir!" she speaks with a slight American twang.

"No thanks!" says Joe, shaking his head vigorously.

Joe turns his back to the woman and jogs down the high street. He builds up speed. People step aside to make way for him. He feels as strong as a warhorse. Someone is running with him.

"Sir, sir, one second!"

The market research lady in her flapping red coat is running alongside him, waving her clipboard. Joe is flabbergasted. He doesn't stop running. *Even if I am the perfect demographic for her research, this behaviour is totally inappropriate.*

The woman keeps pace with him. Joe stops. With his hands on hips he glares at her angrily. The woman gasps for breath.

"Sir!"

"What?"

"Your trouser zip's undone."

"Eh?"

"Your trouser zip is undone!" she repeats loudly. A passer-by looks at Joe's crotch and sniggers. Joe turns his back to the woman and looks down. His flies are not just open, there is a bit of white shirt protruding through the gap. Thank heavens nothing else is showing. Joe wonders how long they've been undone for. It must have been since he got dressed. *How many people on the tube noticed?*

He was stuck in the tunnel for so long. A vision passes before his eyes of all the people on the tube, and on the platform, they are all staring at his crotch, sniggering. He recalls the giggling schoolgirls. He tries to shrug it off but feels hot with embarrassment. It could be worse. He zips up, turns around, lost for words. He offers a genuine big, grateful smile to the market researcher, and jogs off to the coffee shop, a little more humble.

Joe strides into the trendy and busy glass box coffee shop. He immediately notices an immaculate young woman wearing a pin-stripe business suit. She is beautiful and stylish. She is quite short with a curvy figure, has shoulder length red hair, and a pretty face. The top buttons of her blouse are undone revealing ample cleavage. Her legs are crossed. She drinks a cappuccino from a large white cup. It is Cathy. When she spots Joe she puts down her drink and opens her arms for an embrace. Joe rushes over and holds her.

Joe delays letting go for several seconds after Cathy has released him. The poor girl needs a moment to recover from strangulation. When she has her breath back the friends smile warmly at each other. Joe takes a seat upon a stool. His eyes involuntarily wander to Cathy's cleavage. She really does look fantastic.

"Have you got your briefing note Joe?"

The question pulls him back sharply.

"Oh, no, I've left it on the District Line," he jokes.

As soon as the words leave his mouth, he hears them drop on the floor as if someone else has said them. The short run and the sight of Cathy has left him giddy. He concentrates on breathing. Cathy looks concerned. Joe pulls himself together.

"Don't worry Cathy, I've got the paper here for you," he says, rummaging in his briefcase.

Cathy speaks in a business-like tone. "Good. Now then, have you met Bill before?"

"No, I've never met any government ministers."

"Your *Times* article really impressed him. He wants to meet you. Will you ride with us to the House?"

"Whose house?"

"The House of Commons, imbecile."

"Oh, yes, of course," Joe feels his heartbeat quickening again and he senses the landscape of his life is about to change.

"Bill's car will be here any minute."

"Oh, good," Joe squeaks, nervously. He breathes deeply. He gathers his thoughts and turns to Cathy. "Was it your idea for me to meet Bill?"

"No, it wasn't. Bill just called me and mentioned your name out of the blue. Somehow he knows we are friends."

"That's odd. How could he possibly know that?"

"I don't know, I suppose you're famous now, what with articles in *The Times*."

"Hardly. I wonder if Luke's dad, David Rogers, had something to do with it."

"That could be it. Anyway, it's irrelevant. You've got a great opportunity so don't screw it up."

"Okay, I won't."

Cathy's countenance softens. "There's something else Joe, something personal I want to ask you."

Joe's eyebrows are raised. "Oh yes, go on."

"You can tell me to get stuffed if you want, okay?"

"Okay."

"It's about Hannah."

"I haven't seen her for ages."

"I always thought the two of you would get it together,

eventually, you're so well matched." Her tone becomes firmer. "So, is it ever going to happen?"

Joe is flummoxed. For a moment he vainly wonders if Cathy is interested in him. He thinks, *"Is she making sure Hannah's not an obstacle?"*

He realises that is nonsense. Cathy's just got engaged to Jean-Paul. Joe pictures Hannah in his mind. He really does miss her, he would love to see her again.

What Joe does not realise is that Cathy telephoned Hannah the night before, she did this as soon as she knew she would be meeting Joe. The girls plotted for Cathy to ask Joe the probing question to ascertain his intention towards Hannah.

Joe finds himself staring at Cathy's cleavage again.

"Ah, there's the car!" Cathy is pointing through the glass towards a black Mercedes people-carrier on the opposite side of the high street.

"Come along! You can have a think about that question and give me a call later."

Cathy grabs hold of Joe's arm and escorts him out of the café. Together they dart between cars on the heavily trafficked high street and reach the other side. Joe notices a black saloon car parked immediately behind the ministerial vehicle. Two men are sitting in it. Joe steals a look at the back window of the saloon. It flashes words in red, *"STAY BACK!"* Joe relishes the fact he will be riding in a chariot of State along a road used by world leaders for two thousand years. He has arrived. He is already imagining how he will relay the story to Luke and Archie.

Cathy and Joe stand for a moment beside the ministerial vehicle. The passenger door slides open. A suave looking thirty-something civil servant pops his head out.

"Do come in, do come in," he snaps.

Joe pokes his head in cautiously, to see what he is letting

137

himself in for. He instantly recognises the Secretary of State, Bill Robinson. He is a surprisingly short, rotund figure in a grey suit, enthroned upon a cream-coloured leather seat. The interior cabin is spacious but slightly gaudy. The vehicle would better suit a pop star. There are four seats. Two face the direction of travel and are occupied by the Secretary of State and his civil servant, the two seats opposite them are empty. Cathy ducks her head and steps aboard. The Secretary of State collects his papers so she can sit opposite him.

"Do come in," the civil servant snaps again at Joe. His voice doesn't disguise his agitation.

Joe takes a deep breath and climbs aboard. He sits opposite the civil servant.

"Hello, I'm Giles Best. I'm the Secretary of State's Political Secretary." He is very well spoken.

Joe leans forward and shakes his hand.

"Hello, I'm Joe. I'm pleased to meet you."

Bill has his head down, engrossed in his notes. Half-moon spectacles are perched on the end of his nose and slurping noises come from his mouth. He is chewing bubble gum, loudly. Suddenly, to Joe's great surprise, he blows a large bubble. With a "pop" his bubble bursts all over his face and spectacles.

"Oh! Bollocks," he spurts out.

Joe struggles to hold back his laughter. Giles slightly raises an eyebrow. Cathy is about to speak but Bill raises a hand for her to stop. He busies himself with a handkerchief, wiping the pink gum from his spectacles. This done, he repositions his spectacles on the end of his nose and continues to read his notes, as if nothing has happened.

Joe wonders why Bill hasn't even acknowledged him. He takes in his new surroundings with its cream-coloured leather seats, and table with telephonic conferencing facilities. Joe's hand explores the side of his chair, there is an array of buttons that he dare not touch. He wonders about the driver. A dark glass screen separates them from whoever he or she might be.

It feels odd to Joe that he can see all the pedestrians on the street but they can see nothing of him because of the one-way glass. A youth suddenly stares blindly in, wondering who might be there, and then he walks off again.

Joe turns to look at Bill. He notes his grave appearance. He has got bags under his eyes, sagging jowls, and his shoulders are drooped as if he has the world resting on them. He is aged about seventy. Thanks to the bubble gum incident Joe has warmed to him. After a long silence, Bill looks up from his notes. His face is suddenly transformed by a radiant smile. He looks like an old man roused from a snooze who is delighted to find his favourite grandchild has arrived. He speaks with a gruff, smoker's voice, and a strong Midland's accent.

"Alright Cathy, dear, who's this you've brought in to see us? Is this yer new boyfriend?" Bill chuckles to himself.

Cathy adjusts her jacket to cover up any visible cleavage.

"As you know, Bill, he's not my boyfriend, it's Joe, the gentleman you requested a briefing paper from, for your urban renaissance speech this morning." Cathy replies in her crisp, no nonsense tone.

Bill pretends not to hear her. He turns to Giles and mumbles.

"You're still here are yer Giles?"

Giles is dressed immaculately in a pin-stripe suit. He also wears an expression of calm endurance. He nods serenely. Bill turns his gaze to Joe and he gives him a wink.

"Alright son?"

"Yeah, good thanks."

"So, you're the pal of David Rogers's son, Luke, is that it?"

Joe smiles and nods. "Yes, we're old school friends."

"I haven't seen that young man since he was in nappies."

"He hasn't changed much."

"Still incontinent?"

"I think so."

Bill seems to remember something and he looks over his notes again. There is another awkward silence.

The Secretary of State suddenly farts, surprisingly loudly. Joe is taken aback. He wonders if it might have been the sound of something rubbing against something else, but no, it was a fart, released quite triumphantly. Joe looks at Cathy and rolls his eyes. She turns away and stares out of the window, pretending not to have heard it. Joe begins to snigger and he snorts. Now Cathy begins to giggle.

"Alright, alright, settle down, sorry about that," says Bill. "Now then, I'd like to know about the approach to street design that's been championed on Kensington High Street."

Joe pulls himself together. "Oh, right, yes, I've got a note for you in here."

Joe rummages through his briefcase. At last he finds his paper. Bill looks as if he has nodded off again, but then he raises his head and he slides back the dark glass screen so he can speak to his driver.

"Carry on will you please, Simon, but slowly, I want to see what's happening on the high street."

Bill turns to Joe, and he speaks in a more engaging tone. "You know, I've walked up and down this high street thousands of times. I've had a flat 'ere since the seventies. The shops were trading badly but they're doing well now. I'm very impressed with what's been done." He presses a button to lower his electric window and he looks out along the high street.

The vehicle pulls off slowly.

Bill waves his hand in the air, theatrically. "Getting rid of all that highway clutter has made such a difference. It really lifts my spirit."

Giles raises an eyebrow. Bill turns his substantial bulk around in his seat and with considerable effort he crosses his short chubby legs. He emits another squeak. Joe wonders if he might have a medical condition. Bill looks very uncomfortable. He seems to have forgotten just how portly he is. Whilst in this awkward position he turns to Joe.

"But look 'ere, the highways engineers don't like it yer know, because of health and safety. Giles 'ere has tried to stop me from even talking about the improvements to this high street."

Bill's eyes narrow and he stares at Giles. "They're worried about risk assessments all the bloody time." He turns back to Joe. "I tell yer lad, they're obsessed with risk management and bloody health and safety!"

Joe tries to say something but Bill raises his hand to stop him. He continues with a tirade against the obsessions of highway engineers.

"I want to know how the council in Kensington justifies taking out hundreds of metres of guardrail. What about accidents? Are we about to face a major bloodbath? I need hard facts if I'm to support this clutter-free approach."

Joe tries to answer again but Bill raises his hand to stop him.

"Kensington's a wealthy area, everyone knows that, how can poorer areas pay for such improvements?"

Joe is determined to make a point before they arrive at the House of Commons.

"A clutter busting strategy saves a council ten per cent of their highway's budget," he interjects. "I've included hard facts in my note for you."

"Very good."

"We've set up video cameras along Kensington High Street to monitor safety, both before and after the guardrails were removed. They show us how motorists and pedestrians behave."

The Secretary of State nods thoughtfully. "Video monitoring, eh? Would you write that down please Giles?"

Giles's upper lip curls and he snarls very slightly, but then forces a smile when Bill glares at him.

Joe continues. "With the guardrails up, motorists think pedestrians are safely penned in so they drive faster. With the guardrails gone, drivers reduce their speed, they and pedestrians actually look at each other and try to anticipate each other's actions. Everyone takes more responsibility."

"Have you got statistics for the accident rates?"

"Yes, the accident rate is nearly halved when the guardrails are removed."

"It's not just about guardrails though is it?" asks Bill.

"No, we've put in wider stone pavements, human scale street lighting, cycle parking, and pedestrian crossings which follow desire lines. There are better shopfronts too thanks to a new design guide. We've tried to create a high street that's more pleasant than a shopping mall."

Bill is impressed, he nods and smiles. "You're onto something 'ere lad. It's unfair the way pedestrians get left to the mercy of motorists. Fine high streets were one of Britain's great achievements, a legacy from the Victorians. Highway engineers and planners have wrecked them. I struggle to cross the roads. Nobody gives a toss about us old people, or mums with prams. My urban renaissance policy is gonna deal with the highway engineers, head on!"

"Eighty per cent of public open space in cities is highways land," Joe adds. "The engineers have a lot of clout."

Giles looks decidedly bored and he yawns.

Joe continues. "Shouldn't our high streets bring people together for a more positive experience of urban life?"

Bill looks at Giles. "Write all of that down please, Giles, I can use that."

Joe takes a deep breath ready to continue, but Bill raises his hand to stop him.

"We're on the same page lad. Social justice got me into politics."

Due to road works they are forced to take a slight detour. They cruise through a far less salubrious area.

"Just look at that!" Bill says. He slides open the glass screen so he can talk to his driver. "Just stop 'ere a minute will you, Simon."

All that Joe can see of Simon is the back of his short-cropped grey hair. The vehicle pulls over.

Bill turns to Joe. "What do you reckon to this place then kid?" He gestures for Joe to look out of the window. Joe leans forward across Cathy and sees a scene dominated by a traffic junction. There are narrow pavements, rotating adverts, redundant poles, and signs everywhere. There are also rusting guardrails and a discordant range of street furniture. Traffic lights are high up on gantries which peer into living rooms above the shops. An advertising banner flaps in the wind.

Bill pulls a face. "All of this highways crap costs the tax payer billions. It's ruined this place. It's probably a job creation scheme for the fookin Freemasons and I'm not having it!"

Outside, an elderly turbaned man waves his walking stick for the traffic to stop. He needs to cross the road but is going to have a problem. There is a central reservation with a long line of guardrail in the middle of the road. He won't be able cross unless he climbs over the guardrail. A car stops and its headlights flash. The old man waddles forward but his shuffling is too slow and car horns start beeping. He arrives at the central reservation and his bent body leans against the guardrail. He is stuck in the middle of the road, cars are whizzing in front of him and behind. He is trapped.

"What the bloody 'ell's he gonna do now?" asks Bill.

Joe, Cathy, and Giles are all leaning forward, staring out of the window. Another car beeps its horn.

"Shut it!" growls Bill.

The old man grasps the guardrail. He gathers his strength and begins to shuffle along the central reservation. It is very narrow and has pointy paving designed to stop people walking on it. He stumbles, close to the on-coming traffic. Cathy flinches and falls back into her seat.

"I can't bear to watch this. He's not going to be able to cross, not until he gets to that crossing at the junction."

"No, look, he's found a gap!" says Joe.

They watch as the old man forces his large stomach between two sections of broken guardrail. Eventually, he squeezes himself through. There is a break in the traffic on the other side of the road. He hobbles across and reaches safety.

Giles is annoyed. "He knew that gap was there. He misjudged where it was. He should have just used the pedestrian crossing like everyone else."

Bill snaps back with bulging eyeballs. "He shouldn't have to look for a gap. That bloody crossing is in the wrong place, where a highway engineer wanted it, not where an old man needs it!"

Giles falls back timidly into his seat. Bill taps angrily on the glass screen in front of him.

"We've had our practical demonstration, get us out of 'ere please Simon! Quickly now or I'm going to be late!"

After a few minutes they are driving over the River Thames at Westminster Bridge. Joe stares out of the window. A stately, shimmering edifice rises from the lapping waters like a sculpted Atlantis. The Houses of Parliament fill his field of vision. Joe is mesmerised by the sight. He is reminded of the Gothic gatehouse at the entrance to his grandfather's council estate. The gatehouse always spoke to Joe of a more excellent world.

"They say Pugin designed most of it," says Bill with a nod towards Parliament, "but Charles Barry took the credit."

Joe looks up at the thrusting verticals, awe inspired. The first time Joe visited the House of Commons he was a boy on a school trip. He had been fascinated to learn that William the Conqueror was from a line of Vikings who settled in Normandy. William anchored his parliament within the tidal Thames, in reach of sea winds and a quick get away. Joe imagines Elizabeth II as a Viking Queen. After all, she is a direct descendant of the Conqueror. The traffic clears and so does the thought.

The ministerial vehicle pulls in through large ornate gates at the Palace of Westminster, flanked by policemen with machine guns. They pass by the imposing entrance to the ancient Westminster Hall and park in a private courtyard beside a stone cloister. Due to a heightened level of security resulting from a terrorist organization calling itself the Real IRA, they have been escorted all the way by the unmarked police car with its neon sign in its back window flashing, *"STAY BACK!"*

The door to the ministerial vehicle slides open and the passengers quickly disembark. The Secretary of State, Giles and Cathy, don sunglasses for the short walk into Parliament. Joe struggles to get the appendices for his briefing paper into their proper order, ready to give to Bill. The two security men join them, both wear wrap-around shades.

The group walk in a v-formation, like migrating birds. The Secretary of State leads the way and the others following in his slipstream. Joe's awkward flapping with his notes spoils the symmetry. Several other people are in the courtyard including journalists. Heads turn to see a

Secretary of State and his entourage. A man and a woman suddenly turn and head straight towards Bill. Cathy breaks from the formation and greets the couple with handshakes. She makes some hasty introductions.

"Bill, this is the pre-arranged photo-shoot with representatives from the New Urbanism Group. They're visiting from the States."

Bill takes off his shades and pops them into his jacket pocket.

"Ah, yes, I like your approach."

There are handshakes, lively banter, and smiles in front of flashing cameras. The whole exchange lasts for three minutes. Bill puts his shades back on and the party rolls forward. They approach an impressive Gothic porch and another line of armed police officers. Joe calms himself. *You're going to be okay. This will be interesting. Keep breathing.*

There is a loud exchange of "Good morning!" Bill seems to know everyone's first name. Joe wonders how on earth he can remember them all, or is he just making them up?

Suddenly, a gust of wind blows the notes out of Joe's hand. The pages are scattered across the courtyard.

Joe panics. "Hang on! wait for me," he yells as he chases after the papers.

"We've got to press on, Joe," replies Cathy.

Bill shares a few words with an older policeman and he points towards Joe. The policeman nods.

At last, Joe manages to retrieve all of the pages, but when he looks up, the only person left is a younger policeman.

"May I see your pass please?"

"I'm with him," replies Joe pointing through the entrance. The back of the Secretary of State can just be seen at the end of a long corridor. The policeman turns to look, too slowly, Bill and his entourage have disappeared. The policeman shakes his head. Joe remembers the briefing notes in his hand.

He yelps. "I've got to get these to Bill Robinson, immediately!"

The policeman looks decidedly disinterested. "Is he a civil servant?"

Joe's voice is shrill and he stutters and stammers. "No! He's the Secretary of State for Regeneration!" "He needs these papers for a speech he's giving in a few minutes. Can't you let me through?"

The policeman shakes his head. "Not without a pass."

"Don't you have the ability to do anything to help me?" pleads Joe.

The policeman replies coldly. "There's no need to be arsey with me." Then he suddenly stands to attention and his tone of voice changes, he begins to be helpful.

"I'll arrange for your papers to be delivered by hand, sir."

The reason for the change is the return of the older policeman, now standing beside him. Joe hands over his notes to the younger officer. He is resigned to the fact he is not going to be let in.

"Can you tell me how to get out of here, please?"

The young officer points towards the gates where Joe entered a few minutes earlier.

"Just through those gates, sir."

Joe turns around with his head held low. He worked on those blasted notes until late into the night. He doesn't believe for one minute they will get to Bill Robinson in time for his speech. He walks back through the courtyard utterly dejected.

"Excuse me, sir!"

Joe turns around. The older policeman beckons him to come back.

"I do apologise sir, you're requested to report to the

security lodge, my colleague will show you the way." He is referring to the younger policeman who still has Joe's notes in his hand. Joe does not look happy.

"Am I in trouble?"

"I don't know so sir, guilty conscience?"

"No."

"You should be okay then. There are two miles of corridors in there, I don't want you to get lost, so please stay close to this police officer."

Joe is escorted through bustling corridors full of very smartly dressed people. The building is exquisite, all gleaming and soaring with Gothic decoration. There are highly polished tiles; red, blue, green, and gold, and endless oak panelling. Joe resolves to learn more about Pugin, the designer. They pass through the clamour of a crowded Central Lobby and arrive at a small wooden booth. There is a sign that says *Security* above an open window. The police officer turns to Joe.

"Just give your name to the clerk at the window, someone will be along shortly. Sorry I was a bit curt earlier, 'aving a bad morning. I'll deliver your notes to the minister's office." He turns on his heels and Joe is left alone.

Joe feels distinctly uneasy. He gives his name to an elderly male clerk behind the counter who looks as if he hasn't seen the light of day for years. After a few minutes a slightly officious looking young woman arrives.

"*Helloo*, are you Joe?"

She has short, brown hair, a small face, and she speaks in a slightly musical Edinburgh accent.

"Hello, yes I am."

"Pleased to meet you."

A firm handshake is exchanged.

The woman continues. "I'm Fiona, I work for James Montgomery, the Foreign Secretary."

Joe looks baffled.

"I think we have a friend in common. Didn't you go to school with Cathy Baker?"

"Yes, that's right."

"It's a small world isn't it?"

Joe looks anxious. "It is, but what am I doing here, Fiona? I've got no idea what's going on."

"Och, I'm sorry, you do know James Montgomery though, don't you?"

"Well, I met him over ten years ago at a birthday party. He's my friend's cousin. James had just become an MP back then."

"Oh, is that right? He'd have been the youngest MP back then. You'll know he's very friendly, there's nothing to worry about," replies Fiona trying to put Joe at ease.

"I remember him being very down to earth, but there's some mistake, you seem to be suggesting I've got a meeting with him. I haven't. I had a meeting earlier with Bill Robinson, the Secretary of State for Regeneration."

Fiona continues to treat Joe as if he might have learning difficulties. "Ock, as I say, you're not to worry, he's very friendly, would you please follow me now?"

"First of all Fiona, please tell me what's going on?"

"Well, Joe, you've got a meeting with the Foreign Secretary."

"You're serious?"

"Of course."

"What's it about?"

Fiona glances at her watch. "I don't know but come on. We shouldn't keep him waiting.

As they walk along endless corridors Joe tries to guess why the Foreign Secretary wants to see him. It must be mistaken identity. Something else springs to mind.

"I've just had an article published in *The Times*. I wonder if that's what he wants to see me about?"

Fiona looks quite impressed. "You've had an article published in *The Times*?"

"Yes."

"What's it about?"

"High streets, it's nothing to do with foreign policy."

"Och, he's very interested in sustainable development."

"Perhaps that's why he wants to see me then?"

"Could be."

"Actually, I need the loo."

"We'll pass one shortly, dear." Fiona looks a bit worried about Joe. She glances at her watch again and mutters something about keeping the Ambassador to the Netherlands waiting.

"We'll take a shortcut," she adds.

They leave the corridor and climb a narrow back staircase. They walk along another wide, carpeted corridor, then there is another narrow staircase to climb. There is a series of narrow, dark, little corridors. At last they arrive in a very grand, bright hallway flanked by a line of Gothic arched windows.

"I'll never find my way out of here Fiona," says Joe, his heart racing.

"Och, don't worry. I'll make sure you get out all right. There's the loo."

Joe enters the single cubicle toilet. He takes a few deep breaths and gathers his thoughts. He washes his face with cold water at a large porcelain sink and drinks from the tap. He talks to himself in the mirror. *"What's this all about?"*

Joe decides he has two options. Firstly, he can proceed as existing, in a heightened state of anxiety. Secondly, he can relax and enjoy this unexpected tour of Parliament. He opts for the second approach. He joins Fiona. She glances at her watch again and gives Joe a stern look, and then she hurries him onwards.

They soon arrive in a grand anteroom. The Foreign

Secretary's core team are busy on telephones and computers. A couple of them look furtively at Joe and brief smiles are exchanged. The room has a large Gothic window framing an oblique view of Westminster Abbey. One of the assistants approaches Fiona. She gives her a nod and a smile and points towards an inner door. As Joe follows Fiona through this second door he feels the thick pile ruby red carpet give gently beneath his shoes.

"This is Joe, the gentleman you wanted to see, Foreign Secretary!" Fiona projects her voice like an actress on the stage. She touches Joe's arm gently as she leaves the room.

On the other side of the vast room two men are talking intently to each other. They are very smartly dressed in pin-stripe suits. Joe instantly recognises the younger man as James Montgomery, the new Foreign Secretary. His face is little changed from the night of the party, all those years ago. Perhaps he is just a little plumper and he has a few grey hairs now. The Foreign Secretary is perched on the edge of an enormous walnut desk.

"Just a tick, Joe!" he says, giving him a cursory glance.

The older man looks old enough to be the father of James. As they continue their conversation, Joe allows his eyes to wander. The room is palatial. The lower halves of the high walls are dark linen-fold wood panelling. The upper sections are covered in green embossed wallpaper. Large historic maps hang everywhere. Above is a lofty vaulted ceiling with a Victorian painting of the world. The countries of the old British Empire are highlighted in pink. There is an enormous globe in the middle of the room. Most splendid of all, one side of the room has a very tall Gothic window that looks as if it belongs in a cathedral. It reveals a splendid panorama of the River Thames. A yellow tugboat is towing a long line of cargo barges.

James smiles warmly as he steps forward and shakes hands.

"I'm very pleased to meet you again, Joe. We did meet didn't we? At the auspicious occasion of my cousin's eighteenth birthday party, isn't that right?" He speaks quickly and precisely. Joe notes that James's voice has changed. It is deeper and more powerful, every word is clipped. Joe nods and smiles in agreement.

James introduces his colleague. "This is Tristram Fortesque, my Permanent Secretary."

Joe still feels nervous. He opens his mouth to offer a greeting and a surprisingly high-pitched squeak comes out.

"Pleased to meet you."

James continues. "Thanks so much for coming at short notice. I expect you're wondering what this is all about?"

"Yes, I am."

"Okay. I recently visited Lullingdon. I know you're good friends with Luke and the family. Has David mentioned anything to you?"

"No, nothing."

"It's a wonderful place isn't it, Lullingdon?"

"Yes, I love it, but I haven't been there for a long time."

"It's the best bit of Warwickshire." James can see that Joe is distracted by the view of the river, so he guides him over to the massive window. "Let's look at the view."

"This room's very impressive."

"What, this? Oh, it's just a meeting room really. You should see the real Foreign Office, have you been there?"

"No."

"Oh, we'll have to arrange a tour for you Joe, it's quite special."

"I'd like that very much."

"I have got one treasure in here I must show you, it's on loan, it's a Turner, what do you think?"

Joe is ushered towards a remarkable painting of a great inferno.

"Can a fire really be that big?" he asks.

"Yes, and it was, it's the great fire that destroyed the old Palace of Westminster in 1834, if it wasn't for that fire we wouldn't have this building."

Then Joe nearly jumps out of his skin. There is a thunderous, brassy chime from Big Ben. Nine more chimes reverberate around the room. After the last chime, James speaks in a more serious tone.

"Can I speak to you candidly, Joe?"

"Yes."

"I think it was Edmund Burke who said, 'All that's necessary for the triumph of evil is that good men do nothing.' I suppose I became an MP because I wanted to make things better in some way, especially for the worst off. It probably sounds a bit supercilious, but I think we all have a duty to do the right thing. Would you agree?"

"Yes."

James continues. "I've got a proposal and it includes a significant element of personal risk."

Joe now feels hot around his neck, his collar feels too tight and James's voice is becoming more distant.

"I only want you to do this if you absolutely believe it's the right thing for you to do. Is that agreed?"

"Okay," replies Joe and he prepares to say *no* to whatever the request is.

"Have you ever been to Lebanon?"

"I haven't."

"Have you ever been in a refugee camp?"

"No, never."

"Have you seen anything on the news recently about the assassination of the Lebanese Prime Minister?"

"Yes, I did see something about that. I've got a friend who works out there. Actually, she works in a refugee camp. I'm concerned for her."

"Ah, yes, Hannah."

Joe is amazed to hear the Foreign Secretary mention her

name.

James continues. "Do you know anything about the role of Syria with regard to the internal governance of Lebanon, and the implications for the Middle East Peace Process?"

Joe stalls for time. "Could you repeat the question, please?"

8 Escape from Lebanon

It is a dry, pleasantly hot spring day. Friends greet each other in the street with kisses and handshakes. The architecture and the people are all very chic. It could be Paris, but it isn't. A young man leads his girlfriend towards the outdoor photography exhibition. The exhibits are arranged upon tall grey panels, like gravestones they march down a cobbled street. At the bottom of the hill stands a stone clock tower, gleaming white in the sunshine. Bells chime musically for midday. People gather in huddles around the exhibits with beaming faces. Strangers share comments. The photos show images of the earth taken from the air. The exhibition has travelled around the world. It arrived here in downtown Beirut a few days ago.

On the opposite side of the street is a long line of dining tables outside numerous cafés. A heady smell of herbs and grilled meat wafts down the hill. It lures a trickle of shoppers, tourists and office workers. They begin to occupy the seats under canvas parasols, shaded from the sun. Beneath one of these parasols sits Joe. He isn't alone. He is with an elegant middle-aged woman and a similarly-aged man, both from Holland. The three of them sit together as any group of friends might, sipping coffee and chatting.

"How was your meeting with the developers, Joe?" asks

the woman.

"Really good. I'm so impressed with what they've done in the city centre. There's beautiful new architecture, restored historic buildings, investment in streets and squares."

"Will it help strengthen civil society?"

"I think investing in the public realm will certainly help."

The woman is pleased. Her name is Ingrid. She has a regal demeanour, high cheekbones, and perfectly groomed blonde hair. She wears a long thin cotton coat over a beige trouser suit. She looks confident and authoritative and she is. Sitting with her long legs resting together she sips at her hot coffee.

Now Ingrid picks up her papers and holds them at arm's length, so she can read them without putting on her glasses. She speaks in a very refined accent, clipping and cutting every word.

"Do you realise we three are the Anglo-Dutch Committee of Investigation into the Spending of United Nation's Funds for the Relief of Refugee Children in the City of Beirut?"

"Catchy title," says Joe.

"Very grand isn't it? Is it really possible to do all of that in one day, Mike?"

Mike, the distinguished Dutchman sitting next to Ingrid, laughs.

"Nothing happens very quickly in Lebanon, I can assure you of that."

Joe begins to fidget nervously. "She's going to be here any minute now."

"Don't worry. She's going to have a very nice surprise when she sees you, my dear," says Ingrid.

"She's certainly going to have a shock."

"Stay calm, remember what we've agreed," says Ingrid. "Don't tell her any of the details until we're all in the car.

156

Then we tell her about the boy."

Mike interjects. "It's okay to speak in front of Philippe, our driver; he's completely trustworthy. Just say the minimum necessary. Do everything we were told in the briefing."

Joe nods dutifully. Suddenly there is a loud bang. Joe jumps to his feet.

"What was that?" Joe's Dutch colleagues aren't so alarmed. Mike looks very sophisticated in his light summer suit. He slowly pushes his sunglasses up above his thick grey hair and looks around.

"It's just a car exhaust backfiring. Sit down and relax Joe."

"Sorry, I'm so jumpy." He rubs the back of his neck and tries to regain his composure.

"Why don't you tell me some more about the developments you've seen in the city, Joe?" says Ingrid.

Joe is too agitated to chat. Mike tries to help him get over his jitters. He leans forward inquisitorially.

"Tell me more about your young friend, what's she like, exactly? How does she look?"

"She's very pretty."

Mike leans even further forward.

Joe looks pensive.

"I've met her a few times," says Ingrid. "She's good at her job, highly respected by the UN and local embassies. It isn't easy for a single young woman out here."

Ingrid is a member of the Dutch parliament. Her colleague, Mike, is from their Ministry of Foreign Affairs. Joe met them both for the first time the previous day in The Hague. After a day of briefings, they were driven to Amsterdam. They departed from a cold and wet Schiphol Airport late last night. They arrived at a warm, sunny Beirut Airport early this morning.

An old, battered, brown Mercedes strains to reach the top

of the hill. It stops abruptly beside the café. People sitting at the tables stop talking and they turn to look. They have learnt to be wary. The woman passenger sitting in the back of the Mercedes leans forward to speak to her driver then hands him some cash. She wears large sunglasses that almost cover her small face. Her blonde hair is pulled back, covered by a baseball cap. The Mercedes pulls off noisily, leaving the female passenger standing at the roadside. Everyone stares at her because even with unflatteringly baggy clothes, she looks like a film star. There is another bang. Joe jumps again.

"Sorry!" he splutters.

The Mercedes has left an unpleasant trail of black smoke. One of the diners on another table gesticulates angrily with his fist in the air, but the car has already disappeared over the brow of the hill. Joe's Dutch colleagues stand to attention. They are both around six feet tall. Joe takes a few steps backwards so he is hidden by a half-closed green parasol.

Ingrid stretches out her elegant hand to greet the woman, who removes her sunglasses and smiles warmly. She is beautiful. Her bright green eyes sparkle in the sunlight.

"Oh! At last we meet again Hannah, I'm so pleased to see you!" says Ingrid.

"It's so good to see you, Ingrid." Rather than shake Ingrid's hand, Hannah gives her a little hug. A flustered Ingrid kisses Hannah on both cheeks. Ingrid then introduces Mike.

"This is Mike, my colleague from the Ministry of Foreign Affairs. Now, I've got a surprise for you! We need a planner to assess the condition of the camp. We've got someone you know."

"Who?"

Joe steps out from behind the parasol.

"Oh, my goodness, it's Joe! Ooooh!"

Hannah's face is contorted with utter disbelief. Joe opens his arms and Hannah falls into them. It takes them several minutes to get over the shock of seeing each other. They just stare, smiling and shaking their heads in disbelief. It is left to Ingrid to maintain some order.

"Now, Hannah, please pay attention. Thank you so much for agreeing to show us around the refugee camp. I'm so pleased we'll get some time to be with the people, especially the children."

"It's a pleasure."

Hannah turns to Mike. "It's good to meet you, Mike. What do you do in the Ministry?"

"I'm a diplomat."

"Have you been to Beirut before?"

Mike chuckles. "Oh yes, I know the city pretty well. I was based here for a time in the 1980s. It was very lively back then," he says knowingly.

"Mike's from a well to do banking family in The Hague," adds Ingrid.

"There's no need to give away all of my secrets," replies Mike. "Why don't you tell our young friends about your past, Ingrid?"

Ingrid rolls her eyes and looks down at her feet. "They're not interested in my past."

"Oh, yes we are!" says Hannah."

Hannah already knows quite a bit about Ingrid. They first met a few years ago at a fringe event at a Middle East Peace Conference. They sat together at lunch and talked for ages about refugee children. Hannah turns to Joe.

"I can tell you that Ingrid was a pop star in Holland in the seventies."

Ingrid laughs out loud and turns to Joe. "I'm a grandmother now."

"Ingrid's much better known these days for campaigning for refugee children," adds Mike.

Ingrid raises her hands. "That's enough talk about me! Shall we order something to eat?"

Hannah shakes her head. "Please don't eat anything. Lunch is being provided in the camp. They've put a lot of work into it. Don't spoil your appetites."

"Well, can we get you a coffee at least, Hannah?"

"Oh, go on then, yes, that'd be lovely."

Hannah and Ingrid smile at each other. Ingrid repeats the word *lovely* as if she's heard it for the first time and finds it intriguing. Mike is up talking to a waiter.

"Now then, Hannah," Ingrid speaks in a business-like tone, "I was serious you know, when I said we want to get involved in doing something practical. We're agreed on that aren't we?" Ingrid makes a quick sideways glance at Mike. He nods enthusiastically.

"We don't want to get in the way, but we do want to help," Ingrid explains, "We definitely want to meet some of the children too."

"Don't worry, I won't let you down. There's a community hall, well, no, it's a shack really. Anyway, I've spoken to the camp leaders, they've agreed we can help with painting it."

Ingrid puts her hand to her mouth and looks at Mike with wide eyes. He is unsure of how to respond.

"Lovely!" says Ingrid.

Hannah glances at Ingrid's expensive clothes and Mike's summer suit.

"They'll have overalls won't they?" asks Ingrid.

"I'm not sure, sorry."

Mike leans forward with a serious expression.

"Hannah, due to the assassination of the Lebanese Prime Minister, it was very difficult for us to get clearance to come on this trip. Can you tell us what the atmosphere in the city is like?"

Hannah looks equally serious. "People are talking about

the assassination, about links with Syria. It feels as if something's changed in the city."

"How do you mean; what's changed?" asks Mike.

Hannah stares into her coffee for a moment and then looks up.

"Since I first arrived, three years ago, people have been growing in confidence. They talk more about their civil rights. People have been mixing more easily, especially in the city centre. I've seen men from different religious backgrounds playing cards together in the squares." She pauses for a moment. "Since the assassination things have felt uneasy. People are prepared to make a stand for their rights. Just coming here today I passed groups of people carrying the Lebanese flag. I haven't seen anything like that before."

Ingrid looks concerned. "Well, we aren't here to do politics on this trip. We're here to listen and to learn. We want to help the refugee children."

"Yes, that's good," replies Hannah with a smile. "Really, I don't do politics. It's far too confusing. I just try to get on with people whatever their background. Please don't talk about politics at all when we're in the camp."

The others nod earnestly.

Hannah rummages in her bag. "Have you all got your itineraries for the day?"

"Yes, I've got all of my paperwork here," replies Ingrid.

"Good. Shall we order a taxi to the camp?"

"No, no, transportation's all arranged," says Mike. "We have use of my Ambassador's car and his driver for the day."

"Are we all going to fit in, Mike?" asks Ingrid

"Yes, we'll all fit in," he replies. "It's a Range Rover, the best of British. It'll be here any minute."

Joe excuses himself to visit the bathroom.

While they wait, Hannah chats with Ingrid and Mike

about the day's arrangements.

"Will you be able to help us with language translation Hannah?" Ingrid asks.

"Yes, although I'm not fluent in Arabic. I can handle most of the day-to-day stuff."

Mike looks up from his mobile phone. "Please excuse me Hannah, I need to ask Ingrid about a government matter. Ingrid doesn't appear to be particularly pleased about this. Mike begins speaking to her in the guttural tones of the Dutch language. Hannah isn't sure what she should be doing while this conversation is going on. She turns away and goes through her bag again, she finds her morning's post. There is a postcard from Cathy with a picture of two elderly women trying to do an aerobics workout. The greeting says:

"It was so great to see you Hannah. Loads to tell you about marriage plans! Will you be my Chief Bridesmaid? When can we talk? Stay safe. Lots of Love, Cathy (PS: The picture reminded me of us in the school gym)."

Hannah laughs. Her recent London stay-over with Cathy gave her a much-needed break. She worries about things a lot more these days, even getting old and the ticking of her body clock. She works too hard and doesn't see enough of her friends. Hannah is so pleased to have Joe with her now, and here is this postcard from Cathy. She smiles at the thought of Cathy getting married, but doesn't like the title of *Chief Bridesmaid*.

Hannah has one other item of post, it looks official. She opens it carefully. After reading the letter, she sucks in her lips.

Joe returns from the bathroom. "What's up Hannah?"

Ingrid breaks off from Mike's discourse. "Not bad news, I hope?"

Hannah sighs. "Oh, the authorities are making life difficult. I don't want to bother you with this."

"Please, Hannah, tell us if you can, what's wrong?" says Ingrid.

"It's from the British Embassy. It says the Lebanese Foreign Office isn't going to renew my visa. It's bizarre. It says if I want to appeal I have to go to the Lebanese Embassy in London. How much is that going to cost? It's ridiculous. I went to their London Embassy for an interview a few weeks ago. They're getting rid of us. Other aid workers have already been told to leave."

"Do you want to leave, Hannah?" presses Ingrid.

Hannah finds it difficult to answer. She sighs again. She is understandably upset. Ingrid places a hand on her shoulder.

Hannah continues. "I've been in Beirut for a long time. A lot of workers have come and gone in the last three years." She looks down the cobbled street towards the gleaming clock tower and bites her lower lip.

"England seems like another world sometimes, so far away. I haven't seen my parents for ages."

"Tell me Hannah, what do you miss most about England?" asks Ingrid.

"Mum, Dad, friends, the woods."

Hannah turns away for a moment and surreptitiously wipes a tear from her eye. She turns back and forces a defiant smile.

"Most of all, I long for a hot bath. They've only got showers here and the water's rationed!"

Joe looks very concerned. Hannah tries to give him a reassuring smile but then she has to look away again. Tears are streaming down her cheeks now. She apologises for crying.

"I'm sorry, I just love the kids in the camp."

Ingrid nods sympathetically and rubs Hannah's shoulder.

Hannah pulls herself together.

"Anyway, there's no way I can pay for another return flight to London, so that's that.

They are interrupted by the sound of a car horn. A hefty top-specification black Range Rover with blacked out windows pulls up. It purrs on the cobbled street beside their table. It is the Ambassador's car. The driver, Philippe, jumps out. He is aged around forty. He is dark skinned and casually dressed in an open-necked shirt. Philippe is a local man, employed by the Dutch Embassy as chauffeur and guide. Hannah, Ingrid, Joe and Mike get up from their seats; all put on sunglasses.

Ingrid whispers to Hannah. "You must appeal the visa decision. I'll pay for your air fair. It'll be my pleasure to pay for that."

"No, no, definitely not. Ingrid, I wouldn't have mentioned it."

Ingrid's stern look suggests that she is not a woman to be argued with.

"I won't take no for an answer. Even if they don't renew your visa, enjoy the trip to London, go shopping, see your parents."

Joe is already in the front passenger seat of the Range Rover. Hannah, Ingrid and Mike share the back seat.

The car glides over the pristine streets of Beirut's regenerated downtown area. Hannah points out the local landmarks. They pass classical, Italianate buildings with graceful arrangements of windows and balconies. The streets are stunning, gleaming with new and restored stonework. Gaps between them reveal views of distant hills dotted with white buildings and far away villages that merge into a hazy blue horizon. They drive past green, lush peace gardens, palm trees, heroic flights of steps, and the restored cathedral. The conversation in the car is all about the city, how beautiful it is, and how French it feels. For the moment, they have forgotten all about their mission, it is almost like a holiday. The people they pass on the pavements appear wealthy and attractive. Every third car is a Mercedes, but many are old and battered.

Philippe, the driver, looks in the rear view mirror to talk to Mike. "We're going to have to take a slight detour along the coast road."

"Why?"

"There's a demonstration being held in one of the squares. A protest about the assassination."

The others listen carefully.

"I saw people with flags earlier," says Hannah. "They must have been going to the protest."

After driving down a few more streets they approach the edge of the city centre. Ingrid suddenly gasps and swears in Dutch. Beirut's legacy of war is now all too evident. The city's veil has been lifted to show a pockmarked face.

"Every building in this neighbourhood has bullet holes in it," says Hannah.

Joe is speechless. Ingrid repeats another Dutch expletive, then apologises. The others continue to stare out of the windows. They drive along a main road lined with concrete tenement blocks. Dirty curtains are draped across open balconies, blowing mournfully in the wind. All of the buildings have been sprayed with bullets. Chunks of masonry are missing where missiles have hit. This part of the city is almost a ruin and yet many people are living in it.

"It's difficult to imagine what it must have been like isn't it?" says Joe finding his voice.

"It was bloody terrible, believe me," replies Mike.

To their relief the car pulls out into a much wider palm tree boulevard. There is less traffic. To their left, the Mediterranean Sea comes into view, bright aquamarine, calm and inviting. It looks exotic, like the Caribbean Sea.

The mood in the car lightens a little.

"Philippe, does this button make the windows go up?" asks Joe.

"Yes."

After the window is raised, Joe turns around from the front passenger seat to face Ingrid. She nods encouragingly. It is time for him to talk.

"Hannah, there's someone we need to meet in the camp, a young lad."

"Oh yeah, who's he?"

"He's sixteen, he's a virtuoso on the violin."

"You mean Elias. He's lovely. He plays the violin beautifully. He's playing for the Deputy Prime Minister at the cathedral on Friday. So how do you know about Elias? Why do you need to see him?"

"We've got something to offer him," replies Joe cautiously.

"What?"

"An opportunity to study in England, at the best music college."

"That would be amazing but it's impossible. He's a refugee. He doesn't have a passport. He can't leave the camp for a night, let alone leave the country to study. He doesn't officially exist."

"Elias has got friends in high places in the UK. They'll pull out all of the stops for him. They can make it happen. If he'll agree to go with us."

"That's ridiculous, you can't just *take* him," replies Hannah.

A silence follows. Hannah tries to understand what she has just been told. After a while she speaks up.

"Elias is already in a symphony orchestra you know? If he went away, his grandfather would be devastated. The shock would probably kill him. Who are these friends in high places?"

"I can't go into all the details. I don't know all of the details myself. We need to get Elias out for his own personal safety, but also for the peace of Lebanon. His life is in danger, that's why I'm here. Will you trust me on this Hannah?"

Hannah stares into space and remains silent for what feels like an eternity.

Joe speaks again. "If we don't get Elias out the consequences don't bear thinking about, not for the lad and not for Lebanon. Will you help us Hannah?"

Hannah looks agitated. "I've just thought, is this connected to me being called back to London?"

There is another long silence. Now Hannah sounds cross.

"Right! Can we pull over please? I want to get out of this car."

Philippe the driver glances in the rear view mirror to see what Mike's reaction is. Mike nods at him. The car pulls over on the seafront beside the ruin of an old crusader castle. Philippe jumps out first and opens the rear passenger door. Hannah is already out the other side. She stomps off along the promenade. Joe catches her up. He holds onto her arm.

"Look Hannah, we're all taking a risk here. I'm taking a risk for a lad I've never even met. Even if this does mean that your job comes to an end isn't that a sacrifice worth making, if it saves his life?"

Hannah stands still, turns aside, and gazes out to sea. Joe breathes deeply. The sea air is refreshing. For a moment he rests his eyes upon the warm, glowing stones of the castle.

Hannah turns to Joe. "If you aren't going to tell me exactly what's going on that makes things very difficult for me Joe. It feels like a betrayal."

"I'd never betray you Hannah."

There is a long silence.

Eventually, Hannah speaks again. "I have been worried

about Elias. I think he's being watched. Actually, I'm sure of it. Look, I'll do whatever's necessary. Of course I trust you. I'm sorry."

Joe embraces her.

"Thanks Hannah, you're a star. Do you know where we'll find Elias?"

"Yes."

"I'm so relieved. We need to be extremely cautious about what we say. This is really sensitive."

"I realise that."

They join the others who are all standing beside the car, anxiously awaiting Hannah's response.

"Everything's okay," says Joe. "We continue as planned."

Ingrid embraces Hannah. "Well done, this is the right thing to do."

For a moment the group relax. They enjoy the wonderful view of the castle and the tranquil green sea. They breathe the fresh air.

Hannah remains confused and agitated. She takes a few steps away from the group and looks at the horizon alone.

"Hey, that wasn't there the last time I came here," says Mike to Ingrid, pointing to a dazzling glass tower block beside the sea front.

"Yes, a lot of new buildings have gone up."

Joe points out to sea. "There's a big shoal of fish out there."

"Oh, yes, you're right," replies Mike.

"How can you tell?" asks Ingrid.

"Look at the ripples."

"Oh yes, I can see now."

The surface of the sea is glistening with ripples; the water is teeming with fish. Gulls take to the wing and circle the shoal.

Hannah makes her way back to the car, she is still cross.

Joe observes her with some concern. Mike nudges him and he points down the coast.

"Do you see the harbour in the distance, the glistening white masts?"

"Yeah, I can see it," replies Joe.

"You remember the name of the yacht, don't you?"

"*Liberty*."

"A good name."

"Very apt."

Ingrid makes an announcement. "It's time to return to the car! Philippe are you ready to go?"

Philippe jumps into the driver's seat and turns the ignition on. The Range Rover purrs. The passengers climb aboard. They are off again.

They drive along the wide, bright, seaside boulevard. After a while they turn off and enter a maze of narrow, shady, streets. Hannah leans forward and gives directions to Philippe. They are navigating through a poor, densely built-up area. They soon arrive at the modern concrete building where Hannah works and lives. All of Joe's postcards have pride of place in Hannah's bedroom, they are stuck on a mirror above her dressing table.

The Range Rover pulls up. Hannah jumps out and uses the intercom attached to the entrance gates. The gates open. The car descends into the underground car park.

A few minutes later, they are all chatting together on the pavement in front of the gates. Hannah gives a last-minute briefing before they set off for the refugee camp. Standing on the opposite side of the street, beside a café, an Arab man is watching them. He is middle aged and stocky. He has a bald head, thick moustache, and black glistening eyes.

Hannah turns to Philippe. "While you're waiting for us you can get a decent coffee in the café over there." It is then she spots the bald man. "Ah, Sadik, there you are! Come over!"

Sadik crosses the street. He greets Hannah with a handshake and an earnest smile. Hannah explains to everyone that Sadik is a resident of the camp and he is an employee of the aid agency. He is to be their guide for the day.

"The camp's a short five-minute walk away. Is everyone ready to go?" asks Hannah.

There are nods of agreement. Philippe leaves them and heads for the café. Everyone else walks down a narrow street, negotiating a path between street traders. The place is full of life, noise and bustle. Local people turn and stare at Ingrid and Mike because they are so tall and striking. An old battered Mercedes suddenly pulls up. The driver is beeping his horn frantically. Joe jumps and looks alarmed. The driver waves his arms wildly at him.

"Ignore that car, Joe! It's just an illegal taxi touting for business," warns Hannah. This incident with the Mercedes is repeated many times. For some reason they always pull up beside Joe and he jumps every time. Kids on scooters, three on a saddle, are also whizzing by constantly. Their engines sound like exploding hairdryers. No crash helmets are worn. Sadik walks beside the Dutch visitors. His confidence growing, he engages them in conversation, singing Hannah's praises.

"She's helped us to build a new football pitch. It's just outside the camp. You'll see it in a minute."

"Do the children like football?" asks Ingrid.

"They love it. The kids from the camp play with those from outside. It's good for mixing."

Hannah overhears what is being said and joins in.

"It wouldn't have happened without Sadik." She turns to Ingrid. "The thing is there's no space in the camp for football. The new pitch is very rough but it's a great way for our kids to get integrated with the outside world."

They turn a corner and there it is. A dusty red-earth football pitch created out of an old bombsite. High netting surrounds it. There is an informal game going on. Sadik points towards the players like a proud father.

"Look! My boys are on it right now!"

The delegation takes a few minutes to watch the game. Beside the pitch is a single storey breeze-block changing room. Here a group of teenage girls stand, watching the match. Joe spots the girls and he nudges Hannah.

"Look, footballers' wives."

Hannah laughs. There is a broad mix of ages playing in the match.

Ingrid turns to Mike. "Look, one of them is as old as you!"

Mostly they are teenage boys, but there are a couple of middle-aged men too. Several little boys are also chasing around, oblivious to where the ball is. Several of the players wear Manchester United shirts.

Ingrid approves of what she sees. "Sport is good for building confidence."

Hannah is relieved. "Your aid money has helped to pay for this."

"Can I take some photos?"

"Yes, it's okay here, but not in the camp."

Hannah turns to Sadik, he nods in agreement.

"I'll catch you up," says Ingrid. She dashes across the street, miraculously missing a speeding moped. The others walk off, slowly. They are very close to the camp now.

Ingrid returns and Sadik speaks to them all in a very serious tone.

"Please don't take any photos in the camp. The guards have guns. Stay close to me all of the time."

Hannah reiterates the warning. "Stay close together as a group. It's very easy to get lost in the camp."

The others nod dutifully. At the end of the street is a

large, ramshackle gateway made from breezeblocks and salvaged timber. There is a rough sign above the gate made from a plank of wood. The name of the camp is carved onto it in Arabic.

"Okay, this is it everyone," says Hannah. "Stay together, we'll go into the camp now."

They are going to head straight for the school hall, where lunch will be served.

Joe looks pensive. The seriousness of the mission has really sunk in now. He is thinking, *"Why on earth have you got into this situation?"*

The responsibility feels crushing. He isn't sure he can go through with it. Ingrid looks at him and senses his anxiety. She smiles at him reassuringly, although she has butterflies in her own stomach. Together the group walk over to the gateway. There is a sentry post with three armed guards, who enter into a discussion with Sadik. Everyone is ushered into the camp. Ingrid and Mike smile nervously at the guards while Joe just looks at the ground in front of him.

They walk down the main street of the refugee camp leaving behind the everyday world of Beirut. The buildings are almost derelict and their walls are literally covered with bullet holes. Each building has undergone many repairs using random materials. The walls are finished in breezeblock, concrete, salvaged timber, and bits of plastic. Each structure looks as if it is the culmination of many separate building projects. Somehow, they have come together to form somebody's home or a shop. They walk past workmen who are positioning timber roof trusses on top of rubble walls. One of the men waves and shouts at Sadik, who waves back and yells something in Arabic.

"They're friends," says Hannah to Ingrid, who nods and smiles.

Now Sadik says something to Hannah in Arabic and she

laughs.

"Ingrid, they're asking if you're Sadik's new girlfriend."

Ingrid gives a half smile and quickly changes the subject.

"Will the children be in school today, Hannah?"

"No, sorry Ingrid, not today. It's a holiday for them. We'll see them at the community centre though."

"Oh, good, it's just that I've got some gifts in my bag."

"You can always give them to their teachers to pass on. We'll meet a couple of them at lunch."

They continue to walk down the main street. There are a few shops selling rudimentary items. The surface of the road is rough, reddish-brown earth with large potholes containing murky puddles from last night's rain. A few old cars, a van, and several motorcycles are parked along the edge of the street. A jumble of rickety buildings and dark alleys mark the end of it. The place is surprisingly quiet. There are just a few shoppers, people undertaking daily tasks, and children playing in the puddles. It is eerie compared to the bustle outside the camp. The sound of traffic is already a distant murmur.

"So Sadik, is this where you live, here in the camp?" asks Mike.

"Yes, this is where I live, but on the other side."

Mike smiles. He looks as if he could handle any situation. Joe, on the other hand, looks nervous. His bulging eyes are darting this way and that, and he keeps looking over his shoulder. He is overwhelmed by the need to find Elias. Added to this, the armed guards stationed at intervals down the street make him feel edgy. He is thinking about the harrowing stories of the British, Irish and American hostages. He takes little comfort from the blue sky and the warm sun on his face.

Sadik instructs them to stop. They have reached the end of the street. They all gather together and stand beside the mouth of a dark, narrow alleyway.

"Are you all okay?" Sadik asks.

There are nods and strained smiles.

"We must all stay together," Sadik warns them again.

Everyone agrees. They follow Sadik into the dark, ominous alleyway. They are walking down a narrow crevice. Joe walks at the end of the single file line. Towering breezeblock walls and metal sheets rise to either side. This dark, dingy, underworld is almost like a tunnel.

Joe pats Mike on the shoulder, he is looking for some reassurance, but Mike just presses on. It is hard to believe they are still in Beirut, or even in the modern world. It is as if they have stepped back in time. They pass a doorway, a window, a soil vent pipe, another doorway, then a recess with clothes left out to dry in a tiny space, surely it will never get the sun.

There are signs of life in this heap of habitation, but no people. The silence is menacing. They walk upon broken concrete. There are dark puddles and dubious deposits besides holes in pipes. The ground is littered with dead cockroaches. Mike points out an especially large one to Ingrid and she shudders in disgust. They keep walking, slowly, anxiously. Suddenly three small children come running around a corner, like little dancers. They look up at Ingrid, expectantly. Ingrid quickly rummages in her bag to give a gift, but the children run off again, laughing. The sight of the children momentarily lifts their spirits and they are sad to see them go.

Sadik leads the group onwards. They turn another sharp corner and head down an even narrower blind walkway. Then they have to press themselves against a wall to make way for three women. They are wearing long colourful floral clothes and headscarves. The women smile nervously but don't stop.

Joe turns to Hannah. "This is the weirdest place I've ever been in. I've never seen anything like it."

174

"I know what you mean," replies Hannah. "It took me ages to get used to it."

The two of them stand for a moment, looking down the dark, cold passage.

"Look up there," says Joe pointing skywards. "People are actually living up there. Every bit of space is used."

"I know a family that lives up there," replies Hannah.

The place they are looking up at has an upper storey that juts out irregularly into the passageway. Two people in homes on either side of the passage could easily shake hands. Joe marvels how every inch of space is put to use by someone. He is impressed, bewildered, appalled. It is so human and yet so inhumane.

"Where are all the people now?" he asks.

Before Hannah can answer, Ingrid appears beside them. She speaks sternly.

"Come on you two. Sadik wants you to keep up!"

They follow on like scolded school children but soon resume their conversation.

"There's a sense of community in the camp, but the refugees don't live here by choice," says Hannah. "They aren't allowed to live outside of the camp. They don't have rights, can't travel, don't have passports. They can only do certain jobs. Manual things, like cleaning, waiting on tables, the things other people don't want to do. They have to be back in time for the curfew."

They stop walking. Hannah stretches out her hands to emphasise a point. "I just wish they could be assimilated into Beirut society."

Joe looks her in the eye. "I guess they're too politically useful as they are." He shrugs his shoulders, "I'm sorry Hannah."

Hannah rubs the back of her neck. She is agitated.

"Refugees in the Netherlands and Britain don't live like this do they?"

"I doubt it very much, but hey didn't you say *'don't do politics'* in the camp?"

"That's true."

The group continues to walk through a maze of passageways in silence. Joe imagines how he would get out of the place if he really had to. He has to admit to himself that he is utterly dependent upon the local knowledge of Sadik and Hannah. They have been walking for what seems like ages. How big can the camp be? Every now and again Sadik shouts words of encouragement from the front of the line. They turn a corner. At last, they can see an open area, bathed in sunshine. The passageway widens out. On either side are little shops, crudely cut out of the concrete walls. A woman, colourfully dressed, appears at a shop entrance. She is speaking to a little boy. Ingrid recognises the child, it is the one who looked up at her earlier. Sadik leads the group into the little square.

Their eyes sting as they adjust to the bright light, like moles they emerge from the darkness. The sounds of life are all around, children playing, people talking, sparrows chirping. There is the smell of cooking.

The square has the same reddish-brown earth surface as the main street. Breezeblock buildings define the space, varying in height from three to four storeys. Fewer bullets have reached this far into the camp. At ground floor level, some of the buildings have garage doors with closed roller shutters. Incongruous, as no cars can get down here. There are little offices and shops. Old men and children sit in front of them, shielded from the sun by colourful plastic umbrellas.

Projecting bay windows jut out from the upper levels. The windows all have metal shutters on them, decorated with Arabic patterns. Long curtains hang out of the windows and their red stripes make the square appear like an oriental bazaar. Political posters and statements written in Arabic are plastered everywhere.

People's homes are on the upper levels. The staircases leading up to them are hidden in dark passageways, off the square. There are signs of new building work in the far corner of the square, where a group of men are erecting scaffolding. This is the community centre that the visitors are going to help paint.

Joe and Mike stand beside each other with their hands on their hips, surveying their surroundings while Ingrid and Hannah chat. They all look happier now they are in open sunshine.

"The school's just up there, Ingrid," says Hannah. "They'll have lunch ready for us now, so we'd better press on."

Hannah leads the group across the square and up a narrow connecting street. It is covered in muddy puddles but to their relief it is much wider than the alleyways they have walked along. Hannah strides purposefully towards the school. The street becomes wide enough for a car, but none can be seen or heard. The others follow taking in their surroundings. Ingrid waves at a group of children, who wave back cautiously.

They arrive at the school entrance. It is as if they are back in modern times. They are still within sight of the little square down the street and the dark alleyways, but this is a very different place. The school is the most cherished building in the camp and looks as if it might actually comply with modern building standards. It is painted in cheerful bright colours. Hannah pushes open double doors leading into a reception area. The others follow. They walk along a wide blue-painted hall that smells of bleach. The blue walls are covered with children's paintings. Ingrid admires the artwork and then a stark reality hits her.

"This picture is by a child that's been through some kind

of trauma," she says.

Hannah shouts a greeting down the hallway, in Arabic. Immediately, there are squeals of delight from deep within the building. Three Arabic women run down the hallway towards her. They are all wearing aprons over their clothes and one of them carries a large kitchen knife. Joe is relived when the knife is put down before the woman greets Hannah. Two of the women are in their mid-thirties. One wears a yellow headscarf that falls down over her shoulders, she is strikingly pretty. Another wears a one-piece headscarf and her dark round face shines through it. The third woman is much younger. She is dark, radiantly beautiful, with long black hair and no headscarf. She is dressed in a long black robe. Her name is Rubina.

The three faces are aglow. After hugging Hannah they exchange greetings in Arabic with Sadik. Hannah introduces the women to Ingrid, Mike and Joe. The two older Arabic women smile shyly and then look away quickly. The younger woman, Rubina, shakes hands. There is a flash of eye contact with Joe.

Hannah enters into a brief conversation in Arabic with the three women and then she announces lunch is ready.

The group follows her down the blue hall, through a set of double doors into a children's playground. A large canopy held up on poles shelters the main part of the open space from the sun. Enough natural light penetrates for plants to grow along the borders. Walt Disney paintings decorate the walls. The school is quiet as there are no children because of the holiday. In the middle of the playground, under the canopy, is arranged a banquet with a dozen or so dining places. Positioned upon the tables are many foil-covered platters.

Four young adults in their twenties are already seated; two European men and two Arabic women. When they see their guests have arrived they break off from their intense conversation, rise to their feet and stand beside the table. The cooks busy themselves pulling off the foil from the platters, revealing a feast of rice, chicken, lamb, stuffed peppers, mixed nuts, dates, bananas, oranges and unleavened bread. The quantities are overwhelming. Joe's face lights up.

Hannah introduces the two men, Benoit and Johan. They work with her at the aid agency. Benoit is from France and Johan is from Germany. Joe instantly warms to Benoit and they start chatting. Hannah introduces the two Arab women, Mashkura and Noha, who are both teachers in the school. They are initially cautious but Ingrid is very gracious and the ice quickly melts. Everyone is smiling. Introductions made, they take their seats and tuck into the food. Hannah has to drag the three cooks out of the kitchen to join them.

The meal is jovial. Hannah and Sadik translate for some of the time but most of the communication involves an array of facial gestures and hand signs. Joe gets carried away with his gesticulations, which entertains the others. Ingrid whispers to Hannah.

"Doesn't it feel as if everyone's known each other for ages?"

"Yeah, that's the great thing about eating together."

Rubina, the youngest of the cooks, positions herself next to Joe and she keeps flashing smiles at him. Hannah notices and she decides to warn him.

"Joe, come here a minute will you?"

He gets up from his seat. "What's up?"

"Are you impressed with the food?"

"Yes, it's great."

Hannah continues, more covertly. "I think you've made a friend with Rubina, be careful."

"Really? Don't worry."

After the meal there is time for relaxation and digestion.

Ingrid nudges Mike and asks him to give a word of thanks. He gets to his feet, clears his throat, and gives a cordial speech befitting of a diplomat.

"... and I hope one day you'll be able to visit us in Holland and England," he says in closing. Mike directs his words towards Sadik, expecting him to translate, but he just smiles and nods.

Ingrid turns to the cooks. "The fresh fruit and vegetables really were the best I've ever tasted," she says. Then she turns to Hannah, surreptitiously. "What about all of the food that's left over?"

"Don't worry, nothing goes to waste."

Now that Joe has finished eating, there is an anxious flow of thoughts about finding Elias. The meal has been an island of calm but he knows he cannot be too relaxed. They need to move on. Hannah looks at him.

"Do you know where Sadik's disappeared to?"

Joe shakes his head. The double doors suddenly burst open and Sadik's heavy frame lunges through them. He is carrying what looks like a candelabra with a metal dish on top. A long rubber pipe is attached to it. He waddles over to a corner of the yard, sets up his appliance and arranges a little group of chairs around it. Everyone has broken off from their conversations. They stare at Sadik intently. His preparations complete, he gestures for Joe and Mike to join him. Mike gets up first and sits on a chair next to Sadik, who is mumbling under his thick moustache. Joe also joins them. Sadik puffs away at the tube attachment. After a long, deep drag, he emits wafts of smoke. More deep drags follow and then he solemnly passes the tube to Joe, who smiles nervously and whispers to Mike.

"It's nothing dodgy is it?"

Mike checks what is being burned in the dish.

"It's nothing to worry about. This is a shisha pipe, a nargila. It's just burning something fruity. Here, let me have a drag."

Mike takes hold of the pipe and inhales twice.

"What about Ingrid?" says Joe.

"I don't think she'll want any," replies Mike huskily.

"I mean won't you get into trouble with her?"

Mike ignores this further questioning. His whole molecular structure appears to be transformed into a more relaxed state. Joe takes the pipe and takes a single short drag. It tastes sweet. He takes another drag. He is smiling dreamily. He soon feels giddy so he makes his excuses and heads back, unsteadily, to the table. Hannah looks at him quizzically and then she rises to her feet and makes an announcement.

"We need to say goodbye now I'm afraid. It's time for us to go and do our practical work."

"How far is it Hannah?" asks Joe.

"It's just down to the little square again, not far at all. I think you'll make it. The community hall is the building with scaffolding in front of it. That's what we're going to paint. We're running behind schedule though, so we'll have less than two hours of painting."

While everyone is busy getting ready to leave, Hannah pulls Joe aside. Her face is flushed.

"Elias will be in the community centre." Suddenly, Rubina, the young cook, interrupts them.

"Here, my address, write to me," she says, handing Joe a piece of paper.

"Yeah, okay. I'd give you my address, but... I haven't got a pen."

Rubina's face drops. Joe isn't sure what else to say. It has been such a successful lunch, the last thing he wants to do is offend their hosts. He gets his wallet out.

"Here's my business card, my work address is on it." He immediately regrets giving this. What will his work colleagues say when her letters arrive in the post room?

Rubina's face lights up. The Dutch guests are lingering, reluctant to leave. They know they are never likely to see these people again and their goodbyes are fringed with sadness.

Ingrid turns to Mashkura and Noha. "Can't you come with us to paint?"

"No, sorry," replies Mashkura, who speaks excellent English. "We're going to help with the clearing up here. Benoit and Johan are going with you though."

"Can I leave some gifts for your pupils? They're only colouring books and pens."

"Yes, thank you. I'll give them to the children."

Hannah has to practically drag the visitors away. They cross the schoolyard, go through the double doors, along the blue corridor, and then they are all standing on the muddy street. The sun is failing and the shadows are lengthening. There is more noise and bustle as people return from work in the city. Family groups stroll towards the square, carefully avoiding the puddles in the bare earth. Joe turns to Benoit the Frenchman.

"Benoit, does Hannah have a boyfriend?" he asks, covertly.

Benoit grins and shrugs his shoulders. "She's nice isn't she? I think there's someone back in England. I thought it was you."

Hannah walks beside Ingrid who looks very graceful in her flowing white clothes. Given Ingrid's height and her long blonde hair, she looks very conspicuous in the camp.

"I'm afraid we're running well behind schedule now," says Hannah.

"I'm sorry we took so long over lunch. I hope it doesn't create any problems."

Hannah turns around to check on the others. She sees the ungainly frame of Sadik jogging down the hill towards her. When he catches up he is breathless.

"It took me a while to pack everything away," he gasps.

"Oh, Sadik, I'm sorry. I'd forgotten all about you!"

Hannah gathers the group together outside the entrance to the community hall, just off the little square. The sun has disappeared behind the buildings. The air feels cooler. Birds warble and whistle from their roosts up on the roofs. Light shines through the windows of the community hall giving it a comforting glow.

Sadik pops his head through the half-open doorway and gives a greeting in Arabic. After a moment a tall, dark, clean-shaven man in his mid-thirties steps out. He has thick black hair and wears decorating overalls. He smiles nervously and holds a roller brush covered in white paint. Cautiously, Sadik shakes the man's free hand.

"This is Ally," announces Sadik to everyone.

Ally and Sadik speak together in Arabic, and then Hannah joins in. Their talk becomes excitable. The others watch on with growing concern. Two younger men step out from the hall and join in the confab. They are also wearing overalls. One of them waves his paintbrush alarmingly close to Sadik.

Joe turns to Mike and rolls his eyes. "What can we do?"

"Nothing, let's just wait."

The debate seems to be escalating. There is a moment of silence. A resolution has been made. The decorators stare at the smartly-dressed Europeans. They take off their overalls and present them to their guests. Ally ushers the group into the community hall.

He turns to Ingrid. "You too, madam, please you come in, we'll find work for you all if you like?"

"We can't take their overalls off them," says Ingrid turning to Hannah. "What about their clothes?"

"Don't worry Ingrid, it's fine, they'll be upset if we don't take them. Come on, we're running out of time."

The community hall consists of one main room and a number of smaller rooms off it. The place is a hive of activity. Joe chats with Benoit, the Frenchman, while they wait for instructions. Johan, the German, and Mike, the Dutchman, stand beside them. Most of the camp's community appear to be in the building, helping with the decorating. There is a broad mix of men, women, and children of all ages. Ally suddenly appears again. Joe smiles and nods a greeting to him. Ally has given all of his overalls to the visitors and he has only one left. Joe insists that Benoit takes it, and he does.

In the main room, Ingrid whispers to Hannah. "Have you seen Elias?"

Hannah gives a discreet shake of her head. "Not yet."

A group of women are painting in the corner of the room. They catch Hannah's attention. The sight of Ingrid intrigues them. They overcome their shyness and inspect Ingrid's blonde hair and her elegant clothes. Ingrid and Hannah are soon being given practical lessons by the women on how to paint, and laughter fills their corner of the hall.

Ally shouts commands to the men. "Get a partner, work in twos!"

Johan grabs Benoit.

Joe looks at Mike. "Can I be your partner?"

"Of course you can."

Joe and Mike are ushered by Ally into a small side room where a youth is supervising two smaller boys with their painting. Ally shouts at the youth.

"Elias! Come here."

Joe and Mike briefly stare at each other, wide eyed. They turn away quickly and try to act naturally. The very purpose of their mission is standing right in front of them. Elias is a dark, skinny youth, all limbs, big brown eyes, and fluff on his upper lip.

"Elias!" repeats Ally. "Come here now!" The lad puts

down his paintbrush and stands beside Ally. "These are visitors who want to help you paint. You must show them what to do!"

At that point, Ally departs.

Elias smiles cautiously at Joe and Mike. He is curious to know who they are and where they are from. The two smaller boys continue painting and occasionally they glance at the visitors. Joe and Mike feel awkward. After explaining where they are from they get on with some painting.

Elias turns to Joe. "Ruud Gullit?" he enquiries.

"Eh?"

"Ruud Gullit? Do you know him? He's from Holland isn't he?"

Joe laughs out loud. "Ah, you mean the footballer?"

"Yes."

"I know who you mean. He is Dutch. I'm English. Mike here is Dutch."

Elias nods at Mike but turns back to Joe. "Gary Lineker?"

"Ah, yes! He plays for England."

"I love England," says Elias.

Joe is taken aback and he doesn't know what to say. He simply smiles and starts painting again. After a while Joe turns to Elias.

"So, do you like to play football?"

"A bit, yes."

"I also heard that you like music. You play the violin don't you?"

"Yes, I play every day. How did you know that?"

Suddenly, Joe feels something wet brush against his back and he hears a snort of laughter. He turns around. Rubina is standing there holding a paintbrush that is dripping white paint onto the floor. She smiles ironically. A young man stands beside her. He has the physique of a body builder, wild black eyes, and a large scar across his face. Joe turns to inspect the back of his shirt. His fears are confirmed. There is a streak of dripping white paint on his back. The scar-faced youth laughs maliciously. Joe feels anger rising and an adrenalin rush demands a response. He glares at Rubina. The scar-faced youth positions himself in front of her. There is hardness in his eyes. Joe takes a deep breath and controls himself.

"That wasn't a very nice thing to do was it?"

Joe is very cross, but Rubina and the youth show no remorse. Joe bites his lip to stem the anger.

"Bad luck, Joe," says Mike, shaking his head sympathetically. "But look, there's nothing you can do."

Elias has put his paintbrush down. He stands beside Joe with his hands on his hips. He is not impressed with these antics and he yells in Arabic at Rubina and the scar-faced youth.

"It's okay Elias, it's okay," interjects Joe.

Rubina slopes off with her scar-faced friend.

Elias turns to Joe. "I live just around the corner, you come with me. I get you a clean shirt."

Joe glances at Mike, both read each other's face. This is the breakthrough they need. It will be a golden opportunity for Joe to invite Elias to return to England with them.

"It's just an old shirt," says Joe, not wanting to sound over keen. He continues to resist for some time, much to Mike's disbelief.

"Please, really, I'll give you a shirt. It's a Manchester United one. I'd like also for you to meet my grandfather. He's the oldest man in camp. He would like to meet you. It would be an honour."

Eventually, Joe concedes. "Alright then, but I'll have to check with the others first. Is it okay if Hannah comes too?"

"Yes, of course. Hannah's my friend, let's go and get her right now. Your back is dripping."

Hannah is chatting with Sadik in the main hall. Ally

stands nearby, guarding the front door. Joe explains to Hannah what has happened.

"I've got paint all over my back. Elias has very kindly offered me a shirt. Would you like to come with us? His home is just around the corner."

"Yes, of course, I'll come with you."

Ally is listening to their conversation intently and he looks at them suspiciously. He steps over to Sadik and mumbles something under his breath.

"Hannah and Joe, it's okay for you to go with Elias," Sadik announces, "but don't be longer than twenty minutes."

Joe, Hannah and Elias walk out of the community hall into the cool, darkening evening. They cross the little square where a few decorative lights have been turned on. People are standing around chatting and a few children are playing. They leave the square by one of the narrow, dark passageways and take a sharp left turn through a gap in a wall. With caution they climb a very narrow, steep, staircase set within the wall itself. They emerge back into the fading light. They are standing upon a long landing. There is an aroma of baking. The place is littered with pot plants, plastic chairs, drying clothes and other domestic paraphernalia. Joe braces himself. His head is swirling with the order of words he needs to speak to Elias, to offer him a new life in England. The boy is distracted for a moment as two tabby kittens scamper around the plant pots. Joe and Hannah stand together. Joe tries to make sense of their surroundings. It is as if one shanty town has been built on top of another. Hannah places her hand on Joe's shoulder. She can sense his anxiety.

"Are you okay?"

"I think so, how about you?"

"I'm alright."

"I'm really sorry about all of this Hannah, it's been forced upon you. Are you sure you want to go through with it?"

"It's all been decided hasn't it?"

"We could just go back to the community centre, leave rescue missions to the experts."

"Is that really what you want to do?"

"No. Elias is a good lad. It's worth taking a risk to save him.

"I agree."

"So we'll do whatever's necessary?"

"Yes, whatever's necessary," replies Hannah. "Are you going to ask him now if he wants to come to England?"

"I was going to wait until we get to his house."

"We haven't got much time."

Hannah calls Elias and they walk on together, along the landing, passed ramshackle doorways.

"We must go up again, then we're nearly there," says Elias. He continues, in a hushed voice. "We must go through the library first, so please be very quiet, they will be reading."

They turn a corner and by some act of metamorphosis the pathway is transformed into an enclosed, carpeted room, in which a dozen or so chairs are arranged. Five boys are seated with their noses deep in books. The walls are lined with shelves full of books. Elias leads Hannah and Joe through the carpeted room on tiptoe. They come out the other side, back on a scruffy landing. The boys didn't even look up. Joe turns to Hannah, bemused.

She smiles back. "It's a homework club."

Elias leads them around another corner. They climb a second steep, narrow, covered staircase and step out onto a more spacious landing.

It is almost twilight and the crisp air is tingling with expectation. This higher level extends over the flat roofs of the homes below. When Joe sees the view, he gasps out loud. There is a panorama over the vast city. The refugee camp is littered with layers of makeshift roofs. There are hundreds of television aerials that look like crooked, bony fingers, wagging at the sky. Beyond the camp stretches Beirut and thousands of twinkling lights under a darkening sky. Further away is the outline of deep purple hills and a hint of mountains. The western horizon is streaked cobalt blue and burnt orange.

The sun withdraws and night floods in from the east. Joe is awestruck. It is a stunning sunset. Elias and Hannah join him. Together they stare reverently at the heroic landscape. They are losing track of time.

Beside them stands an incongruous, red-panelled front door. It is odd because it could be the front door of a rather ordinary house, but it is surrounded by stained concrete, salvaged pieces of timber, metal sheeting, and a confusing array of dripping pipe work.

"Please come in, this is my home," says Elias cheerfully.

They enter through the unlocked door. At the threshold a strong smell of mildew hits Joe. He steadies himself and ducks his head as the ceiling is slightly lower than he is tall.

"One minute please, I'll get things ready," says Elias rushing off through a connecting doorway.

"He'll make us some tea," says Hannah and then she taps her watch.

"I'm going to ask him when he comes back," whispers Joe.

Joe and Hannah are standing in a tiny living room. There is a thin, stained carpet under their feet. A television set plays in the corner with the sound turned low. Instead of a staircase, there is a ladder in the corner of the room, up to a loft hatch. Joe is pensive. His arms are tightly folded.

"It's interesting to see how people actually live in the camp," he says.

189

Arabic voices can be heard from the next room. Elias reappears. He helps a very old, unsteady man into the room. He has a wizened brown face that is full of wrinkles. He is carrying a tray upon which rattle two glasses of tea. They shake violently. Hannah rushes over and takes the tray, saving a spillage. She gives one of the drinks to Joe and takes the other for herself.

"Thank you," says Joe earnestly, nodding towards the old man.

"He's the oldest man in the camp," announces Elias proudly.

The old man takes Joe's hand and he enfolds it in both of his hands. His deep, dark eyes are fixed onto Joe.

"I'm very pleased to meet you, sir," says Joe. "It's a great honour."

The old man nods graciously. Joe tries to begin a conversation.

"May I ask how old you are, sir?"

The old man does not understand. Joe turns to Elias.

"Do you know how old your grandfather is, Elias?"

Elias shrugs his shoulders, he doesn't seem to know. Joe is curious. He turns to Hannah.

"I wonder how they know he's the oldest person, if they don't know how old he is? Is it impolite to ask?"

"Not really," says Hannah. "I'll try to ask." She speaks to the old man in Arabic and they are soon engaged in an animated discussion. Whilst this is going on, Elias pulls at Joe's arm.

"Come and see my room. I'll get you the shirt. I'll show you my garden too."

Joe is keen to take the opportunity to talk alone with Elias. He follows him up the wooden ladder. Hannah and the old man are engrossed in a conversation about genealogy.

"Be careful," says Elias.

He and Joe have climbed into an almost pitch-black space. Elias turns on a light. They are in a small bedroom that has no windows. It is a very restricted space. Joe holds his head at an awkward angle to keep it from banging against the low ceiling. The room contains two beds. The walls are lined with posters of footballers and military helicopters. There is a very strong smell of mildew and the walls are stained dark green with damp.

"This is the room of my two cousins," says Elias. "Come on, up again!"

There is another wooden ladder in the corner of the room, which they climb. The building seems to become smaller the higher up they go. Now they are standing in a tiny bedroom at the top of the building. There is a single mattress on the floor and in the corner of the room is a white plastic chest of draws.

"This is my room!" says Elias triumphantly. "Through there is my garden."

Fading natural light penetrates the room through a half-glazed door, which leads onto a flat roof terrace. Elias rummages through his chest of drawers and he finds what he is looking for. He proudly presents it to Joe. It is a red Manchester United T-shirt.

"Here it is!"

"Really, I can't take that from you, Elias," says Joe.

Elias grimaces. "It's my gift for you to take back to England, a souvenir!"

"They're expensive, really, it's too much."

Joe wants to offer Elias the new life in England now, but from the disappointed look on the lad's face, the timing isn't right. Joe needs to accept the gift.

"Thanks Elias, I'll treasure it."

Elias steps outside. Joe quickly changes into the shirt and then he joins Elias on the roof.

Elias laughs. "It's too small for you, Joe."

"Eh? No, it's okay."

"It's too small!"

They are standing upon a roof terrace with carefully arranged pots containing an array of herbs.

"What's that?" Joe asks, looking towards a rickety timber structure at the far end of the terrace.

"That's our bathroom. The toilet."

"Bit cold!" says Joe.

"Very cold!"

"Joe, you're the only friend that's been up here, apart from my cousins." Elias guides Joe to the end of the roof. "I think you'll like to see the view, come, look."

They stand looking between makeshift buildings as Beirut shimmers under the darkening Mediterranean sky. Again, they see the faint outline of the distant mountains.

"Have you ever been to the mountains?" asks Joe.

Elias looks thoughtful. "I've been to the mountains once, with school, not long ago. We went to see the cedars of Lebanon. It's the forest used by King Solomon to build the temple in Jerusalem. England's Queen Victoria paid for the wall that protects the trees."

"Really?" Joe is impressed.

On the school trip, Elias had walked further into the forest than the others. He delighted in the sight of the thick grey tree trunks, bunches of blue-green needles, and the smell of resin. His sensitive ears picked up the crackling of the seed cones in the heat. He told their guide the cedars were singing. The guide told him not to wander off again as grey wolves hunt in the forest.

Elias's smile drops and he suddenly looks upset.

"What's wrong?" asks Joe.

"Oh, it doesn't matter."

"Come on, what's up?"

"Well, when we were getting back into the school bus, there was this man. He said he wanted to sponsor me in the orchestra. His family want to watch me play in the cathedral. He was scary. My teacher had to tell him to go away."

"What did he look like?"

"Very tall, thin, and dark. My teacher said he had a Syrian accent. She said I should never speak to him again. When we left in the bus, I saw the man get into a car. There was another man, he looked exactly the same, maybe they are twin brothers."

"That sounds strange."

"What scares me is I saw them both in the camp, this morning."

"This morning?"

"Yes, I definitely saw them, in a shop. I just ran to the community centre."

"You did the right thing. I don't think it's safe for you to stay here, Elias."

Elias looks distracted. "Apart from that trip, I've never left the city before."

"You've never left the city?"

"No, I mostly stay in the camp. Sometimes, I go downtown, but I never leave Beirut. I can see the mountains from my garden. That's enough."

Joe wants to steer the conversation towards getting Elias out of the camp. He notices a violin case leaning against one of the pots.

"So, Elias, I hear you play the violin, very well."

"I meant to ask you, how do you know I play the violin?"

"Some important people in London have heard about you. Some have even heard you play."

"Really? I'd like to go to London."

"Well, I have an offer for you."

"An offer?"

"Yes, to study music in London, would you like that?"

"Err…"

"You could study under the best teachers. You'd be sponsored, so money wouldn't be a problem."

"Somebody else that wants to sponsor me?" says Elias doubtfully. He looks at Joe directly. "But how could I travel to London?"

"We'll sail to Cyprus, then fly to London."

Elias opens his violin case and positions the instrument against his chin, poised to play.

"If you'd like to take up the offer, everything is already arranged, but because of the politics around here we'd have to go in secret, and we'd have to go now. Hannah will come too."

Elias smiles and nods cautiously. "Are you from London, Joe?"

"I live there now."

"Where did you grow up?"

"Birmingham, right in the middle of England. That's where Hannah's from too. We went to school together."

"Is it nice there?"

"Yes, the people are very friendly. We've got the Forest of Arden nearby, even some Cedars of Lebanon. I'd like to show them to you."

"So, would I be able to see you, if I moved to London?"

"Yes, of course. Everything will be sorted out for you Elias, somewhere nice to live, money, a place at the college."

Elias furrows his brow and sucks in his lips. "I really need to think for a minute. If I play it will help me to think."

Elias tunes his violin. Joe feels butterflies of anxiety in his stomach as he considers practical next steps. If Elias says yes, they will need to get him out of the camp without any awkward questions, then to the marina and onto the yacht.

Elias plays sonorous chords and Joe soon finds himself

smiling. He recognises *Spring* from Vivaldi's *Four Seasons*. He is listening to a brilliant musician. Joe feels his anxieties lifting off him. He looks out over the darkening city and feels his own spirit lifting over the landscape. Elias finishes a note abruptly.

"I will come to London with you."

Joe beams and he wants to punch the air, but then his countenance changes. There is a distant roaring from the city, it sounds like a medieval battle. It diminishes and then it rises again, even louder. It sends a shiver down his spine.

"What on earth's that?"

Elias shakes his head. "It's the people. They are angry because their Prime Minister was killed."

There is another roar. The hairs on Joe's arms all stand up as if electrocuted.

"We've got to go now, Elias!"

"Okay, I'll pack my violin."

"I'm sorry, but you've just got to leave everything."

"What about my grandfather? I must say goodbye to him."

Joe looks anguished. "But what if he tells anyone? If he does, we won't be able to take you."

"He loves me, he won't tell anyone."

"I'm really sorry Elias, but you mustn't tell him, otherwise it'll be too dangerous for us."

They climb back down the wooden ladder. Hannah and the old man look very convivial sitting on the sofa in front of the television.

Joe is panic stricken. "Hannah! We need to leave now. There's civil unrest in the city."

Hannah springs up from her seat. Joe gives a swift little bow towards the old man, who struggles to get up from the sofa, but gives up. Elias falls to his grandfather's knees and hugs him. He looks into the old man's eyes with tears. At the sight of his grandson's tears the old man's face crumbles. Joe puts his hand on Elias's shoulder.

"Come on, we've got to go, now."

Joe, Hannah and Elias step out through the front door into the chill night. They run back along the pathway heading for the narrow staircase. Hannah leads the way with her baggy clothes flapping in the wind. They proceed cautiously in pitch darkness down the covered stairs. They arrive back on the first floor landing. They run around the corner and dash through the library room. It is empty, the boys have gone. They run along the cluttered passage, the kittens dart out of the way. They take great care going down the last narrow covered staircase, again in complete darkness. They are back at ground level, breathing heavily. Drums are beating.

"What's going on?" asks Joe.

Hannah shrugs. "I don't know, come on."

Joe and Elias follow her into the little square where the lights are twinkling. The sound of drums is coming from the far side by the school building. People are gathered around a fire burning in a metal bin. Orange flames flicker high revealing glowing faces. The flames recede and the faces vanish.

"I think it's a celebration for you lot," says Hannah.

The flames rise high again and Joe spots Mike standing apart from the crowd, talking on a mobile phone.

"There's Mike, come on!"

Mike is just finishing his telephone conversation and he looks agitated.

"At last you're here!"

"Elias is coming with us."

"That's terrific."

Mike offers Elias a quick handshake and a warm smile. Elias takes the handshake awkwardly.

"Mike, something serious has happened in the city," says

Joe. "It sounds like major crowd trouble."

"I know. I've just spoken to the embassy, there are massive crowds in the streets and Martyr Square." Mike glances at his watch. "The car's been delayed. It should be here soon. Let's join the others by the fire. Try to look as if you're enjoying the party."

The local women have been teaching Ingrid the steps of a folk dance. Sadik has been giving a more advanced lesson to Benoit and Johan. The younger men from the camp watch on. Suddenly one of the women in the crowd shrieks with her tongue rattling on the top of her mouth. People in the crowd link arms and form a human circle around the fire. The two men playing the drums slow their rhythm. The human circle begins to rotate, clumsily at first. A gentle pace allows the beginners to get to grips with their moves. Snorts of laughter are heard from Ingrid.

Elias nudges Joe's arm and together with Hannah they join the dancing circle. Joe has one arm around Hannah and the other arm around Elias. They are all moving in time to the quickening beat of the drums. Joe kicks his legs out awkwardly, trying to mimic what Elias is doing. Their faces are lit up by the warm, orange glow of the fire.

"Isn't this great Joe?" shouts Ingrid, forgetting herself. "They've put this party on for us, to say thanks. Our dancing is even worse than our decorating!"

Ingrid gasps for breath and her face is flushed. She has not forgotten their mission and she stares at Elias, intrigued to know if he is the one. She tries to read Joe's face. At that point, one of the women standing outside the circle shrieks again, her tongue rattling on the top of her mouth. The drums and the dancing pick up a swifter pace. Soon they are hurtling around the fire at an alarming speed. Everyone is laughing, enjoying themselves, apart from Mike. He is the only one not in the circle. Joe snatches a glance towards him. Mike points at him and then he points up the hill. It is time to go.

Joe is suddenly, violently, catapulted forward. He falls to the ground hard on his knees, miraculously missing the fire. Hannah rushes forward to help Joe. The dancing circle is broken. Joe looks up with wild frightened eyes. He is startled to see the stocky youth with the scar face staring at him, frenziedly.

"You're an American! You've been spying on Elias!" screams the youth.

Joe struggles to his feet. He stretches out his arms defensively and shakes his head. Mike rushes over and puts his arm around Joe's shoulder.

"Are you okay?" he asks.

"Yes, I'm not really hurt, just a bit shaken."

"Okay, it's time to go."

"How are we going to get out of here?" Joe asks as he brushes the dust off his knees. Mike points to the black outline of the Range Rover. It is parked on the prow of the hill beside the school with its headlights switched on. In the narrow spaces it looks like something from another world. Joe breathes a sigh of relief.

"Get everyone together, quickly!" orders Mike. "We'll drop Benoit and Johan off too, it'll be a squeeze."

Mike turns to face the scar-faced youth. "You stay back! We're going now, we don't want any trouble from you."

"Get back to Texas," snarls the youth.

"Actually, I'm from Texel, it sounds the same but it's an island in the Netherlands. We came here because we want to help you."

"I've got friends, they'll kill you." The youth spits and slopes off.

Hannah is standing beside Joe with her arm around him.

"Are you sure you're okay?"

"Yeah, I'm alright, come on, we need to get the others."

Mike turns to Joe and Hannah. "Get everyone together!"

he snaps.

Hannah pulls Ingrid away from a group of local women who are apologising for the incident with the youth. Joe retrieves Benoit and Johan who have been talking to a group of men beside the fire. Mike explains the situation to Sadik, their Arab guide. Within a few minutes they are all gathered at the Range Rover. Philippe, their driver, greets them and ushers them into the Ambassador's car. Hannah and Ingrid occupy the back seat with Elias sandwiched between them. The Range Rover has black tinted windows but they still try to conceal Elias.

"Try to sit down as low as you can, so you're not seen," whispers Ingrid.

"Okay," whispers Elias, snuggling down between the beautiful women.

Johan and Benoit clamber into the boot where there is a rear-facing bench seat.

The stocky youth with the scar suddenly reappears. He is walking towards the Range Rover. He is not alone. Two tall, thin, dark, suited men accompany him. They are the Syrians. Elias hasn't seen them yet but Mike has.

Ingrid presses a button accidentally. The rear passenger window is electrically lowered, revealing the occupants. Before she can work out how to raise the window, Sadik takes the opportunity to peer in. He takes Ingrid's hand and kisses it. He spots Elias in the car beside her.

"Where are you taking him?" he asks, with a look of surprise.

"We're taking him for a ride," says Hannah. "We'll see you later."

Sadik is lost for words. Joe realises what has happened, he squeezes Sadik's arm to distract him.

"I'll always remember this day, Sadik. Thanks for everything you've done for us."

Mike is flustered. He is holding up the door to the boot.

"Come on Joe, you've got to get in."

Joe quickly clambers into the boot and squeezes between Johan and Benoit on the bench. Mike slams the boot door and he rushes around to the front of the car, pushing the scar-faced youth out of his way. The youth suddenly throws a punch at him. Mike ducks and the youth misses. Sadik sees what is happening. He grabs the youth from behind and gets him in a headlock. Now the Syrians run forward. Mike gets into the Range Rover and locks the door.

"Go! Go! Go!" he yells.

The car is weighed down with eight people in it. The Syrians are leering through the back window. They look deranged. Joe is face to face with them. One of them is forcing the lock. The other is thumping the glass with a knuckleduster on his fist. The glass is cracking. He is smashing a way in. The engine roars into life. The Range Rover accelerates off at speed.

With large wheels and a bouncing suspension the Range Rover glides over the potholes. Joe stares back at the Syrians as their faces retreat into the night. Joe feels as if he is floating above everything, safely ensconced in that warm, safe carriage, separate from the cruel world.

People jump out of the way and press themselves against makeshift buildings as the Range Rover roars up the mud street. They are approaching the sentry post.

"The barrier's up, that's good," says Mike. He turns to Philippe. "Don't stop, we've got diplomatic immunity, just drive through."

Now Mike turns to the others. "Don't lower any windows, keep silent. If any talking needs to be done, I'll do it. Keep Elias hidden."

Two guards stand with guns at the gateway. Mike lowers his window and casually gives the okay sign to the guards as they drive past.

"Stop!" shouts the guard.

It is too late, they have passed the barrier.

"Drive on," says Mike calmly.

Philippe accelerates hard. They speed out of the darkness of the camp and back into modern Beirut with its wide tarmac streets, humming traffic, and electric lights.

Joe looks out of the broken rear window of the Range Rover, he feels elevated above the street in a strange tranquillity. They drive past groups of people carrying banners and the Lebanese flag. The sounds, sights and smells of the camp have faded like a dream. Mike, in the front passenger seat is distracted by the dangers of the present situation. He is busy on his mobile phone trying to ensure the yacht is ready to leave. He turns back to face the passengers.

"We'll drop off Joe, Hannah, and Elias at the marina first. The rest of us will go back to our embassy. We'll take Benoit and Johan home later, when the city's quieter."

Benoit and Johan remain silent. They are shocked and confused about what is going on.

"How will you get through the crowds in the city?" asks Hannah.

"Don't worry, nobody knows the city like Philippe, and we're in radio contact with the police. We'll go back the way we came, along the coast road."

"Okay," replies Hannah. "Isn't it best for me to go back to your embassy too?"

"What do you mean, Hannah? You need to go with Joe and Elias to Cyprus," replies Mike.

"What? You want me to go to Cyprus too?"

"Yes, I thought Joe had explained everything to you."

"I hadn't realised I was expected to go to Cyprus, tonight! What about all my stuff?"

"Don't worry, everything will be shipped back to you."

There is a long silence.

Joe turns around from the boot. "I'm sorry if I didn't explain things well. There's no way we're going without you, Hannah."

They are approaching the main boulevard beside the Mediterranean Sea. There is less traffic here.

Ingrid turns to Elias. "How do you feel?"

"Excited, sad, but happy too."

Through the damaged rear window, Joe notices the headlights of two motorbikes approaching. The riders are not wearing helmets. Their suit jackets are flapping in the wind. Suddenly, Benoit elbows Joe in the ribs.

"Those guys on motorbikes, they've got guns!"

One of the motorcyclists accelerates hard and comes level with the Range Rover. It is one of the Syrians, waving a pistol, shouting at Philippe.

"Pull over! Pull over!"

Philippe turns to Mike for instructions.

"Can you burn them off?" asks Mike.

"I think so."

"Go for it."

"Hold on!"

The passengers in the main part of the car are thrust backwards. Those in the boot are thrown forwards with their faces nearly smashing against the rear window. The Range Rover accelerates to an incredible speed. They go straight through a set of red lights and hurtle down the main boulevard. Joe is sandwiched between Benoit and Johan. The three of them now have their feet pressed against the broken back window. Through his feet, Joe can see the lights of the motorbikes receding into the distance. He expects to hear a gun blast, but there is none. All of the passengers cling onto each other. Everything is a blur. Elias opens his eyes as the speedometer passes 110mph. He feels both terrified and delighted.

"Okay, pay attention everyone," says Mike, sounding

deadly serious. "We've lost those guys. Joe, Hannah, Elias, get ready to get out. Here's the marina. There's no time for anyone to say goodbye. Find the *Liberty*. It'll be the biggest yacht. You'll set sail immediately."

The Range Rover screeches off the boulevard, down a dark, narrow track. They are driving over a cobbled quayside. As soon as the car stops, Mike rushes out and opens the boot. Joe clambers out. Hannah and Elias join him.

"Go well," says Mike.

He gets straight back into the Range Rover and it speeds off.

Joe, Hannah and Elias stand upon the quayside with their hearts beating frantically. Their eyes adjust to the darkness. All around in the shadows are dozens of yachts moored beside a maze of boardwalks. Metal masts clang and chime manically in the fresh sea breeze.

"Okay, let's find the biggest yacht, fitting for Luke isn't it?"

"Luke?" gasps Hannah. "Is he here?"

"Yes, sorry, didn't I mention that either?"

"No."

"Luke is sailing the *Liberty* for us. She will be flying the Cypriot flag. It shows the outline of the island. Not that we'll be able to see it in the pitch black."

"Shush. Stop talking," whispers Hannah.

There is the sound of motorbikes. Their hearts freeze.

"There's no other way to do this," says Joe. He puts his hands to his mouth and shouts. "Luke! Luke! Luke!"

"Is that him?" Elias is pointing towards the main boardwalk where someone is flashing a torch at them.

The motorbikes are approaching and their headlights beam across the quayside. Joe pushes Hannah and Elias to the ground to avoid being seen, and he falls on top of them.

"We're going to have to run for it. Come on, get up,

run!"

The three of them scramble to their feet. They run as fast as they dare in the darkness, along the main boardwalk. By the time they reach the torch, they are gasping for breath.

"Three singles for Cyprus is it?" enquires Luke jovially, a bodiless face illuminated by the torch. His demeanour suggests a day trip on the Thames.

"Turn off your torch!" orders Joe. "We're being followed. We need to go immediately!"

"Okay mate," replies Luke. "The steps are just over there, come aboard. We got a call, we're all ready to go."

They climb up the narrow steps to board the enormous yacht. As soon as Joe is on deck, Luke grabs his arm.

"So, is this Elias?"

"Yes, it is."

Luke clenches his fist. "Well done."

"We're not safe yet. Let's go!"

Suddenly, Luke's father, David appears. "Shall I cast off?" he asks calmly.

Joe doesn't have time to ask any questions. "Yes! Yes! Go! Go! We're being followed!"

"Take a seat please everyone," replies David coolly. "As soon as we clear the harbour walls, I will accelerate hard. You will need to hold on tight!"

Joe, Hannah and Elias scramble to seats on the deck. They stay low, not daring to look overboard. The motorbikes are on the boardwalk, directly beneath them. The engines of the yacht roar into life. The huge vessel lunges forwards. BANG! A gunshot. They all hit the deck. BANG! Another gunshot. The engine screams. The yacht propels forward like a speedboat at an incredible speed. Joe, Hannah and Elias have to wedge their limbs between items of furniture so they don't roll away. The open sea before them is black and mercurial. They disappear into the abyss.

Later that night, when the yacht is many miles away in the open Mediterranean Sea, the friends stand together on the upper deck. The salty air blows in their faces. They yell triumphantly, punch the air and hug each other. When they have celebrated enough, the friends make themselves comfortable on deckchairs and talk about their tumultuous day.

"I feel as if I'm in a dream," says Hannah. "I'm still expecting to wake up any minute."

They discuss practical details.

"We'll enter Pathos harbour at dawn," explains David. "Then we'll get a taxi to the airport and fly back to Heathrow."

"From there we'll get on a tube train, go home, put the kettle on, and have a nice cup of tea," adds Luke.

"Or have a pint," says Joe.

"I have got some questions," says Hannah, "about tickets and passports, or rather the lack of them."

"I've got tickets for everyone and a passport for Elias," says Luke.

"I haven't got my passport, Luke," says Hannah.

"Don't worry, my cousin's the Foreign Secretary. Everything's going to be all right."

Hannah decides to trust Luke, he has never let her down before and anyway there is nothing else she can do.

She turns to Luke. "Who does this yacht belong to? It's incredible."

"A toothpaste tycoon. Thankfully, he doesn't ask too many questions. He wanted his yacht moved from Beirut to Pathos, and that's what we're doing.

They enjoy a simple late-night meal together. Shortly afterwards they go to bed, exhausted. Each is given their own birth and a bathroom with a degree of luxury they could only ever have dreamt about.

Joe sleeps deeply for a few hours and then he finds

himself awake. Sleepily, he pulls back the curtain over a porthole above his bed. There is a grey, choppy sea. A faint pinkish line marks the horizon with the first glimmers of dawn. Splash! Initially he is too sleepy to give the sound another thought. He lies back on his bed. Splash! What could it be? Various scenarios go through his mind. *Are the crew throwing themselves overboard?*

Splash! There it is again. Curiosity gets the better of him. Wearing boxer shorts and his tight Manchester United T-shirt, he goes on deck. David is standing there alone, wind swept, in a long dressing gown. He is pointing out to the side of the yacht. All Joe can see are circling white gulls. Suddenly, a great shape springs up out of the water.

"Whoa! As big as a whale!" Joe yells.

"Dolphins!" shouts David.

For almost half an hour, David and Joe watch the spectacle of dolphins escorting them towards land.

The dark green outline of mountains comes into view. The fresh sea-salt air is already mixing with the scent of pine forests.

9 Chequers

It is a Friday morning at the end of March, in the last year of the Twentieth Century. The cheerful sound of Scottish folk singing echoes through the offices of the Regeneration Company. Jock is singing in a rasping yet musical voice. Sketching on his drawing board he is in a happy little world of his own. On the other side of the office, Joe sits at his desk admiring the view out of the window. A new e-mail pings on his computer. He pulls a face. It is from his boss, Vernon Flemel, who has recently returned from a long placement in China. He is requesting an urgent meeting at midday. Joe wonders what it is about. *Is this going to be another rollicking?*

He imagines what Vernon will say.

"It's this article of yours in The Times. I didn't agree it. Self-aggrandisement just won't do. It's not all about you, Joe. It's all about me!"

Joe imagines being assertive. *"I agreed it with the public relations team when you were in China. I'm not taking any crap from you over this!"*

Vernon would blow a gasket if Joe spoke to him like that, so he tries a softer approach.

"Look Vern, it's all good publicity for the company."

Vernon laughs spitefully so Joe goes for the nuclear

option.

"You can stuff your job where the sun don't shine, I'm leaving!"

Joe comes back to reality with a shudder. Jock is shouting at him.

"Time!"

Joe looks at the clock, it is dead on twelve. He adjusts his tie and makes his way towards Vernon's office. Before entering, he looks up and notices the fresh paint above the doorway. The damaged plasterwork has all been repaired. Joe knocks on the door and enters Vernon's cubicle. The office is pristine, not a single piece of paper, not even a paper clip can be seen. It is like an immaculate rabbit hutch. Vernon does have some interesting photographs of cities and copies of classical paintings on the walls.

"Ah, Joe! Do come in. Make yourself comfortable. Are you alright?"

"I'm fine thanks, Vernon. How was your stay in China?"

"Remarkable! Planning these new settlements for the Chinese government is so stimulating. I'll be giving a presentation to everyone next week."

"I'll look forward to that."

Vernon looks apprehensive. He is biting his bottom lip. He runs his hand through his flop of dyed black hair and glares at Joe.

"Congratulations on your article in *The Times*!" Vernon bites his lower lip again, harder, before continuing. "I understand it created quite a stir?"

"Well, a bit."

Vernon waves his hand in the air. "We're both very busy, Joe, so look, I've got some good news for you. I'm offering you a significant promotion."

Joe's ears prick up. "Really?"

Vernon continues. "I'm inviting you to be the head of the urbanism team."

Vernon can't stand making direct eye contact. He looks to the side of Joe's head. It is as if he is addressing some imaginary person. Joe finds this unnerving. He makes a quick sideways glance, just to make sure no-one else is there.

"The urbanism team?" asks Joe, hesitantly. For a split second the two men make direct eye contact, then Vernon looks to the side of Joe's head.

"Yes, urbanism is so *now*, it's part of my rebranding," he continues.

The sound of Jock's singing is heard as he passes by the closed door. Vernon frowns and mumbles his thoughts out loud.

"Some dead wood will be cut."

Joe looks startled. Vernon realises he shouldn't have said that, he looks frightened. He pulls himself together.

"There'll be winners Joe, and you can be one of them!"

Joe wants to leave this hot, airless room but after a moment's reflection he decides to play along with Vernon for a little while.

"Can I ask what the salary package will be?"

"I'm offering you a fantastic opportunity, Joe. It's a great career move. I'm giving you the opportunity to manage your own team. This is something you need to get under your belt."

Joe presses his point. "But there'd be a salary increase, wouldn't there?"

Vernon looks disappointed. He briefly makes eye contact but then his eyes narrow, gaze drifts sideways and he bites his lower lip even harder.

"Most staff won't be getting an increase this year," he hisses.

Joe opens his mouth but no sound comes out. He tries again.

"Will there be any other benefits? Will my contract of

employment be any different?"

"It will be different, Joe. It'll be a much more professional contract. You won't be paid overtime anymore. The modern world doesn't work like that. Oh, I should say there's also one week less annual leave, and you'll need to give four months' notice to quit instead of one."

Joe's face drops.

Vernon continues. "Don't worry about the details, Joe. You won't miss a week's holiday. You'll be having a good time here with me. We'll travel. You'll be involved with the new settlements in China!"

Again, Vernon bites his lower lip, his nose curls into a snarl and perspiration drips from his forehead. He presses his chin into his neck, giving the unflattering appearance of multiple chins.

Joe is silent, his thoughts are drifting. *Has Vernon ever taken a holiday? He looks as if he needs one.*

Jock's singing drifts past the office again. It is too much for Vernon. He springs up from his chair and claps his hands nervously. Joe stands up too.

"Do you want to give me your answer in principle now, Joe?"

Direct eye contact is being made and it is placing an enormous strain on Vernon. He is anxious for Joe to leave his office.

"Why don't you sleep on it?"

Before Joe can give an answer, he is being shown the door.

"Let me know in the morning then," says Vernon, ushering Joe out. "I do have others who are interested you know?"

As Joe walks down the corridor he resolves that he will leave the Regeneration Company, but in his own timing. He returns to his desk and feels weighed down. He decides to go for a walk, and grabs his jacket. As he passes Jock's desk the old Scot looks at him, concerned.

"Is everything okay, son?"

"Yeah, well, nothing to worry about, I'll tell you later. I need to get some fresh air."

Joe walks out of the office leaving Jock scratching the back of his head.

Joe gets a beef sandwich with horseradish from a deli bar on Kensington High Street. That done, he walks up the street towards Holland Park. The fresh, spring breeze rustles the last of winter out of the trees. It has become a warm, sunny day. All the nationalities of the world seem to be on the high street, there are so many different accents and languages. Joe navigates his way along the pavement. He weaves between businessmen in suits and elegant ladies with their hands full of colourful shopping bags. Many people are sitting outside at the pavement cafés. Some youths dressed in sports gear are hanging around a Ferrari, casually parked on double yellow lines. Everyone is happy to be on the street, to watch and to be watched.

Every now and again Joe nods to someone he knows. He passes a group of people being escorted up the high street by a council official. They have come from provincial towns on a study tour. They are learning how the improvements to Kensington High Street have been implemented. The council officer points to a lamp column.

"It's designed to avoid light pollution, it uses white light so true colours can be seen at night."

A very stately elderly lady, a Kensington resident, prods the officer.

"You're causing an obstruction, move along!"

Joe turns off the high street and enters through the ornate gates into Holland Park. The park is full of people, walking, playing, sitting, eating their lunch. Joe heads for his favourite place, the rose garden, where there is usually a free bench. He wants some peace and quiet to plan his exit strategy from work. Suddenly, someone grabs his shoulders forcibly from behind. For a moment, he thinks he is being mugged.

"Argh!"

"Hey Joe, it's me!"

"Eh? Luke! Don't do that!"

Joe catches his breath and recovers. He is glad to see his old friend.

"How you doing, Joe?"

"Okay, Luke, how you doing?"

"Great thanks! Have you got time for a coffee?"

Luke is pointing towards the café in the middle of the park.

"Yeah, I've got time, that's a good idea."

They stroll over to the café, which is very busy. They are fortunate to find an empty table outside. The other dozen or so tables are all occupied. The atmosphere is open and affable, almost like a garden party. Joe and Luke gossip about the characters sitting around them. There is a whole pack of dogs sitting and lying nearby while their owners socialise over drinks. Most of the dogs are well behaved. A couple of them jump up at each other resulting in loud chastisements from their masters. Luke points out the group of nannies, he winks at Joe; some of them are very attractive. Behind them sits a group of older men playing chess. There is a small group of spectators gathered around. Luke points to them.

"Have you seen the grand masters? Look, the porter from our apartment block is playing with them."

Joe muses that Luke uses the word *apartment* rather than *flat*. Then he recognises the old man with the red face and bushy side-burns.

"I've got something to tell you," says Luke.

Joe leans forward with his elbows resting on the table.

He gives Luke his full attention.

"Go on then."

"I heard Elias play last night at the Barbican. He's become quite a celebrity. The Prime Minister's wife was there. I got to speak to her, briefly. She's very friendly and a big fan of Elias."

"Who did you go with?" asks Joe, covering up the hurt at not being invited.

"Serena and her parents."

"Ah, was Elias good?"

"Yeah, everyone in the orchestra is excellent."

Joe wonders how Luke could tell that *everyone* in the orchestra was excellent. His thoughts drift on. *After all we've been through, couldn't I have been invited too?*

Joe and Luke have met up fairly frequently since their Cyprus mission, almost a year ago.

"Elias really looks the part in his tuxedo," adds Luke.

"How's he getting on with staying at Serena's parents?"

"Fine, they're mad about him. We drove him back last night. He says *hello* by the way."

"It would have been nice to have been invited to the concert."

"Yeah, I'm surprised he didn't tell you about it. He asked about you, wanted to know how you are."

Joe can't be bothered to be offended anymore.

"I'll give him a call, perhaps we can meet up in town at the weekend."

"Let me know if you do."

"What, like you let me know about things?"

"Sorry!"

After a discussion about Elias and the progress he is making, Joe decides it is his turn to share some news.

"I've got something to tell you, Luke."

"I'm listening."

"I'm leaving my job. I'm thinking of leaving London

213

too."

Luke spurts his coffee back into his cup. "What?"

Joe hands Luke a napkin. "Sorry, was that a shock?"

"Are you serious?"

"Yeah."

"Will you go back home?"

"I think so."

"How could you leave all this?"

"I don't live in Kensington, remember, I live in Clapham."

Luke thinks for a moment. "Do you want to go back home because Hannah's there?"

Joe looks puzzled. "Well, I suppose that might be a part of it."

"You should definitely make a move there."

"Hmmm." Joe considers the possibility before continuing. "You know when we fed the homeless people together, do you remember the lanky lad that was going off to Cornwall?"

"You mean Phil."

"Yeah, that's the one. I felt envious about his new adventure. Then there's Elias starting a new life in London. I think it's time for me to start something new. I can't remember the last time I saw my grandad. That's bad isn't it? He's getting on."

Luke nods sympathetically. "I know what you mean. I can't believe my dad's seventy. So, when do you think you'll leave?"

"In a month."

"Can you really go so soon, just like that?"

"I can't think of any reason why not. I've got to pay my rent to the end of the month, give a month's notice at work, then I'm free."

"I'll miss you," says Luke and then his eyes light up. "Hey, I've got to drive my dad's old Bentley back home for him; it's being serviced down here. If the timing's right, I might be able to give you a lift home in it."

"It'd be great to travel home in style."

Luke and Joe get up, pat each other on the back, and head off in opposite directions. As Joe passes the dog owners, he notices a poodle sniffing the backside of a bulldog. The bulldog is so fat it can hardly breathe.

"That's not a very nice thing to do, Bunny, is it?" says the lady owner of the poodle.

"For goodness sake be a gentleman, George!" commands the male owner of the bulldog.

It is eight o'clock in the morning on the last Saturday of April. The weather is blustery and fresh. Joe stands on the grey pavement in front of the Victorian terraced house where he has rented a room in a basement flat for several years. All of his worldly possessions are packed into a few cardboard boxes and plastic bags, piled up by the kerbside. Joe glances at his watch again. When he looks up, he sees the shiny metal grill at the front of an elegant Bentley. It looks like an upturned nose gliding towards him. The car pulls up. Luke is behind the wheel of the beautiful, highly polished 1969 black Bentley. Serena sits next to him. They look like a picture from a fashion magazine. Serena waves at Joe, she has a beaming smile. She gets out of the car and greets Joe with a kiss on the cheek. The thought of spending some time with Serena is appealing.

Serena is to be dropped off at her parents' house in Hertfordshire, from where Elias will be collected. From there, Joe, Luke and Elias will drive over the Chiltern Hills into Buckinghamshire for an auspicious cup of tea at Chequers, the official country residence of the Prime Minister. Their invitation from the Prime Minister's wife was sent via Luke's cousin, James Montgomery. James informed them he will also be at Chequers with his wife Hilary, having stayed overnight following a dinner party for the French President. James has also said there is a remote chance of them meeting the Prime Minister himself, although he is due to fly out to Washington. The Prime Minister's wife has requested that Elias bring his violin.

Joe and Serena stand behind the Bentley, chatting about Elias.

"My mum adores him. I think she wants to adopt him," says Serena.

Joe smiles and turns to Luke. "There is definitely something about Elias and people's mums. They all want to take him home."

"Come on, we'll help you get your gear into the car," replies Luke, opening the cavernous boot.

The luxurious scent of the leather interior combines with Serena's perfume to form a heady mix. Joe breathes it in.

"Is this all you've got?" asks Luke, bringing Joe back to earth.

"Yeah, not much is it?"

Luke shrugs his shoulders.

Serena turns to Joe. "Do you want to sit upfront?"

"No, it's okay, I'll do the royal wave from the back."

All aboard, they drive off. The Bentley purrs. They reach Kensington High Street surprisingly quickly. Looking out of the window, there is a slender tower rising above a gleaming Art Deco department store. At the top of the tower the wind ripples through the canvas of a Union Jack flag. Joe notices the interesting patterns of light and shade and how vivid the red, white and blue is against the pale sky.

"Joe, you're right about taking out the clutter along the high street, it looks so much better."

"I agree," says Serena. "Do you reckon it'll serve as a model for other places?"

Joe is pleased to hear that Luke and Serena are interested in his work. He leans forward, his head between them.

"I hope so."

"My dad was asking questions about you recently," Luke adds. "Since we got back from Cyprus you're a bit of hero with him."

"What was he asking about?"

"He wants to know what your work situation is."

"What did you tell him?"

"Unemployed."

"That doesn't sound so good."

Joe changes the subject. "I'll miss Kensington."

"Are you having second thoughts about leaving?" Luke asks this just as they drive past Joe's old office.

"No, I'm doing the right thing, but I do feel quite sad though. I'll miss some of the people I've worked with."

"You can always stay over in our Kensington apartment," says Luke.

"Thanks mate," replies Joe falling back into the soft leather seat. It seems bizarre to him that he is gliding down Kensington High Street in the back of a Bentley.

The traffic is surprisingly light for central London and they are soon heading north up the Edgware Road.

"I need to get some petrol," says Luke, "in fact, with what this does to the gallon, we might have to stop a few times."

Joe wonders if it is a hint. He rummages in his pockets and reveals a ten pound note which he waves by Luke's head.

"Here, for the petrol."

"No, it's okay, put it away. I'm doing my dad a favour, he'll pay for this."

The Bentley stops at a bright yellow petrol station. Luke gets out and fills up the tank. Inside the car, Serena turns to Joe.

"Are you excited about going to Chequers? It's a great privilege, it's never open to the public."

"I know. It's a shame you can't come."

"Yes, I'm a bit annoyed about it," replies Serena, glancing at her watch. "I'm on stage in a few hours. The show must go on."

Joe nods.

Serena continues. "Your friend Hannah isn't going either, I hear."

"That's right, she's in New York for her mum's sixtieth birthday treat."

"Where are you going to be living, Joe?"

"I'm going to stay with my grandfather until I find somewhere to rent. I like the idea of having my own place. I've been sharing for years."

"Do you think it's going to be a cultural adjustment for you, after so long in London? I love doing rep theatre, places are so different, but it can be a culture shock."

The question flummoxes Joe. He thinks for a moment.

"Home's, home. I don't think it'll be a culture shock."

"What work will you do?"

Joe doesn't know, he feels slightly embarrassed.

"I've got some savings. I can afford to take a couple of months off. I don't want to rush into anything." He pauses, giving himself time to choose the right words. "I know it probably doesn't make sense, just leaving like this, without a job to go to, but I feel I'm doing the right thing."

"I think you're very brave."

Joe smiles back at Serena. It is impossible not to notice how perfectly formed her lips are or how bright her blue eyes are.

Suddenly, a group of lads gather around the Bentley. One of them knocks on the windscreen. Joe shudders at the memory of the Syrians bashing the window of the Range Rover in Beirut.

"Just ignore them," he says, feeling vulnerable.

The youths leer at them through the windows. Luke returns from the shop, engages the lads, and they quickly back off. Soon the engine is purring again. As they pull away, Joe waves at the youths. One of them gives him the finger. The Bentley resumes its stately progress northwards.

Luke beeps the horn long and hard when they cross over the M25. They have left the metropolis.

"You've done it Joe, you're a free man!" says Luke, triumphantly.

A comfortable silence fills the Bentley as they pass woods, hills, and drive down a cutting through a chalk ridge. Beech trees climb the steep slopes, thrusting branches towards the car. The verdant leaves are as soft as baby's skin. The Bentley turns a corner and there is a blinding burst of sunshine.

"I can't see a thing through this windscreen! Where's the road gone?" yells Luke.

"Watch out!"

The wheels go over rough ground.

"Argh!" They all cry out as one.

Luke regains control of the car.

"Careful honey!" gasps Serena.

"That was close! I thought I was going to lose it then. My dad would not be happy."

Serena turns to Joe. "Fortunately, my parents' home is just over there. I think we'll make it alive."

Joe pulls himself forward and looks to where Serena is pointing. Between the trees is a pair of substantial Victorian villas. They stand well back from the lane, isolated from any village. The Bentley turns into the private drive.

"You're coming in to say hello aren't you?" asks Serena.

Luke turns around to Joe. "Is that okay with you? We've got some spare time."

"Yeah, sure."

Serena rushes out of the car and up the garden path, excited to be home. Joe and Luke follow at a more leisurely pace. They breathe the invigorating country air. A lamb bleats further up the hill and there is only the whisper of a trafficked road, very far away. A dog is barking within the house.

The dark green front door is wide open. Joe and Luke step into the lobby and walk over a black and white ceramic floor, which continues into the hallway. The dog is barking madly. The smell of home cooking greets them. Serena embraces her mum while a small golden dog runs around at their feet, beside itself with joy, jumping up at Serena, trying to get in on the hug. Serena's mum comes over to Luke and greets him with a kiss on the cheek. Joe stands awkwardly, waiting to be introduced. His eyes drift up to the ornate cornices and then down at the pictures. The house feels antiquated but very homely.

"Oh, Liz, this is Joe," says Luke.

"Ah, Joe, it's good to meet you at last! Are you excited about going to Chequers? I hear you might even meet the Prime Minister."

"Yes, I'm looking forward to it. It's good to meet you too."

Liz smiles kindly, she takes Joe's arm and speaks in a confidential tone.

"I don't know all the details of Elias's trip to England, but I just want to say we're really enjoying him living with us, he's no trouble at all."

Joe smiles back. "I'm pleased he's settled so well."

Liz ushers them all into her enormous kitchen.

"I've just cooked a lasagne. I was going to freeze it, but are you boys hungry?"

Joe nods, he warms to Liz and her rolling rural accent.

"Mum! You can't give visitors lasagne for breakfast,"

interjects Serena, looking at her watch.

Liz glances at her daughter. "Boys can eat lasagne at any time. I don't want them meeting the Prime Minister on empty stomachs."

"I wouldn't mind some," says Luke. "We've got twenty five minutes."

"Okay, it'll be ready soon," replies Liz. She turns to Serena. "Would you be a love and take some around to Mrs Williams next-door? The poor old dear doesn't know what day of the week it is anymore, she won't mind having lasagne for breakfast."

Elias's lanky frame comes trundling down the stairs. He enters the kitchen with a smile. He has put on weight and shines with good health. His big brown eyes are as wide as saucers. He gives Joe a hug, and then Luke and Serena are given one too.

Elias wants to be show where Lullingdon is on the map. He is going to be staying there with Luke for the weekend.

Serena turns to Joe. "Can I introduce you to my dad, Joe?"

"Sure."

"Come on, I think he's hiding in the lounge." Serena escorts Joe back down the hall. They hesitate beside a half-open door. A man's voice can be heard within, he is engaged in a telephone conversation.

Liz shouts from the kitchen. "Serena! Can you help me please?"

"Hang on!"

Serena turns to Joe. "My dad's name is Henry, go in and say hello. I think you'll get on really well."

Joe is now left standing alone in the hall, feeling awkward. The golden dog appears and sits down on his foot. After a full minute of waiting, Serena's dad emerges with an air of puzzlement. He has a short beard and a kind face. He wears a long knitted cardigan that borders on being interesting.

"Hello, I'm Henry," he says offering a handshake.

"Hello, I'm Joe. I'm a friend of Serena and Luke. We've just arrived from London."

"Ah, the great Babylon. You're going on to Chequers aren't you?"

"Yeah."

"Do come in."

Henry ushers Joe into a spacious lounge. Sunshine streams in through a big bay window. There is a pleasant view over a country garden. The dog follows Joe like a shadow. Henry stands beside the window as Joe makes himself comfortable on the enormous, floral-patterned settee.

Henry proceeds to tell Joe about his cricket team, country walks, and good pubs near to Chequers. Joe feels the warm sun on his face and his concentration drifts. His eyes wander over the family photographs hanging on the walls. Henry and Liz were clearly childhood sweethearts, and very good looking in their younger days. All the photos are of the family and the dog. One of the photos makes Joe smile, it is of Henry and Liz as teenage hippies sitting on the roof of a canal barge, with flowers in their hair.

Henry fetches a battered road atlas from a homemade magazine rack and sits on the settee beside Joe. The blue cover has a date embossed upon it in gold, *1968*. It is the first road atlas Henry ever owned, purchased after he passed his driving test. He gives Joe detailed advice about the route to Chequers. Joe is perplexed. He sees the yellow blob of Hemel Hempstead, but it is far too small. The M1 is shown but the M25 does not exist. Henry looks at the maps as if they were a hoard of treasure. His fingers follow roads through the Chilterns and he mumbles about short cuts and landmarks. Joe wonders if Henry is in denial that the country has changed.

"So, where do you play cricket, Joe?" asks Henry.

Before Joe can reply there is a yell from the kitchen.

"Lasagne's ready!"

The dog, which has been lying beside Joe with one paw resting on his shoe, bolts to the kitchen. Luke and Elias are tearing down the stairs. Joe stands to attention but restrains himself, trying to keep some decorum in front of Henry.

"After you," he says, gesturing towards the door.

"No, no, you go ahead, it's far too early for me to eat anything."

"Okay," says Joe, already out of the door. He takes a seat beside Luke at the big family breakfast table. Behind them are French doors overlooking a lawn in need of mowing, and dark green woods marching up hills. Luke, Joe and Elias tuck into lasagne. The rest of the family sit with them, drinking tea.

After the lasagne is devoured, Luke clutches his belly.

"Thanks, Liz, my stomach hurts now I'm so full."

"There's homemade chocolate cake, yet" replies Liz.

"Can we take it with us? We'd better go now."

"Of course you can. I'll wrap some slices for you."

Joe is wondering if it was wise for them to have eaten quite so much prior to their propitious meeting. He feels he could easily stay in that homely house and is glad that Elias is living there. He looks at his watch.

"We mustn't be late for the PM!" he forces himself to say.

Goodbyes are said and then Joe, Luke and Elias make their way out to the Bentley. Elias is carrying an overnight bag and his violin case. Joe sits upfront with Luke, and Elias has the spacious backseat to himself. The car pulls off. They chat in an easy way as they glide through the Chilterns.

Joe turns to Elias. "How do you feel about going to the Prime Minister's house?"

"Okay," he replies nonchalantly, "his wife is nice, I met her after a concert." Then in a much keener tone, "I'm excited about going to Birmingham afterwards."

Joe and Luke turn to each other and chuckle. They have agreed that after Chequers they will take Elias to Birmingham for the weekend. He will stay with Luke and his family at Lullingdon. They have got surprise tickets for him to visit the City of Birmingham Symphony Orchestra. They are also going to take him to the pub.

It is a short drive to Chequers along quiet, country roads. They pass a bold green sign with an ornate coat of arms proclaiming, *Buckinghamshire.* Overhead, red kites follow performing acrobatics in the sky. They are large birds of prey with long fingered wings and wedge-shaped tails. Sometimes they swoop low and seem to be inquisitive about the car. They remain in view all the way to Chequers; an aerial escort.

The Bentley is climbing now. The landscape around them is a bright picture of farmland and wooded ridgeway. The soil is chalky.

The friends chat about what they will to say to the Prime Minister if he hasn't left for Washington. Luke reckons he will know about their Lebanon expedition.

"I'm sure my cousin James has told him."

Joe turns back to Elias. "Have you been able to get in touch with your grandad yet, Elias?"

Elias's face drops. "No, I never get a reply to my letters."

Joe regrets that he didn't allow Elias to say goodbye to his grandad.

"I'm sure he's okay," he says hoping desperately that the old man hasn't died of a broken heart.

They approach a village with white painted gates either side of a welcome sign. It is clearly a cherished place. Cottages are built from decorative brickwork, speckled flint that looks like crushed diamonds, and thatched roofs. A stately grandmother walks behind a child on a shaky bicycle. A pack of serious cyclists whizzes by in colourful, figure-hugging Lycra. The driver of a vintage car waves in acknowledgement of the Bentley and Luke indulges in the camaraderie by beeping the horn twice.

They are on higher ground now, following the ridgeway. It is England's most ancient route, used by tribes since the dawn of time. There are no more villages to be seen. A red kite swoops low, flying parallel to the car. A very large crow flies towards the kite like a fighter jet coming out of the sun so it can't be seen. At the last moment, in mid flight the kite turns upside down and its talons reach for the crow; it just misses. The crow turns on its wing and disappears. The kite gives a piercing, shrill call. Joe and Luke have seen what happened and they stare at each other, wide eyed.

The beech woods are closing in now and the Bentley is lost to view under the trees. They descend a steep country lane, slowly.

"The brakes aren't brilliant," says Luke, anxiously.

They stop at a T-junction. There are no other cars around.

"I think this is it," says Luke, with some relief.

They have emerged into an open valley. In front of them is a picturesque Victorian gatehouse, a folly, made from the familiar crushed diamond flint and decorative red brick. The gates are low and they can see over them, across the pastoral lands of Chequers. It is a rural idyll, bathed in soft sunlight. The only discordant features are security cameras on poles, a surgical reminder this is no ordinary country estate.

"We need to drive around to the main entrance," says, Luke struggling with a map on his lap.

"I think it's left," says Joe.

"Okay."

They follow a country road between woods and the ancient red brick estate walls. They soon arrive at a grand gateway flanked by Tudor-style cottages. The gates stand open between enormous brick piers but they cannot proceed. In their way are bollards that would stop a tank and two policemen with machine guns.

"I think the PM's still in residence," whispers Luke. "They wouldn't have this level of security if he'd gone."

A policeman steps forward to greet them. They are relived to hear they are expected. The practicalities of the security check-in take a while.

At last, they are released to drive up to the house. They drive slowly with the windows down. The avenue of lime trees rustles in the breeze. The red kites are replaced by a pair of black and white lapwings, which show off with extravagant swirling wing beats. The park is dotted with ancient oak trees and a herd of small black cattle completes the bucolic scene.

"There it is, Chequers!"

The solid gables and massive stone mullion windows give it a resolute appearance, and yet the rustic bricks also speak of restfulness and of England at peace with itself. It is a fitting country residence for the Prime Minister.

The driveway takes them to the East Front where they pass under a stone archway, into a gravel courtyard and arrive at the main entrance.

Joe turns to Luke. "I can't believe we're here. I'd love to look around."

As soon as they are out of the car a smartly dressed middle-aged woman greets them.

"Hello and welcome to Chequers," she says shaking their hands warmly. "I'm Marion, the housekeeper. Would you like a brief tour of the house? You have about twenty minutes to spare before tea."

"That'd be great," replies Joe. "Are you two up for it?"

Luke and Elias definitely want to go on the tour too.

"Wonderful," says Marion. "After the tour, I'll take you to the Rose Garden for tea with the family and their guests."

Marion whisks them through opulent rooms and corridors. She explains that Chequers is a mix of historic periods. It was remodelled by the Elizabethans but parts of the building are nearly a thousand years old. The interiors have light oak panelling, embossed silk wallpaper, antique furniture, and stone floors. It is grand but it is also a relaxed family home. The Prime Minister and his family have made every room comfortable.

They arrive at the Great Hall with its soaring ceiling, enormous chandelier, and clerestory windows that provide a perfect light for viewing the masterpieces upon the walls.

"This Great Hall is actually quite new," Marion tells them. "It was created in the nineteenth century from an inner courtyard."

"It looks as if it's always been here," says Joe.

Elias has to be dragged away from the painting of a lion caught in a net before they can press on to the Long Gallery with its extensive library. They are shown artefacts that once belonged to Oliver Cromwell and Churchill.

Marion times the tour to perfection, as might be expected, she has done it a thousand times.

"Right, follow me, it's time for tea!"

They follow Marion outside to a Gothic archway set within the walls of the Rose Garden, they pause to read a stone tablet set in the wall.

"ALL CARE, ABANDON YE, WHO ENTER HERE."

Entering the Rose Garden they are greeted by a riot of colour and delightful scent. Thousands of roses are in bloom within beds surrounded by topiary. A long terrace runs the length of the house and beside it are great swathes of flowering lavender, alive with buzzing bees. Beneath the terrace and surrounding the rose beds are immaculate green lawns. Beyond the formal garden is the park with its stately oak trees and grazing cattle. Further away still are gently rising forested hills. All of this is under a clear blue sky and warm sun. It is heavenly. To the far side of the garden is a large conservatory containing a swimming pool.

The Prime Minister and his wife are sitting out at a table and chairs beside the conservatory. The Foreign Secretary, James Montgomery, and his wife Hilary, sit opposite them. The Prime Minister's two teenage sons are kicking a ball around. The Prime Minister looks rather incongruous in jogging bottoms and a sweatshirt. He has just returned from a run in the woods. The friends follow Marion along the terrace. Joe glances at the Prime Minister's wife, she has an unexpected beauty that doesn't conform to conventional good looks, but is quite radiant. Joe is reminded of a photo of Jackie Kennedy. The Prime Minister has spotted them. He gets up and shouts over.

"I panicked when I saw your car, I thought I'd forgotten Her Majesty was coming for tea."

The friends laugh.

Soon they are all sitting around a table piled high with cakes. The Prime Minister and his family are very down to earth and they are easy to be with.

"What do you do for a living?" the Prime Minister asks Joe.

"I'm a landscape architect."

The Prime Minister's eyes light up. "I'm very interested in the public realm, let me show you something."

Joe gets up and follows the Prime Minister across the garden. They stand together beside the house. The Prime Minister points towards a Latin inscription sculpted into a stone balustrade. He pronounces the words slowly.

"*JUSTITIAE TENAX*. Do you know what it means?"

"No, can you give me a translation?"

The Prime Minister smiles, revealing a near perfect row of shiny teeth.

"It means *tenacious of justice*. I hope we can both live up to it, Joe."

Luke is catching up on family gossip with his cousin James and looks completely at ease. Elias is enjoying a relaxed conversation with the Prime Minister's wife.

"I did enjoy your concert at the Barbican," she says.

"Thanks," replies Elias. "I have tried to learn about art. I noticed your painting of the lion, by Rubens. We did a concert in the Banqueting House, it has a ceiling painted by Rubens. Is it the same artist?"

"Gosh! It is. I'm impressed. I also saw that same ceiling very recently. It is magnificent. I was at a dinner to honour the queen."

"Ah, I like Rubens."

"I wonder, Elias, if you might like to play for us, but don't feel you have to. My husband will have to leave shortly for the airport."

"I would love to play for you."

Elias unpacks his violin and places it to his chin. He plays Greensleeves, the sixteenth century English song. It is perfect for the setting. The Prime Minister's boys stop playing football and come over to listen. Their father closes his eyes and feels as if a boat has scooped him up and is sailing off along the fields in the valley and over the forest. England is blessed and bountiful. The music stops and after a long pause, the Prime Minister speaks.

"I'll be going to Washington feeling very refreshed. Thank you, Elias."

The Bentley makes steady progress northwards on the M40. Luke calls it the scenic route. After an hour and a half they turn off the motorway and then travel through miles of gently rolling, green countryside. The roads become more familiar as they approach their hometown. Luke turns to Joe.

"You can store your stuff at my parents' house if you like, there's loads of space."

"Thanks, that's a good idea, although I haven't got much," replies Joe.

"What time is your grandad expecting you?"

"I just said early afternoon."

"I hope you're not going to get another feed."

"Me too, I'm still stuffed with lasagne and cakes."

They enter the suburban fringe. Elias has nodded off. Joe points out of the window at a new block of flats.

"I don't remember them being there."

"You've been away a long time, haven't you?"

They continue in silence and Joe stares into his memories.

Luke pulls the Bentley in towards the kerb. They park on a main road, beside an alleyway that leads into the housing estate. Elias has woken up and is confused about where he is.

"Could you open the boot please, Luke?" asks Joe.

"Sure."

Luke flicks a switch. They hear the lock open. Without saying another word Joe gets out of the car and sorts through the bags and boxes in the boot. Luke and Elias join him. Joe explains which items can be stored at Lullingdon.

"I'll give you a call later about going out," says Luke. "Give my regards to your grandad."

"I will. Thanks again for the lift!"

Joe leaves clutching his holdall and a Sainsbury's plastic bag. A stooped, elderly man has come over to look at the Bentley.

"Dawn't make 'em like that iny more do thay, son?"

For a moment, Joe is taken aback by the man's accent. He smiles back at him. "You're right there."

230

Elias has walked off down the pavement. He stands with one arm wrapped around a lamppost as he takes in the housing estate. Joe walks over to him, drops his bags to the ground, and braces himself. The low grey sky moves swiftly over the surface of the earth. The air is acrid. It is an overwhelmingly drab scene. All colour has drained away. There is litter, glass, graffiti and abandoned furniture everywhere. Most of the fences have been pulled down. The charred remains of fire stains the tarmac. At the end of the estate road, beyond the maisonettes, stands the empty tower block. All of its windows are broken. For almost a decade it has been empty, awaiting demolition. Unbelievably, it is still there, surrounded by spiked palisade fencing. Crowning the summit of the tower are immense telecommunications structures. It is a mocking landmark to abandonment.

Elias turns to Joe. "I didn't know England was like this."

From the look on Joe's face, Elias realises he has been too blunt. He puts his hand on Joe's shoulder.

"Can I come and meet your grandad? I'd like to see your home."

"Yeah, sure, but later, if that's okay?"

"No problem, Joe. I'll see you later."

Elias joins Luke in the Bentley and they drive off. Joe remains standing for a moment. Is this really the same England as Chequers? Joe begins walking towards his grandad's home. There is a burnt out car in one of the parking bays. His spirit lifts a little when he spots his own brown Skoda, apparently intact. He makes his way over and inspects it. Joe left the car with his grandad because there was nowhere to park it in London. The Skoda's paintwork is in surprisingly good condition. Joe peers through the side window and frowns. There are exposed wires where the stereo should be.

Joe straightens himself up and looks down the road.

There are very few other cars to be seen. A large removal truck turns into the estate and it approaches Joe. The driver and his mate are open-mouthed, grimacing. The driver has a large potato-like head, he shakes his sagging jowls as he lowers his window.

"Do yaw live 'ere mate? Dawn't suppose yaw know where number seventy-four is do ya?"

Joe wonders if he looks as if he lives there. He tries to remember where number seventy-four might be. The driver turns to his mate, rolls his eyes, and mumbles something about the locals.

"No, sorry mate, I don't live here."

"I didn't think yer did. Blimey, it's like Beirut in it? Are you a social worker?"

Joe wonders if he looks like a social worker. He wonders if the estate is better or worse than the refugee camp in Beirut. The mystified driver pulls off and the truck disappears around a corner. The place falls back into a lonely silence.

Joe decides to have a look around the estate, to get orientated. He walks towards one of the inner courtyards, behind a maisonette block. When Joe was a boy he played in these inner courtyards with his friends. He remembers them being a hive of activity with kids running about everywhere. But now the courtyard is desolate. The homes are empty and boarded up. He wonders where everyone has gone.

The place appears to be ready for demolition. A solitary washing line is fixed into the earth. A white sweatshirt blows in the rain like a flag of surrender. Suddenly, a boy aged about eight with a runny nose appears. Behind him, his older sister follows on a little bicycle. The boy forces a nervous smile.

"What ya doing ere mate?"

Joe can't believe these children are living in such an abandoned place. He smiles at the boy. His eyes scan around to see where his home might be. There is one front door that is not boarded up. Suddenly, faces appear. People are standing in the shadows, huddled together, muttering, staring at Joe. He feels very uncomfortable. The huddle breaks up and a woman steps forward. She looks directly at Joe and sniffs the air with her sharp nose. She is about twenty years old, dressed in a white shell-suit. Her bleached hair is pulled back tightly into a ponytail, accentuating a shrunken, weasel-like face. An older woman appears in a pink dressing gown holding a baby in her arms, she is accompanied by two young men, also in shell-suits.

A Rottweiler suddenly brushes past the men's legs and bounds over to Joe barking fiercely.

Joe yells to the young woman. "Can you call him off, please?"

The woman doesn't respond. The men are laughing.

Joe speaks again, assertively. "Call him off please!"

The dog stops growling. Its jowls slobber over Joe's shoes. Joe is shaking, his heart is racing. Fortunately, the Rottweiler isn't in attack mode and Joe decides to ignore it. He takes a deep breath and looks at the young woman. He tries to make a connection.

"I wonder if you know my grandad?"

The woman takes a moment to digest Joe's words. She sniffs the air again, as if to get some clue about his identity. The boy, still with his sister by his side, looks up at Joe.

"So what are ya doin around 'ere?" He sounds much bolder now he has got serious back up.

"I used to live on the estate. I've come back to visit my grandad. You might know him. He's very friendly." Joe points in the direction of Grandad's home. "He lives in the block over by the alley."

The woman in the white shell-suit responds at last.

"Oh, ang on, d'ya mean Ted, the very old bloke?"

Joe has never heard Grandad be referred to as *very old* before. He feels more anxious to see him. The woman seems to soften a little.

"He fixes the kids bikes, ain't that right bab?" she says, turning to her daughter.

The little girl nods in agreement. The woman continues.

"We're the last family with kids to be living on the estate. It's a right dump, init?"

"Yeah," Joe agrees with her.

"What was it like, when you lived 'ere?"

"It was alright, it was friendly."

One of the young men butts in. "Yawl get a knife in yer back around 'ere now."

The other young man cackles with laughter only to be smacked on the back of the head by the older woman in the pink dressing gown.

"Shut it!" she snaps and then she turns to Joe. "You're a bit posh to be from around 'ere ain't yer, kid?"

Joe forces a smile at her and then he looks down at the runny-nosed boy. He feels overwhelmed by hopelessness.

Joe asks himself a question: *Why have you abandoned your own grandfather?*

Joe feels a lump in his throat and his eyes begin to water. He tries to pull himself together.

"How come you're still living here?" he asks the younger woman in a broken voice.

"We're moving today."

"Where are you going to?"

"The council's got us a proper 'ouse. It ain't far away. The kids'll be able to go to the same school. That's important, if y'knaw what I mean?"

Joe nods. The young woman continues. "I feel a bit bad leaving old Ted. D'ya reckon he'll be alright? Can't yer fix him up somewhere else?"

Joe remains silent for a moment, lost in thought, and then he remembers something.

"There's a removal truck driving around the estate, is it looking for you?"

"Eh? Yeah it is."

The rain begins to fall from the black sky. The Rottweiler runs back indoors.

"Ah, it's pissing it down. C'mon yaw kids. In! Now! I'll go and find that truck."

The children stand gazing up at Joe.

"See ya mate," says the little boy and he runs inside with his sister. Joe grabs his bags and walks off, downcast, along the estate road, towards his grandad's home.

Joe lifts his heavy head and sees a small bit of garden is still cared for. The cherry tree planted by his grandparents in 1969 is in the middle of it. Its pink blossom brings a smile to Joe's face but then a gust of wind brings cold rain smashing against his cheeks. There is a distant rumble of thunder. He walks on against the wind and the rain and arrives at the back of Grandad's block. In the courtyard, it is a scene of desolation. Only two out of a dozen front doors are not boarded up. The rain is pouring down hard. Joe goes through the gate.

His wet knuckles hurt as he pounds against the front door. The voice from within sounds frail and confused.

"Who's there?"

"It's Joe, Grandad, it's Joe!"

"Hang on Joe, hang on son!"

Several locks are turned and a chain is released. The front door is set within a heavy steel frame, it opens slowly. Joe does not move. Grandad stumbles out into the rain and fading light. His bright green eyes look into Joe's blue eyes, drinking him in. He grabs hold of Joe's shoulders. Joe searches the contours of Grandad's face. He has lost too much weight and his cheekbones are pronounced. His stature may be diminished but those bright eyes are reassuring. They speak of a gentle intelligence. Joe can see his father's face in those eyes, a life that might have been but never was.

Joe's eyes fill with tears. He tries to smile but the ends of his mouth are trembling. His emotions overtake him like a river bursting its banks. He collapses to his knees and clings to his grandad's legs. The old man's countenance crumbles and he holds onto Joe's shoulders with both hands. That is how they remain, oblivious to the drenching rain.

They are both soaked through.

"Come on Joe, come on son, come inside now. It's so good to see you."

Grandad and Joe come in from the rain, wiping away tears from their eyes. They stand in the hallway.

"I'm so sorry it's been so long, Grandad. I had no idea the estate was like this, what's happened?"

"Oh, don't worry about that now, it's just so good to see you. Come on, I want to show you what your Auntie Rosie's done."

Joe is standing upon new white ceramic floor tiles, which he hasn't really noticed yet. They enter the living room.

"Blimey, Grandad! This is amazing!"

"It's not too glitzy is it? Now your Auntie Rosie's an interior designer she wanted somewhere to practise on."

Rosie is living in Spain, but she spent two weeks with Grandad at Christmas. That is when she refurbished the place.

"Rosie so wanted to see you, Joe. She's still waiting for you to visit her in Madrid. She's got a lovely place out there. Does it look like a boudoir with all these cushions?"

Joe pulls a face. "No, it looks wonderful. I love the new fireplace."

"Real gas flame! I'll put it on so you can warm yourself."

"Thanks Grandad."

Grandad squats down to get the fire on and then he turns to Joe.

"When I can find a space between all those cushions, I lie on the sofa and watch the flames. It's better than a telly!"

"Where is the telly?"

"I got rid of it, complete rubbish!"

"Don't blame you."

Joe helps Grandad up and then he stands beside the fire with his hands on his hips. His expression is stern.

"What Auntie Rosie's done is great, but what's happened to the estate?"

Grandad's face drops. He takes a deep breath and steadies himself, resting a hand on the back of the settee. "Shocking isn't it? But look, do you want to get changed? You should get out of those wet things. I'll put the kettle on. Where's all of your stuff?"

"I'm storing a few boxes at Luke's parents."

"Oh, right. His dad's in the paper all the time now with the football club. Good they got promoted. How's young Luke getting on?"

"Fine, he sends you his regards. He gave me a lift up. I've got something amazing to tell you Grandad, you'll never guess who we've had tea with…"

"Who?"

"First, I want to talk about the estate then I'll tell you who we visited on the way up."

Joe sits down beside Grandad on the large colourful sofa, richly decorated in an Aztec pattern. Cushions surround them and the fire roars.

Grandad sighs. "Do you remember the little market garden that stood here before the estate was finished?"

"Not really," Joe replies.

"Well, there was a broad avenue of trees leading to

where an old manor house once stood, next to a lake."

"I don't remember any of that."

"The manor house was knocked down and the lake was drained before you were born. A few of the old trees remain."

Joe is pensive, he wants to talk about the estate as it is now, not as it used to be, but he doesn't want to rush Grandad.

"Who owned the market garden?" he asks.

"It was a smashing old couple, they doted on you when you were little. They used to let you play in their orchard. Don't you remember them?"

"Not really."

"They were good people. Your nan and I used to love watching you play out there, happy days."

"But Grandad, looking at the estate now, it looks as if you've been through a war. What on earth's been going on? Why have you got a steel doorframe for goodness sake? Why didn't you tell me about any of this?"

"Well, you've been so busy and rightly so, doing your work in London. What could you have done anyway? What could anyone have done?"

Joe looks down at his feet. "Have drugs been an issue here?"

Grandad nods slowly. "Yes, drugs have been a major cause of the problems. It's the addicts that do the burglaries." He thinks for a moment. "It's housing management or lack of it that opened the door to the drug problems in the first place." Grandad looks forlorn. "I've tried to be the caretaker, even after I lost the job, that's what Nan would have wanted. We promised each other from the beginning that we'd do our bit to look after this place. As you can see, I've failed." He is visibly upset.

Joe leans across and puts his hand upon Grandad's arm.

"You haven't failed. I was just speaking to some kids out

there whose bike you've fixed. You've always looked after the kids around here."

"Thanks. So you've met the owners of the Rottweiler, have you?"

"That dog frightened the life out of me."

"They've got a lot of problems, that family. The Rottweiler's known to be dangerous."

Joe takes a sharp intake of breath. "When did the estate take a turn for the worse?"

"When the heroin addicts moved in, about eighteen months ago. They will steal anything, that's why I've got the steel doorframe. The buggers didn't get in 'ere. They had a go at your car though, Joe. They had the stereo out of it. My mate Bob from the Guards was visiting; he scared them off before they did too much damage. It's still working pretty well by the way, your car."

Joe doesn't want Grandad to get distracted. "Go on, what's it been like living here?"

"The drug addicts were the icing on the cake really. Things began to go seriously wrong several years ago, when the council made me retire. That's when they started moving in the problem people. The antisocial behaviour began then. Do you remember, Joe?"

"Yeah, I do. The games stopped and the fighting began."

"That's right. You kids used to have good games before then. Do you remember the cricket matches on the green? You were quite good in bat."

"I wasn't good in bat, Grandad."

"You weren't bad, you could have been good. You just needed to practise more. Well, really you needed coaching."

Joe is lost in thought for a moment. He stares into the flames. "Why is the empty tower block still standing after all these years?"

Grandad's face reddens. "Someone at the council signed

a bloody contract with the mobile phone companies to let them put their equipment on the roof. They've given them a twenty-year lease, even though another council department signed a demolition order for it!" Grandad sighs. "What can you do?"

Joe shakes his head. "So the council makes money from the mobile phone companies at the expense of everyone who has to live next to that monstrosity."

Joe takes a deep breath and sighs. "Are any of the addicts still around?"

"They've all gone." Grandad breathes out heavily, demonstrating his relief. "All the antics have stopped."

"What kind of antics? Go on, Grandad, please tell me, what did they do?"

"The usual things, I guess. Mattresses and shopping trolleys were thrown about the place. I used to take them off to the tip in the car. We had the fire brigade around most days. One day some of them had a bonfire. They smashed up all the fencing. Jason Cookson was one of them. Do you remember him from school?"

"Yes I do, he was always rough."

"His mum could never cope, but he was a smashing little boy. Breaks your heart to see what can happen." For a moment Grandad looks lost. Then he picks up his story again. "It wasn't right, the council never replaced those burnt down fences. The people in the private houses at the back had to pay for them." Grandad shakes his head. "The druggies would scream at each other and some of them had kids. I hated it when they screamed at their kids."

"Didn't the police do anything?"

"They don't respond to simple criminal acts around here anymore, son, or they turn up a day late. They did a big drugs raids though. We had helicopters and everything. It was pretty frightening and I'm an old soldier!"

Grandad pauses, trying to make sense of all he has lived

through.

"I'm not sure why the druggies suddenly left, it's strange. There was this lad, Simeon, unusual name. He's a trainee priest, I think. A proper bloke though, not how you'd expect them to be. He came over and spoke to the druggies. I had a nice chat with him, too. Anyway, they've all gone. It's quiet again."

"Most of the place is boarded up."

"We'll be alright here. I wonder what the future's got in store for us. There's talk of redevelopment. Some fat cat's buying everything up. I called the council to find out what's going on. I couldn't get any sense out of them."

Joe is deep in thought, staring into the fire again. "What about all the wasted lives?"

Grandad grabs a cushion. He is also staring into the fire. "Yes, what about the wasted lives? Like little Jason Cookson?"

"Why don't you move, Grandad? I don't believe Nan would want you to stay here now. You're not the caretaker anymore and you're not getting any younger. I hope you don't mind me saying that."

"This is our home, it's where my memories are. Having you live here with me was a real blessing. It was a difficult time when your parents died, and then Nan died too. You made this a home again, you and Rosie, and that daft old cat. Good old Scruff, he lived to be twenty-three. He was a good cat."

Joe and his grandad have never really talked openly about their past before.

"I hear what you're saying, Grandad, but I don't know, there must be more than this for you."

Grandad smiles. "Well, I do have a recurring dream."

"What of?"

"Of a little cottage where I just have the earth beneath me and the sky above me, and my own little garden.

Complete peace!"

Grandad looks dreamily across the room towards a photograph on the wall of his daughter, Rosie, standing in the garden of her Spanish villa. He suddenly remembers something. "There is one problem of antisocial behaviour that remains."

"What's that?"

"Old Beryl from next door has gone very deaf. She wakes up in the middle of the night and listens to those bloody story tapes for hours, very loudly! The old girl's going into a nursing home, soon."

"Don't worry, I'm used to it. I've been living in a basement flat for the last few years, people above and all around me."

Grandad gets up from the sofa with some difficulty. He pats Joe on the back.

"Get some dry clothes on. Your old bedroom is all ready for you." Grandad looks at Joe quizzically. "Have you grown?"

"I don't think so. You don't grow when you're thirty, do you?"

"I've probably shrunk. Your feet will dangle over the end of that little bed. I got you some new bed linen."

"Thanks."

Grandad remembers something else. "So, who did you have tea with?"

"Ah, you're not going to believe this?"

"Go on, try me."

"We had tea with the Prime Minister at Chequers."

Grandad looks at Joe with utter disbelief. "You're joking, right?"

"No Grandad, it's for real."

Grandad leans forward and looks into Joe's eyes as if checking for signs of insanity, but he looks normal.

"Well, I definitely want to hear about that," says

Grandad straightening up. "You're going to be staying with me aren't you, Joe?"

"Yeah, if that's alright with you, at least until I find somewhere to rent."

Grandad's face lights up; he wants Joe to stay for as long as he likes.

"It'll be great to have you around, putting a bit of life back into the old place. Now, tell me about the Prime Minister.

10 Return to Arden

It is the following Monday at nine o'clock in the morning. Joe leaps out of his little bed. He scrambles through his clothes and the bags left scattered across his bedroom floor. He is searching for his mobile phone, which is ringing.

"Gotcha!" He presses the answer button.

A woman speaks down the line. "Good morning sir, I have a call for you from David Rogers's office. Will you take the call?"

The only David Rogers that Joe knows is Luke's father. Why would he be calling? Various possibilities flash through his mind. "Yes, I'll take the call."

Now a very posh woman speaks. "Good morning. Is that you Joe?"

"Yes, speaking."

"It's Janet Steers here, David Rogers's secretary. David would like to invite you to lunch tomorrow, if you're available, at one o'clock."

Joe is silent for a moment.

"I apologise it's such short notice, do you need to check your diary?"

"I've got my diary in front of me," Joe lies. "Yes, I can do lunch tomorrow."

"That's wonderful. David has suggested lunch at the

Boat House, next to the pool, not far from Lullingdon. He said you'd know where it is; is that right?"

There's a longer silence. Joe's thoughts drift back to the boathouse, the pool and the night when he and his friends took the rowing boat out to the island.

"Are you still there, Joe?"

"Yeah."

"Would you rather I book somewhere else, in town perhaps?"

"No, I'm sure the Boat House will be fine, it's just that I remember it being, well, an old shed really."

Janet laughs down the phone. "I guess you haven't been there for a while have you?"

"Not for about ten years, actually."

"I think you'll be pleasantly surprised. It's quite smart now."

Joe thanks Janet for the call and hangs up. He is dumbfounded. Why would a busy man like David Rogers want to invite him to lunch? Surely he wouldn't just want to welcome him back, would he? There must be something else. Joe wonders if it might have something to do with Elias. He is intrigued. He is also keen to see the pool again, after all these years.

Joe pulls back his thick bedroom curtains, he is greeted by bright sunshine and the grotesque tower block. He looks further on and rests his eyes upon the Gothic gatehouse. He would explore the woods behind it if it wasn't for the spiked railings. He lets his weight fall down upon his little bed and relishes the thought of a free day. Grandad is clambering down the narrow staircase, slowly, with a lot of huffing and puffing.

"Are you alright, Grandad?"

"Yeah, just my back giving me jip. Did you sleep alright?"

"I slept like a log. I feel great."

"Good! I'm doing a cooked breakfast, special treat." The words are like music to Joe's ears. He rushes down to their little Spanish-style kitchen. Two places are set at the breakfast bar. The tantalising smell and sound of sizzling eggs, sausages, and bacon fill the place. Grandad cracks open another egg on the edge of the frying pan.

"Have you got any plans for today?" he asks.

"I'm going to go into town to buy a new shirt. I've got a lunch appointment tomorrow, with David Rogers."

"Really? What's that about?" Grandad is impressed.

"I haven't got a clue."

"He's an important man, although I bet he doesn't see the Prime Minister as often as you do."

Joe nods back with a grin.

"The papers are going on about him standing for the new elected city mayor thing," says Grandad before he seamlessly changes the subject. "The Skoda's been serviced, so you've got wheels."

Joe smiles keenly from behind the wheel of his old brown Skoda as it rattles down the forest road towards Lullingdon Manor. He is on his way to have lunch with David Rogers. The car's engine ticks over nicely but it does have several botched repairs. Black tape holds the wing mirrors together and part of the front bumper.

At last the suburban houses give way to the Warwickshire countryside. Joe lowers his window and takes a sideway glance at fields and hedgerows basking in the glorious sunshine. After a shorter distance than he expected, he is approaching the ornamental trees and the red brick garden walls of Lullingdon. He slows the car down to a crawl. The old lodge with its colourful cottage garden stands where it always has, and beside it are the lichen-covered granite gateposts. The scene is undoubtedly beautiful, yet smaller than Joe remembers it being. The fresh, earthy smell of the place stirs his senses. Joe catches a glimpse up the gravel drive, but trees screen the manor house. He wonders if Luke is in. It feels as if he has only been away for a few days rather than a decade, then he reminds himself that he is meeting with Luke's dad not Luke, and that significant events have passed since he last visited Lullingdon.

The Skoda trundles on, under the sturdy limbs of oak trees which seem to be ushering Joe back into the forest. The way is lost in shadows. Joe presses his nose against the windscreen. After a while he stops the car for no particular reason and turns the engine off. He sticks his head out of the window and looks up into the canopy of leaves and dappled sunlight. There are white flowers on the tips of the trees. He breathes deeply. The forest air is full of oxygen and a pleasant woody fragrance. There is copious birdsong all around. He would like to stay there drinking it in, but he needs to press on.

Joe restarts the engine and follows the forest road. A little further on he takes a tight right turn and descends down a hill towards the pool. Dark holly trees, oaks and rowans loom over the car. The lane becomes a narrow track. The leaf canopy is so thick it creates an underworld, hidden from the sky. The track widens out again and Joe is surprised to find he is in a car park, exhibiting several very smart cars. He parks the Skoda nonchalantly beside a Porsche and tries to close the door. It is jammed. There is a knack to closing the driver's door. It requires a lift and a slam. It takes Joe three attempts. Fortunately, nobody is watching. Joe breathes deep the forest air again and takes a moment to listen to the birds chattering in the trees. He decides to take a quick look at the pool.

Joe walks between the lofty beech trees, meandering around their silky, smooth, grey and green trunks. A carpet of russet, copper leaves, crunches beneath his black brogues. He emerges from the shadows into the bright open air beside the pool. His breathing is steady and he feels a great sense of wellbeing. He lifts his gaze beyond the water. There is nothing to offend his eye. He is so happy to be here. As if awakening from a pleasant dream he becomes aware of the sound of a motorcycle, it is getting louder.

He turns around and looks at the old boathouse. He never really appreciated what an attractive building it is, with its over-hanging eaves and Gothic style windows. It certainly isn't a shed, more like a picturesque folly, and now it is a smart restaurant. A sympathetic extension has been built and French windows open onto a terrace with tables and chairs, all taking advantage of the magnificent view over the pool. Nobody is sitting out, but people can be seen within the building. The conversion has been done sympathetically. The beauty of the place is intact. Joe thinks, a little grudgingly, perhaps it is good others can enjoy what was a secret place.

Joe's attention turns to the motorcycle that has appeared at the end of the track. There are two riders on it. The rear passenger, a particularly large figure, climbs off unsteadily. He takes his crash helmet off and reveals a mop of white hair. The helmet and jacket are stuffed into a pannier box. He pats the rider on his back and then with a growl from the engine and a wheel spin the motorcycle disappears into the forest. Joe's face lights up when he realises the passenger is David Rogers. He pulls up his tie, runs his hand through his hair, and strolls over to Luke's dad.

Joe and David greet each other warmly. Then David looks at Joe quizzically. "Now you weren't thinking about going for a swim, were you?"

Joe looks confused for a moment and then he remembers his appearance at Lullingdon in his paisley underpants.

"No, not before lunch."

They stand together for a few minutes, chatting about the motorbike and then about the dolphins they watched from the yacht off the coast of Cyprus.

"Have you heard the exciting news from Elias?" asks David.

The expression on Joe's face suggests he hasn't.

"He's been accepted into the City of Birmingham Symphony Orchestra, Simon Rattle's done a wonderful job as conductor."

Joe is dumbfounded. He wonders why Elias hasn't told him, or Luke for that matter. He pulls himself together.

"Wow. Does that mean he'll move to Birmingham?"

"Yes, of course. He might stay with us at Lullingdon."

Joe concludes that negotiations between David and Elias must be quite advanced.

David continues. "I'm sponsoring Elias to make sure he gets the support he needs. He's going to be a great asset for the city. He's one of the best violinists."

Joe nods and rubs the back of his neck. He seriously wonders if Elias has a grudge against him, for not letting him say goodbye to his grandfather. Why else wouldn't he have told Joe that he is relocating to his town?

David senses that Joe is put out by the news and he changes tack.

"Elias wouldn't be in the country if it wasn't for you, Joe. I'm very impressed with what you and Hannah have done for the lad, you took a big risk for him."

Joe smiles. "It was worth it. We couldn't have done it without you and Luke. Thanks for sailing the yacht. Do you remember the gunshots?"

"I do." David reels as he recalls the danger they had been in.

Joe touches David on the shoulder to steady him and he shifts the conversation.

"So how are you and Annie?

"We're both as well as you could expect at our age. Annie's looking forward to making sure Elias is properly looked after."

Joe wonders what it is with Elias and people's mums.

"Are you hungry, Joe?"

"I am, yes."

"Come on, I'd value your thoughts on the conversion. We've had a nightmare with English Heritage. I think they're happy now though. Antonio runs the restaurant for me. He's a bit over the top but an excellent chef."

They enter the refurbished boathouse and Joe looks about the place. A few of the tables are occupied by ladies that lunch and a scattering of business people. The atmosphere is sophisticated and restrained, until Antonio bounds over to them. He gives them a verbose welcome, gesticulating wildly with his arms in the air. Antonio is very Italian, he is in his mid-forties and has a wonderful moustache with turned-up ends.

"Ah, David, it's been too long!"

"It's only been a couple of days, Antonio."

"That's too long!"

"How are you? How is Annie? How is Luke?"

"We're all fine thanks and how are you?"

"Very well thank you, David."

David introduces Joe to Antonio and then he takes Antonio aside and whispers. "It's a bit quiet in here today, isn't it?"

"It is a little quiet, yes," Antonio confesses, and then he continues defiantly. "Yesterday was very busy, you should have seen it, the car park was overflowing!"

That seems to cheer David up.

"I've reserved your favourite table, by the window," adds Antonio.

"Very good, we'll be joined by Peter later, so we'll need

a table for three."

Joe wonders who Peter is.

"I hope you don't mind, Joe," David says as they take their seats, "I've asked Peter Caruthers to join us. He's the chief executive of Richmond Investments, my property company. I want you to meet him."

"Okay."

Joe manages not to show it, but he is flabbergasted. He is officially unemployed, so why is he having lunch with such exalted company? He is desperate to find out what is going on. He feels nervous and out of his depth. He reassures himself with the thought that he has nothing to lose so he might as well sit back and enjoy the journey.

David's eyes scan around the restaurant. He looks very pleased with himself, it is all just as he wanted it to be.

"So, what do you think of the place, Joe?"

Joe hesitates to answer as he gathers his thoughts.

"Are you all right?" David asks in a rather forthright manner.

"I'm fine, thanks," replies Joe. Inwardly, he feels uneasy and he hates it when people ask him if he is all right, like that. It makes him wonder if they know of some reason why he shouldn't be all right. Now he gives David the answer to his previous question.

"The pool used to be our secret place when we were teenagers. I'd have liked for it to remain as it was."

Great disappointment flashes across David's face.

"The conversion is very impressive, though," Joe quickly adds. "It's good that other people can enjoy the place. Does Luke like it?"

"I think he's in two minds, a bit like you really. Would you like a drink? You do drink don't you?" asks David in a slightly belligerent way.

"Only alcohol," replies Joe.

David laughs. "Glad to hear it! We do an excellent house

red."

"Ah, perfect." Joe immediately regrets his choice; he should have stuck to water, he is going to need a clear head.

"Antonio!" shouts David. "Two large glasses of your excellent house red please!"

David turns in his chair so he can take in the view of the pool through the French windows.

"Isn't that the prettiest of views, Joe?"

"Yes. This is definitely one of my favourite places."

David looks pleased. He begins to tell Joe about the history of the boathouse.

"The main building is in Victorian Gothic, but it's built upon an ancient watermill. You could hear the water running under us if it wasn't for the chatter." David turns away and stares at the pool. A smile brushes across his face. "Antonio found some kids swimming in the pool the other day." He chuckles. "I must confess, Annie and I used to swim in the pool when we were young. Swam all the way to the island once."

"Really? That's a long way."

"I didn't think Annie was going to make it. She got cramp. It was quite a scare, but she managed it in the end, with a bit of help. I was very fit back then."

Joe warms to David, their conversation is going well. David positions his half-moon spectacles on the end of his nose, he looks like a headmaster. He looks Joe squarely in the eye and adopts a serious tone.

"Now, Joe, I'd like to talk to you about a business proposition, if I may. I'd like you to treat it as confidential, is that agreed?"

Joe has been slouching in his chair, he pulls himself up and straightens his back. His heart begins to beat a little faster. The purpose of their meeting is about to be revealed.

"Yes, I'll treat it as confidential."

David nods solemnly.

"Thank you. Richmond Investments, my development company, is going to be involved in rebuilding rundown council estates. I'm currently negotiating to buy the worst ones." David looks Joe in the eye. "I have to confess that I built many of those estates back in the 1960s."

David cannot hold Joe's piercing gaze, he looks down and fumbles with his napkin. His voice sounds a little shaky. "I don't want my legacy to be broken communities. I always wanted to build decent places. I'm going to rebuild the estates."

There is a moment's pause. Joe wonders if Grandad's estate might be on David's list. He breaks the silence.

"How are you going to achieve your objective?"

"Well, the council accepts that some of the estates will have to be demolished. Several of them are already half empty. They look awful but that means land values are low, which means they can be purchased relatively cheaply. Once the legal work is done, we are going to rebuild on a large scale, but this time with streets, squares, and parks. I want to create the kind of places that people actually choose to live in."

David pauses, he wants to gauge Joe's opinion. He leans back in his chair with his hands cupping the back of his head.

Joe leans forward with his elbows on the table. He is wide eyed. "What will happen to the people already living on the estates?

Now David leans forward and his grey eyes briefly meet Joe's intense, bright blue eyes. "Existing tenants will be given new homes in the new developments. First of all, we'll build on the existing open spaces, they are currently covered in dog mess, syringes, and burnt out cars. Existing residents will go into those new homes. The buildings they vacate will then be demolished and redeveloped. Simple decanting."

"What will the new developments look like?" asks Joe.

"They will have a traditional urban character with a mix of homes, shops, workspace and leisure uses. Imagine it, no more commuting! We can double the number of homes on each estate and still provide a network of squares and little parks."

Joe is touching the end of his nose, anxious to make a point. "I don't know if you remember, but I've got direct experience of what it's like to live on one of the estates."

"Yes, of course, I remember, when you were at school, you lived on the Broadway estate."

Joe nods. "Some good people still live on the estates."

"I want to work with those people."

"There are some rotten apples too. How will you stop them from spoiling your vision?"

"There will be no more renting from the council. We'll follow the Scandinavian model and subsidise mortgages so even the poorest residents can own a share in their home. Residents in flats will form a cooperative to own their block. If people own a stake in their environment, they'll look after it. We'll also have resident porters."

"I met the porter from your Kensington block," says Joe.

"An excellent man!"

Now David cuts to the chase. "I'm interested in you having a role to play in delivering these redevelopment projects, Joe."

Joe sits to attention.

David continues. "I've been very impressed with your articles and your work in London. Redeveloping the housing estates will give you an opportunity to apply what you've been writing about."

Before Joe can answer, David is getting up from his seat. He is welcoming a middle-aged man, immaculately dressed in a beige suit.

"Ah, Peter, I'm glad you could make it. Let me introduce

Joe to you. This is the young man I was telling you about."

"Hello. I'm Peter Caruthers, pleased to meet you, Joe. I've heard good things about you."

Joe gets to his feet and shakes hands with Peter.

David shouts over to Antonio. "More wine!" Now he turns to Peter. "I've told Joe about our plans for the housing estates and that he might have a role to play."

Joe's heart beats faster again.

David continues. "Peter, explain to Joe how the new venture will work."

Peter fixes his black eyes upon Joe. "We'll start with the Broadway estate."

Joe wonders if the others notice the jolt of his body at the mention of his grandad's estate. He concentrates on breathing.

Peter continues. "I've just come from a meeting at the council to discuss it. We've been involved in painfully slow negotiations. At last, we've found a new site for the mobile phone masts that were stuck on a derelict tower block." Peter's eyes narrow and fix on Joe. "Some twit gave the mobile phone operators a twenty-year lease to put their equipment on top of a building that was due for demolition."

Joe makes a tutting sound and rolls his eyes.

Peter continues. "It should be relatively easy to clear the estate now. The council's got most of the people out. There's just one owner-occupier left on it. There's always one awkward sod that's used their right-to-buy from the council. We'll have to deal with him."

Joe shifts uneasily in his chair as he wonders what *deal with him* means.

Peter turns to David and he speaks in a hushed voice. "We'll probably need to come up with the right package to convince him to move. He's the only stumbling block now. I don't want to do a compulsory purchase order for just one homeowner. The time delays and lawyers' fees won't stack up. It is very annoying."

Joe realises they are talking about his grandfather. He wonders if David Rogers has orchestrated the whole meeting to get to his property. But David wouldn't exploit one of his son's best friends, would he? Joe is about to speak up but then he stops himself. He will let them reveal the full extent of their plans.

David is talking. "Offer him a new house somewhere else."

"He's an old bloke, he probably wants to rest his bones there," replies Peter.

"Well, if that's the case send him on a long holiday during the construction works. When he gets back, we'll have a new home ready for him."

Peter Caruthers looks mean.

Joe speaks up in a faltering voice. "The owner occupier you're talking about, that's my grandfather. At least, I'm pretty sure it's him you're talking about."

Peter Caruthers looks genuinely astounded. "Really? Joe, if I've spoken out of turn I do apologise. I had no idea." He appears to be genuinely troubled.

Joe looks David in the eye but it is impossible to make out what he is thinking.

After an agonising silence, David speaks. "There is no need to look so worried, Joe. I do apologise. I hadn't realised your grandfather still lives on the estate. I meant what I said though. If it takes a new home, or a long holiday during construction works, it'll be worth it for us. What do you think your grandfather would say to that?"

Joe takes a moment to think about his response. "He wants to stay where he is, although…"

"Yes, although what?"

"Well, the other day, he said he wanted to have the earth beneath him and the sky above him. That sounds like a bungalow, doesn't it?"

David raises an eyebrow at the mention of *bungalow* and he exchanges a furtive glance with Peter.

Joe resolves to be bold. "My grandfather would probably accept a new detached bungalow and a long holiday in Spain during construction works." Joe pauses for breath, and then he continues. "There's a cherry tree that would have to be retained too, it's got sentimental value."

David raises both eyebrows. He looks as if the world has fallen upon his shoulders. He sighs. "Well, if that's what it takes, we'll have to look into it. But I must say, a *bungalow* does concern me. I've never built such a thing."

"There's always a first time, David," chips in Peter.

"What on earth would it look like?"

David turns to Joe for an answer.

Joe thinks for a moment. "This old boathouse is rather like a bungalow. Could it look like this?" Joe gestures with his hand and looks about the place. In the corner of his eye he notices an attractive waitress standing beside the bar. He quickly looks back to gauge David's response.

David is warming to the idea. "Yes, it could be designed as a lodge house, perhaps in a new garden square."

"I can see that working," replies Peter.

David looks at his watch; he wants to wrap things up. He looks Joe in the eye. "Any role that you have to play, Joe, is completely independent of a deal with your grandfather. So, are you still interested in working with us?"

"Yes, I'm definitely interested, although the scale of it does sound a bit overwhelming." Joe is about to elaborate on his concerns but then the attractive waitress arrives at their table. She is wearing a black skirt, white blouse, and black apron. "Are you ready to order gentlemen?" she asks.

Once the orders are taken, the waitress departs.

"Antonio is very good at recruitment," says David. Joe and Peter nod earnestly.

Their lunch consists of excellent Italian food, good wine, and stimulating conversation.

"So, it's agreed!" booms David so loudly that everyone in the restaurant turns to look at him.

They have agreed that Joe will work with them on redeveloping the housing estates, subject to agreement on remuneration. There are nods and smiles around the table.

David turns to Peter. "Any chance of a lift to Lullingdon?"

"Of course, but I'll need to leave now, I've got a meeting with the lawyers."

David gets to his feet and presses his hand on Joe's shoulder. "The bill's taken care of. If there's anything else you'd like, just ask the delightful waitress."

Joe gets up and shakes hands with David and Peter. David wanders off to have a quick word with Antonio.

Joe is now sitting alone, staring out of the window. David suddenly turns on his heels and heads back to the table. Joe looks up with a start to find David looming over him.

"My glasses! I can't read a thing without them these days." He picks up his spectacles, which are resting upon the crisp white tablecloth.

Joe appears to be pensive. "David, the job sounds great, but…"

"But what?"

"It's not something that Luke should be offered first is it?"

David is emphatic in his reply. "The job matches your skills and experience, not Luke's." David looks down at the floor for a moment and then he looks directly at Joe with an unnerving directness. "That strange dream I had years ago of you and Luke crossing a river between the old gatehouse and your estate, you did make it to the other side. Weird things, dreams." He winks at Joe and turns to leave. Before he reaches the door he turns back yet again and bellows across the restaurant. "You'll be great on our team, Joe!"

Joe smiles and waves goodbye, and then he is left to his thoughts. He runs his finger around the rim of his wine glass until it hums. He looks up and smiles as he catches the eye of the pretty waitress.

11 Pugin's Gatehouse

Winter and spring have been battling in the sky for some time but spring appears to be winning. It is quite cold, bright and sunny. A large crowd is gathered in front of a stage. There is cheerful chatter and the smell of fresh paint.

Bill Robinson, still Secretary of State, snaps at Giles Best, his long-suffering Political Secretary. "Have you got a bit of tissue? Quickly! I've got to get rid of this gum."

Giles's upper lip quivers with disgust as he explains that he does not have a receptacle for his boss's gum.

Cathy, who has become plumper, is wrapped up warm in colourful scarves. She rummages in her handbag for a tissue.

The three of them are standing behind greenery in the wings of a temporary open-air stage. It has been erected for the grand opening of phase one of Broadway Place, Joe's reborn housing estate.

David Rogers beckons the Secretary of State to join him on the main stage. Bill's face reddens, he forces a quick smile, gives a little wave, and then turns his back.

"That's it! I'm being called on, now."

David looks a little anxious, and then he formally introduces the Rt. Hon. Bill Robinson MP. The sound of restrained applause breaks out from a crowd of two hundred people. They are all gathered in a beautiful new garden square. Many people are attending from David Rogers's companies, together with council workers, contractors, curious local residents and potential homebuyers.

There is a large floral display standing on the edge of the stage. The Secretary of State breaks off a leaf, spits his gum into it, and hands it to Giles. Without further ado, his short, rotund figure bounds onto the main stage. His reddened jowls shake violently when David gives him a firm handshake. Given their difference in size, the two men look rather odd standing side by side. David's large frame resembles a grizzly bear whilst the diminutive stature of the Secretary of State is closer to a koala. The crowd settles down.

Looking flustered, Bill grabs hold of the lectern with both hands. He is like the captain of a ship holding the wheel in a storm. He pulls down the microphone to his height and winces when it whistles back at him. He takes a deep breath, regains his composure, and looks over the square. The expectant crowd is hushed except for a few squeals from overexcited children who are being dragged off a bouncy castle on the far side of the square. A large white marquee stands beside it, guarded by Antonio, the manager of the Boat House restaurant. He is doing the catering for the day.

Beside the marquee is a bandstand where cool-looking musicians loiter, including Elias, clutching his violin to his chest. David asked if he would play at the opening ceremony and he was happy to agree. Elias has grown. Physically, he looks more like a man now that he has put on weight and muscle. He has grown in confidence too. Living and studying in London, and then moving to the Midlands to play with the City of Birmingham Symphony Orchestra, he has become sophisticated. He wears a cap, pulled down on one side of his face. It marks him out as an artist, all be it in a slightly affected way.

Bill suddenly scowls. Some commotion has distracted him. He looks down with sharp eyes like an old owl. Cathy and Giles are navigating their way around the side of the stage, between reporters and a television news camera. Cathy has spotted Joe and she wants to greet him. She elbows her way through the crowd to exclamations of "Oi!" and "Watch it!"

Cathy needs a hug, she and Jean-Paul have been experiencing difficulties in conceiving a child. Jean-Paul is away a lot, working in Paris. Cathy has been seeking solace by over-eating and listening to her old Tori Amos albums, loudly. The frown on the Secretary of State's face becomes a smile when he sees her embrace Joe.

Grandad stands beside Joe, looking older, but glowing with a Spanish suntan. The other friends are nearby. Luke stands with his girlfriend, Serena, and his mum, Annie. Archie is no longer a copper top; his short-cropped receding hair is bleached and he is wearing wrap-around sunglasses. Right at the back of the crowd is the old Scot, Jock, from the Regeneration Company. He has driven up from London for the day, keen to find out what his young apprentice has been up to.

Bill waits for silence. He looks beyond the expectant faces. Connecting with the square are new streets lined with town houses with brightly painted doors behind neat front gardens. There is even a little corner shop. The new garden square is at the heart of it all. Within the square itself is a charming single-storey cream rendered lodge. Its steeply-pitched slate roof shimmers blue in the sunlight. Beneath overhanging eaves are ornate Gothic style windows. There is a cottage garden. Grandad moved in just two weeks ago.

The Secretary of State clears his throat and begins his speech. "It's been my privilege to serve as your Member of Parliament for three decades."

"When are you going to retire?" shouts a heckler.

Bill ignores him. "My old dad is ninety-four now. He delivered the milk to the old manor house that stood here, not so very long ago. It was a very pleasant place."

He explains about the housing shortage after the war and how they tried to build homes fit for heroes but followed untested ideas. He speaks passionately.

"I'm not going to tolerate failed housing estates, not on my watch! Look around you. Why don't we use this transformation as a model? Squares like the one we're gathered in can bring people together. I'm not going to go on."

The heckler cheers loudly and some in the crowd laugh. Bill takes this as a cue to wrap up.

"We're all invited to partake of refreshments in that impressive marquee over there and it's all free!"

The crowd turns towards the marquee. Antonio stops twisting his moustache and braces himself like a rugby player.

David suddenly lunges across the stage in an ungainly way. He holds a pair of scissors in one hand and a red ribbon in the other. He leans down and mutters something into Bill's ear.

"Can I have your attention again please, ladies and gentlemen?" says Bill. "Shssh, this way please. Thank you. Right, I'm delighted to declare this new square and Broadway Place is OPEN!"

There is applause. The band starts playing. The lead singer bursts into a rendition of *Is this the way to Amarillo?* The Secretary of State is now boogying on the stage. He turns to David and mouths the words. "Was-that-okay?"

David nods back emphatically, gives the thumbs up sign, and starts dancing in a rather alarming fashion. His son, Luke, puts his hand to his forehead and shakes his head in embarrassment. His father is flapping his arms on the stage like a seagull on acid. Both David and Bill are singing:

"Sha la la la la la la la ... Sha la la la la la la la ... Sha la la la la la la la ... and Marie who waits for me ... "

David spots his wife, Annie, and he beckons her to join him. As soon as she is on the stage the Secretary of State grabs hold of her. They dance together as if back in the sixties. All decorum has gone. The Lord Mayor, his wife and other dignitaries are all on stage, twisting and turning. Joe takes Hannah by the hand and they lose themselves in the bopping crowd.

Luke and Archie are standing next to the buffet tables in the marquee, laughing.

Joe joins them. "What are you laughing at?"

"Shush, he's here," says Archie covertly to Luke.

Luke places a hand upon Joe's shoulder.

"We're laughing at you! Do you remember when you came to my house in your paisley y-fronts?"

"He looks very different these days in that dapper suit. Your dad must be paying him too much," says Archie looking very cool with his sunglasses pulled over the top of his head.

Cathy joins the boys with more snacks after her third visit to the buffet table. Hannah is standing nearby, engrossed in a conversation with Luke's mum. Joe picks up the conversation where Luke left it.

He turns to Cathy. "Do you remember when we were eighteen we went swimming in the forest and you drove off with my clothes? I never got them back, what did you do with them?"

"Yikes! That was a long time ago, sweetie. I didn't drive off with your clothes though. I'm pretty sure I left them on the roof of Luke's mighty Mini. Didn't you find them?"

"No. I never did!"

Everyone tucks into more food. Amicable chatter and

laughter fills the friend's corner of the marquee. Then Joe spots Archie drifting off. He decides to follow him.

Joe finds Archie staring at Grandad's beautiful lodge house. Joe taps him on the shoulder and points out the cherry tree, which is full of pink blossom.

"My grandparents planted it in 1969 when they moved into the old council estate."

"Very pretty," replies Archie. "Your grandad's house looks great. That old estate was such a dump."

"I know, I lived on it for years."

"I didn't mean to be rude."

"You weren't, you were just honest."

"Honesty's important isn't it, between friends?"

Joe suspects something is up. "How're things going with you, Archie?"

"So, so."

"Why not good?"

Archie doesn't answer.

Joe continues. "Have you ever thought about moving back home? It'd be great to have you around."

"You're joking aren't you? I hate coming back here," replies Archie, tersely.

Joe is taken aback.

Archie's voice is getting louder. "I hate things like this event. People are so smug and small-minded. I can't wait to get back to London."

Joe takes a moment to gather his thoughts. "You looked as if you were having a good time last night, in the pub."

Joe, Archie, and Luke had taken Elias out to one of their old teenage drinking haunts.

"That was the drink," replies Archie.

Joe looks annoyed. "So, you weren't having a good time with your mates?"

"It was nice to catch up. Elias is a good lad. It's amazing

how many girls appear when he's around."

Joe nods, that is certainly true, but he wants to get to the bottom of what is making Archie unhappy. He pushes further. "So, what's going on in your life?"

"I don't know, I don't enjoy people's company anymore."

"What about Sam? I thought you were going to bring her."

"She's got a new boyfriend. They're very serious. Everyone's become a couple. I seem to be the only one left, on the shelf." He looks forlorn. "Sometimes I wonder where everybody's gone."

Archie has been introspective since he turned thirty. The other friends all had thirtieth birthday parties, but not Archie. His friends didn't even give him a card.

Joe tries to say something helpful. "Perhaps you need a holiday."

Archie's demeanour becomes harder. "You need to be careful, Joe."

"That sounds ominous, what do you mean?"

"You've changed, in some ways for the better. It's good to see you and Hannah together, you certainly took your time there, but…"

"But what?"

"You've also changed for the worse."

"How d'you mean?"

"You've become, well, what's the word? Smug. You'd be crazy to stay in this backwater. Haven't you at least thought about coming back to London? I've been seeing a bit more of Luke recently, we sometimes meet up for a pint."

"I don't want to move back to London," replies Joe. "I feel different since I returned home, not smug, but settled. I've been unlearning a lot of the rubbish I thought was important. Do you know what I mean?"

"No. Enlighten me."

"How can I put it?" Joe thinks for a moment, and then he continues. "Kensington High Street used to have orange sodium streetlights, which meant people couldn't see true colours. When we put white light in, people could see true colour. It looked completely different, much better. I've been going through a similar process. Trying to see true colour."

Archie doesn't reply. He turns his back on Joe and stares at the cherry tree. Joe talks to the back of Archie's head.

"I love this place. I thought you did. It's where we grew up."

Archie turns around, his eyes are slightly bulging. "Yes, but Joe, you're supposed to move on aren't you rather than going backwards? Otherwise, it's entropy. You become a loser."

"Eh? You think I'm a loser?" Joe feels that Archie has overstepped the line now. Archie stares at Joe, unnervingly. Joe tries not to show how hurt he feels. He looks down at the ground.

"I think you're a loser if you stay here," adds Archie coldly.

Joe cannot believe what Archie has just said. He feels angry. "I need to go," he says calmly. "I need to find Elias. I'm giving him a lift back to Lullingdon."

"Remember what I said," says Archie, as if knocking a nail into the coffin. They flash a look into each other's eyes and go their separate ways.

A few minutes later, Joe is leaning against the bandstand trying not to feel offended. He is waiting for Elias who is helping his fellow musicians pack away their gear. The lead singer from the band puts his guitar into its case. He offers a friendly nod to Joe.

"Hello, I'm Simeon." He is tall, thin, and aged around

thirty. He seems familiar to Joe, but he can't quite place him.

"Hello, I'm Joe. Thanks for the music. I liked the mix of classical and pop."

"I'm glad you liked it. It's an honour to play with Elias. You're a friend of his aren't you?"

"Yeah, that's right."

"And don't you work with the developer?"

"Yes."

"What'd you do?"

"Project manger, I oversaw this redevelopment."

With that response Joe seems to go up in Simeon's estimation. He is searching for a question, but before he can find it Joe asks him one.

"What do you do for a living?"

"I'm studying at the college, just over there, through the woods."

"What, you mean behind the gatehouse?"

"That's it."

"Isn't that some kind of religious institution?"

Simeon nods. 'It's a seminary."

Joe looks perplexed. "I don't mean to be rude but you look more hoody than clergy."

Simeon laughs. "Thanks, I think."

"I've always wanted to see the building beyond those woods, what's it like over there?"

"It's certainly impressive. There's a great view. You take it for granted after a while. I'm heading back now. I could show you the building if you like, there's a great view from the top of the tower."

Joe can't believe his luck. "Can I bring some others?"

"How many?"

"There's Hannah, Grandad, Elias and me, four of us."

"That's fine but I heard Elias was going for a drink with some of the band."

Joe is annoyed to discover that Elias has planned to go for an afternoon drink without telling him. He agreed to give Elias a lift back to his digs at Lullingdon because Elias's motor scooter is broken. Now he finds himself hanging around as Elias's chauffeur. To add insult to injury, Simeon says that Archie is also going for a drink with them. Simeon and Joe agree to meet back at the bandstand in ten minutes.

Joe eventually finds Elias and he speaks to him in a rather unfriendly tone.

"Would you like to see an historic building?"

"No thanks, I'd rather go to the pub."

Some quick negotiations follow. It is agreed that Joe will go and see the seminary and Elias will go to the pub. Joe will give Elias a lift back to Lullingdon, but only if he is back at the bandstand in an hour.

"I won't wait for you if you're late," says Joe.

Joe scans around the thinning crowd, searching for Hannah and Grandad. He knows they will want to see the seminary and its view. He cannot find either of them. He spots David and Bill engrossed in conversation beside the bandstand. He makes his way over and loiters next to them.

The Secretary of State is explaining that the renaissance of the city centre is fine but there is a lot more work to be done in Birmingham. "David, I want you to stand as the candidate!" he says emphatically. He is referring to the new position of the city's elected mayor. He hammers his point. "You'll have real power. You can roll out what you've learnt about regeneration and football. You can take the whole city into the Premier League."

David looks uncomfortable.

Bill continues undeterred. "Just look what you've done with this housing estate. Don't you want to roll this out as best practice?"

David frowns. "No, I don't think I do want to roll it out."

"Why not?" Bill looks confused.

"I'm seventy-three years old and I'm still learning so much. Rebuilding whole neighbourhoods is not sustainable. We had to start again with the Broadway estate because it was a catastrophic failure, but retrofitting is the future, working with people to improve their existing homes and streets. You're right to mention the football club though. There are some lessons to learn. It starts with hearts and minds and installing some belief."

Bill looks very determined. "If you become mayor, you can champion a grassroots approach, empower communities, be at the cutting edge."

"Be at the cutting edge? I think you said that to me on this very spot forty years ago."

"Oh, come on David!"

David looks concerned. "I'm too old for the cutting edge, now."

"Pah! That's nonsense. I'm the same age as you and I'm practically running the country! You just need to have the right team with some young talent in it." He spots Joe and ushers him over.

"This lad's learnt a lot working with you, and he's done a stint in London. The two of you work well together."

David looks a little unsteady. He turns away and leans against the bandstand. His mop of white hair blows across his pale face.

Bill cuts in again. "You're not one for sitting on your arse in retirement, David. You'd drive poor Annie mad. So what'd you say?"

There is no reply.

Bill turns to Joe and rolls his eyes. "It's nice to see you again, young man. I've been hearing good things about you!"

Joe's face beams. "Thanks very much." Now he turns to David. "I'm sorry to interrupt, but have you seen Hannah?"

"No. I'm afraid not."

At that point Simeon joins them. Joe introduces him to David and Bill

"We're going on to see the seminary building," Joe explains.

"Do you mean the old college beyond the gatehouse?" asks Bill. "I've always wanted to see that building, the interiors are by Pugin, he designed the gatehouse too."

Joe looks shocked. "Do you mean the same Pugin who did the Houses of Parliament?"

"Yes, that's right."

"I can't believe I didn't know that."

David suddenly looks more attentive. "Could I come with you?"

"Yes, if it's okay with Simeon," replies Joe.

Simeon nods. "That's fine."

David's face lights up.

Bill frowns. "I wish I could join you but I've got to leave for London and a meeting with the Prime Minister."

Simeon looks at his watch. "Are you ready to go?"

David and Joe nod keenly. Then Joe spots Grandad returning home. He excuses himself for a moment and runs over to get him. Grandad is now eighty-three years old, but he is sprightly enough. His suntan disguises the chill he has caught, which he dismisses with his usual bravado. He is more bent over than usual, due to backache. He soon perks up when Joe explains the gatehouse was designed by the same architect who did the Houses of Parliament, and that they have been invited to see the seminary.

"I wouldn't miss this for the world!" exclaims Grandad as he fetches his overcoat. He remembers he has a message for Joe from Hannah; she has gone shopping with Cathy.

Grandad greets Simeon with a handshake.

"Hello, we've met before, do you remember when you spoke with the druggies on the old estate?"

"Yes, of course, how are you?"

"Fine, thanks. It's quite a different place now isn't it?"

"It certainly is a transformation."

As the afternoon wanes, winter begins a fight back and the air temperature drops. A few dark bottomed clouds roll over the sky. David and Grandad are both wearing thick overcoats but Joe is just wearing his rather thin beige suit. Simeon wears a thick grey hoody over his clothes. He pulls the hood over his head giving him the appearance of a monk. The four men make their way across the garden square and then up a smart new street fronted by red brick town houses, green verges, and recently planted trees.

They arrive at Pugin's magnificent gatehouse with its buttresses and arches. Its weathered, fiery orange bricks look like the gnarled bark of an ancient tree. It has the appearance of a living thing. In all the years that Joe and Grandad have known the gatehouse, they have never seen its grey wooden door open. Now Simeon produces an enormous medieval-looking key.

"Apart from today, I've never come through this gatehouse," he says. "It took ages to find this key."

He unlocks the door and presses his shoulder against it. It opens slowly. They all step into a cold, dark passageway, with a high stone vaulted ceiling. The heavy door closes behind them with a thud.

At last, Joe has entered into the mysterious woods. The veil of secrecy is being lifted. There is a rough path before him carpeted in crunchy, golden leaves. He is relieved to have Grandad and David with him. The path continues around majestic beech trees. In the distance are swathes of bluebells, their luminous blue colour contrasts with the lime-green leaf buds and golden carpet. The woods are alive with birdsong. The four men walk without talking.

Too soon, they are out of the woods, standing on the

edge of an open expanse. In front of them is a mown sports field surrounded by a belt of wild grass. In a commanding position at the far end of the field is the magnificent Victorian seminary. The turreted main tower thrusts into a patch of blue sky. Simeon glances at his watch again, but Joe needs more time to absorb this amazing sight. The others move on. Joe drags his feet. His eyes are feasting on the surroundings. He is awestruck and amazed that such a beautiful place exists so close to where he has grown up.

"I really can't believe I've never been here before," says David, with a bewildered look.

There is a burst of song from a bird flushed out of the tall grass.

"That's a lark!" Its song reminds David of when he was a boy.

Simeon mutters half to himself. "Look at the birds of the air, they don't sow or reap or store away in barns, and yet your heavenly Father feeds them."

Joe is still looking upwards but the others have walked off. The sun streams down through a gap in the rolling clouds. It feels a little warmer. Joe drags himself away from the view and he jogs over to join the others. They have already crossed the sports field.

Now they all walk together past an ornate chapel designed by Pugin, and then they are in front of the main seminary building. They are standing upon an elevated plateau. To one side the land drops steeply, westwards, towards the city. There would be a fine view but for the trees. The seminary building is made from the same fiery, orange bricks as the gatehouse. It has tall, pointed windows, soaring chimneys and a tower. It is bursting with dynamic energy.

"What's the view like from the upper windows?" asks Joe.

"Don't worry, you'll see the view in a minute," replies

Simeon.

In silence they walk though splendid formal gardens and across a gravel driveway. Simeon leads them on, underneath an impressive portico entrance, and then they are in a richly furnished reception area. The walls are lined with a cream limestone which is as soft and warm as skin. From deep within the building comes the sound of men singing. The songs from centuries past are resonating through the walls. The visitors follow Simeon along a corridor where fine paintings hang on the walls.

David's eyes are darting around taking in wondrous things. He stops in front of a painting. "That's an Italian masterpiece," he gasps.

Simeon looks at his watch again. "You're more than welcome to come back another time to have a proper look around."

They turn a corner and follow a long corridor lined with well-polished wood panelling. There is a strong smell of beeswax. Simeon stops and leans against a small, polished door. "I should warn you, it's pretty cramped and dusty in here. It's a long way to the top of the tower, are you sure you want to do it?" He looks with some concern at the smart clothes of his guests. He is also a little concerned about Grandad's age.

"I wouldn't miss this for the world!" says Grandad, a little less convincingly than when he first said those words.

Simeon steps through the doorway into the tight confines of a stairwell. The narrow spiral, stone steps will take them to the top of the tower. The four men climb slowly. Joe is at the back of the line. They keep going for ages. David is breathing heavily.

"Are you okay, David?" asks Joe.

"I'm quite alright, thank you," he gasps back.

"Actually, I could do with a breather, can we rest for a minute?" puffs Grandad.

"No, come on, we can all have a good rest at the top," replies David.

Grandad continues his climb, very slowly. At last, they reach the top of the staircase.

Joe steps through a tiny arched doorway and he joins the others in the brightness of the afternoon. They are all standing upon the middle section of a lead roof, which is almost flat, but not quite. It consists of a central ridge from which there are two gentle slopes towards waist high battlements. Even though it is a gentle slope it is vertigo inducing. Joe turns his collar jacket up against the strong wind which is buffeting his face and ears. In the sky above them floats tall clouds against patches of blue. The men bravely walk over to the battlements. They look in wonderment at the expansive view before them.

Joe spots a kestrel demonstrating perfect aerodynamics. It hovers effortlessly, holding its position in the air just a few metres away. Its reddish brown feathers are ruffled by the wind. The kestrel turns, folds back its wings and soars away. Joe's eyes now wander over the new Broadway Place. It has a rich grain of streets, squares, and intricate roofs, it all looks as if they belong there. He spots Hannah's house on top of the adjacent hill. Joe breathes deeply and he feels energised. He would like to lift his arms and feel the wind under them, but then David taps him on the shoulder. David looks a little shaky. As he speaks a gust of wind takes his words away. He is pointing at the dark woodland haze on the horizon.

"Do you see the forest?" he shouts

Joe smiles back. "Yes, Lullingdon!"

Joe notices a deck chair positioned in the corner of the tower. Beside it is an empty bottle of wine. He turns to Simeon. "Is that deckchair for sunbathing?"

"It's my prayer chair."

Joe's quizzical face suggests some further explanation is needed.

"I've been praying for the Broadway estate since I first arrived," adds Simeon.

"When did you first arrive?"

"About five years ago. I'd never seen anywhere quite as bad as the estate. I thought it needed all the help it could get."

"Do you mind me asking, what made you choose to be a priest?"

"I don't mind you asking, Joe. I was living an ordinary life, training to be an accountant and living with my girlfriend. One morning I woke up with a particularly bad hangover, and a revelation. There are two paths in life. Salvation and damnation; it was time for me to choose."

"Accountancy often has that affect on people," interjects David.

Joe looks puzzled. He wants to ask Simeon what happened to his girlfriend, but it doesn't seem to be an appropriate question.

"Do you think your prayers have resulted in the rebuilding?" he asks instead.

"Well, you've put a lot of hard work into that, haven't you?"

"Yeah."

"Maybe it's been like a partnership."

There is a slightly awkward silence.

"The works have gone a lot quicker than I thought they would," says David picking up the empty bottle of wine. "Is it thirsty work, praying?"

"We take communion up here too," replies Simeon.

"Oh, of course, sorry."

"No need to apologise," says Simeon and he quietly stares into space, lost in thought for a moment. Without further explanation, he ushers them to the other side of the tower. "Look at this view. You can see all of Birmingham and beyond."

The men all follow Simeon's instructions and lean against the battlements. They are looking beyond the trees that Joe and Hannah could see from their childhood windows. Stretched out before them is a great bowl containing a city region. Rising in the far distance are the Shropshire hills in a bluish haze. In the mid distance shafts of white light illuminate a cluster of tall buildings, glittering like jewels upon a ridge of land. It is the city centre, about seven miles away.

An uncanny silence descends and they stare at the city as if through a dream. It is unimaginably beautiful.

Joe leans against the parapet and sighs. "It's like a garden, how can there be so many trees? It's gone so silent. What's happening? Is this real?"

"I'm seeing it too," says Simeon. "This is what the city could be like."

"It's the old Forest of Arden," says Grandad, grasping for an explanation. His knuckles turn white as he grips the parapet, tightly.

Now another reality becomes evident. Coming into focus is a multitude of randomly dotted council tower blocks. Swathes of the city are grey and uninspiring. They can hear the traffic again.

Joe turns to Simeon. "What's happening? Where's the vision gone?"

"For the want of grace, this is reality for now, Joe."

Joe recalls the verse David spoke to him, before he left for university, all those years ago: *Above all else, guard your heart, for it is the wellspring of life.*

He turns to David. He wants to remind him of it, but David is talking to Grandad. He is pointing over the city.

"Look! There's our football stadium," says David, "now that's hallowed ground."

Grandad suddenly flinches and turns away quickly. His body is shaking as if he is weeping. Joe moves over to him and places a hand on his shoulder. "Are you okay Grandad?"

Grandad flinches again. His face is horribly contorted and is turning blue. He is in agony.

"Grandad!" The hairs on Joe's arms are standing on edge. "Grandad! What's wrong with you?"

"My God! I think he's having a heart attack," gasps David. "Quickly, loosen his collar! Help him to lie down!"

Joe and Simeon help Grandad to lie on the cold lead roof. They loosen his clothes. Simeon takes off his hoody top and gently places it under Grandad's head as a pillow.

David is shouting into his mobile phone. "I need an ambulance, immediately!"

Grandad stares into Joe's eyes. He takes a sharp intake of breath. "I'm dying?" he gasps.

Joe doesn't know what to say. He tries to cover his own terror. A seizure grips hold of Grandad and he rolls into a foetus position. There is froth around his lips. His ribcage heaves, up, down. He is gasping for breath and making dreadful noises. His body is straining to pump air into a broken chamber.

"Lie flat!" instructs Simeon and then he administers first aid, pressing down hard upon Grandad's chest. Joe catches another look from Grandad's frightened eyes. A wave of compassion overwhelms him. He so loves this old man.

Simeon is speaking but his words are only half heard. Joe's one concern is to affirm Grandad, in case these really are his last moments. The rest of the world vanishes into inconsequence. Joe rests a hand upon his grandad's forehead. Grandad manages a broken smile. He looks into Joe's bright blue eyes. Mustering all of his remaining strength, he speaks. "I've...prayed for you...every day, Joe"

Tears are streaming down Joe's face. He places a tear-drenched palm onto Grandad's forehead. Grandad tries to say another word but he can't get it out, there is a terrible gurgling in his throat.

Joe desperately turns to Simeon. "Would you pray for him?"

David is crouched down beside them. "We're losing him, you should give him the last rites, Simeon."

Simeon panics. "I haven't been ordained, yet."

"Does that matter?"

Simeon moves closer to Grandad and takes his hand in his own. "Do you want to be anointed, so that you are ready to meet Christ? Do you accept him as your saviour?"

Grandad's throat is still gurgling, terribly. "Yes."

Simeon reveals a tiny vial of oil. He uses it to mark a cross on Grandad's head. He prays over him. "Through this holy anointing may the Lord in his love and mercy help you with the grace of the Holy Spirit..."

Joe and David bow their heads.

Simeon finishes. "Everything is going to be alright now, he is in the safest place."

Grandad lies motionless upon the lead roof with his eyes closed. There is silence. Joe lies beside his grandad, their bodies touching.

"You're the best grandad I could have had."

Grandad's bright green eyes open and stare up at the blue sky. He looks serene. The years fall off him. His eyes begin to fade and like a boat drifting away from these shores, he utters his last words.

"God bless you Joe, my dear grandson."

"Don't go Grandad!"

Joe rests his face on Grandad's chest.

Simeon places his hand on Joe's shoulder. "The Lord is taking him now, Joe."

12 Epilogue

Joe and Hannah walk around the slender tree trunks, headed towards the sandy beach. The early May sun is warm on their faces. The pool is a wonderful prospect before them. It takes their breath away, just as it did when they were eighteen years old. Hannah, now thirty-five, is still stunningly beautiful. Her skin is smooth and without blemish. Her blonde hair shines in the sunlight.

High above them, cotton clouds go sailing by in a bright blue sky. The pool is like a great reflecting mirror. At its edges are bright green reed beds dotted with yellow flowers. Beyond the reeds, the Forest of Arden rises and it forms an unbroken, rolling canopy, like a green velvet curtain draped around the pool. A few pine trees soar high like spires, greeting the sky. At the far side of the pool the canopy dips low forming a window on infinity. On the horizon, huge cumulus resemble heavenly mountains. This vision of clouds, reeds and trees is intense and all is reflected in the mirror of the pool. A light breeze blows across the water, ripples dart this way and that, and then everything melts into a glittery gold.

The dark shadows under Joe's eyes reveal his lack of sleep. Grandad's passing on has brought back childhood memories, the loss of his parents and feelings not yet dealt with. It was Hannah's idea to visit the pool. She thought the beauty of the place might bring Joe peace. He has been looking troubled since the funeral.

Joe tells Hannah about Grandad's last moments and then his lower lip begins to tremble. He finds a patch of grass amongst the rough ground and sits down. He stays there for a while, head bowed. He clutches his knees under his chin like a schoolboy. Hannah remains beside him, silent. Her presence is comfort enough. He just needs her to be with him, to wait in the silence.

Joe speaks in a faltering voice. "We've all played a role in saving Elias."

Hannah sits down on the grass beside him, bodies touching. "How do you mean?"

"Luke and his dad, their contacts, they sailed the yacht."

"That's true."

"But you were key to it all, Hannah. Without you, Elias wouldn't have got out of the camp. You sacrificed your job for him."

Hannah lowers her head and smiles. "Even Archie's helped Elias to settle in."

"How'd you mean?"

"He's taken him to all the pubs."

Joe manages a smile. He gets up to his feet and helps Hannah up. He leans against a tree for support. Hannah can sense that something new is flickering in Joe and she is intrigued by it. She rubs his back and smiles reassuringly.

"Let's walk around the pool," says Joe, and then after a few steps he adds, "I wonder if David prays."

"What would he pray for?"

"Keeping his club in the Premier League, mending the mistakes of the past, rebuilding my council estate."

Hannah looks thoughtful. "The estate was his mistake to mend. It sounds to me as if Simeon's prayers got answered."

Joe smiles and nods. "It made Grandad so happy to see the estate rebuilt and to get his new house. I just wish he could have enjoyed it for a few years." Joe turns to Hannah. "I've got something important to say."

Hannah's heartbeat quickens.

Joe looks her in the eye. "I hope David has learnt from his mistakes."

"Why?"

"He's going to stand for mayor."

Hannah feels disappointed. It isn't that she doesn't want David to be mayor, she does, but she thought Joe might have been about to propose to her.

Joe continues. "David's asked me to get involved with his campaign."

Hannah tries to look pleased. "Doing what?"

"He wants me to lead with urban regeneration."

"That's wonderful, Joe! Right up your street."

Hannah looks distracted. "I think it's time for us to go back to the boathouse. Cathy and Luke will be there any minute."

Joe isn't ready to leave just yet. He doesn't look well. His eyes are bloodshot. Hannah looks at him with concern.

"Joe, do you really want to meet up with the others?"

"I'd rather be with friends. I'll be okay. You know, Hannah, I was so fortunate to be with my grandad at the end of his life, to receive his blessing. How could I have denied Elias that? That was a bad mistake."

Joe catches sudden movement from the corner of his watery eye. A tiny flash of turquoise darts across the water and then disappears between the reeds.

Joe blinks. "That was a Kingfisher!"

"Where?"

"Too late, it's gone."

"I wish I'd seen it."

Joe looks across the pool and he spots something else.

"Look, Hannah, there are two Arctic terns up there," he says, smiling.

The terns are circling the little island. They perform aerial acrobatics, diving, swooping, and ascending again. One of them suddenly swoops into a nosedive and plunges into the water. Plop! In an instant it takes off again with a tiny fish in its bright orange beak. The birds are like tiny actors performing on a great stage. Joe and Hannah watch every move. The birds fly closer to them, revealing their forked tails and sharply sculpted wings. Their shrill trumpet call echoes across the water.

Then a distant but more familiar sound is heard, human voices are calling them. Joe and Hannah turn around. On the other side of the pool are Luke and Cathy. A third person also stands beside the boathouse. They are all waving their hands.

"Who's that with them?" asks Joe. He hopes it is Archie as they haven't spoken since their quarrel.

"It's Elias," replies Hannah. She turns to Joe. "If you had let him say goodbye to his grandfather he wouldn't be here today, he'd be dead. He asked if he could come and see you. He doesn't hold a grudge or anything like that."

Hannah's bright green eyes are fixed upon Joe's blue eyes. "I know you really loved your grandad, this is a difficult time for you. I just want you to know, you don't have to go through it alone. I love you, Joe."

Joe looks deep into Hannah's dazzling green eyes. They are irresistible. "I love you too, Hannah."

Made in the USA
Charleston, SC
30 May 2013